QUICKSILVER

QUICKSILVER

MYSTERY IN THE WILD

THE FORENSIC GEOLOGY SERIES
BOOK 1

TONI DWIGGINS

Copyright © 2013 by Toni Dwiggins

All rights reserved.

No part of this book may be reproduced in any form or by any electronic or mechanical means, including information storage and retrieval systems, without written permission from the author, except for the use of brief quotations in a book review.

All characters and events portrayed in this work are fictitious. Certain geographical features have been slightly altered.

Cover design: Wicked Good Book Covers

— To be notified of new releases, sign up for my mailing list:

https://eepurl.com/GtdZn

— Contact me at:

Website: tonidwiggins.com

Facebook: facebook.com/ToniDwigginsBooks

EPIGRAPH

I said, "We don't do treasure hunts."

He raised an eyebrow. "How about to save a life?"

"That, we do." I folded my arms. "Should there be a life in danger."

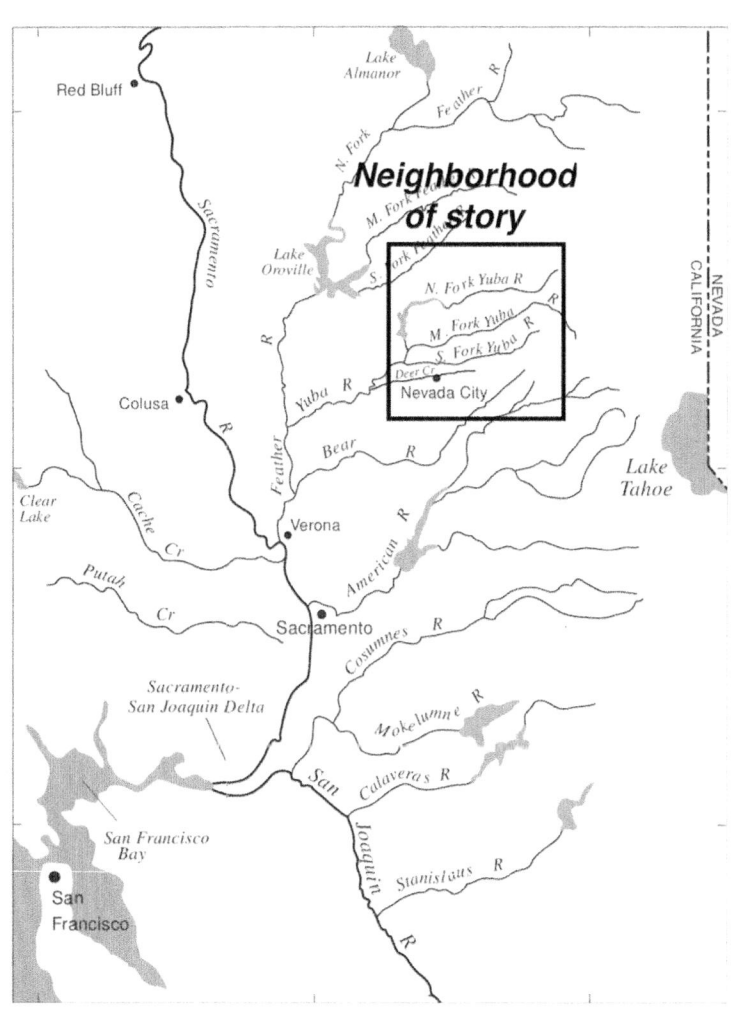

1

THE MAN who had hired us took the lead.

His name was Robert Shelburne and he was as sure of himself as he was of this path. Indeed, he had a name for this way up the mountain--the *rogue route*.

That it was.

No trailhead marked the beginning. The path did not exist on any map. It had been blazed decades ago, surviving today as little more than a hint. It shot straight up the slope and was so thickly haired with trees and brush that we were nearly hiking blind.

I heard my partner Walter Shaws, a couple dozen feet behind me, muttering words he would not normally speak aloud. Walter and I had certainly hiked plenty of unofficial trails and exploited the terrain where no trails ran at all, in rougher country than this—we're geologists who read earth evidence from scenes of crime, environmental crisis, or in this case a missing person--and that usually takes us deep into the field. Still, we weren't in the habit of bushwhacking up a mountain without good reason.

Robert had given a reason, good enough that we'd signed on

to this case, good enough that we'd become a team, the three of us on a first-name basis, but that did not stop Walter from grumbling about the topography.

And it didn't stop me from keeping an eye on the landscape.

As we climbed, a breeze kicked up and brought an odd vegetative odor, which I could not identify. Clearly, it didn't come from the rangy manzanita or deer brush that infested the path. It came from deeper into these oak-and-pine wooded slopes, or perhaps up higher.

Up ahead, Robert picked up his pace and then disappeared into the timber as if he'd been consumed.

I began to grow annoyed. What if he took a turn that Walter and I, in turn, missed? What if the path branched left and we went right? Bad form for two geologists to lose the client in the field. I shouted, "Slow down!"

After a long moment, a reply came from the woods above. "Up ahead, Cassie. I've stopped."

I picked up my pace and called to Walter to pick up his and a half-minute later I crashed through the brush and found Robert kneeling on the path.

I could not see around him and so I asked, "Find something of interest?"

He got to his feet and brushed dirt off the knees of his stylish hiking pants and adjusted the hip belt of his backpack and then, almost in afterthought, he stood aside to reveal the ground where he'd knelt. On the trail was a bandana, moon-silver and dirt-smeared. If this had been a proper trail I would have assumed that a random hiker had wiped grime from his face and gotten careless stashing the bandana, dropping it.

The chance of a random hiker, here and now, was not worth discussing.

Walter drew up, winded, and crowded in beside Robert. Walter in his battered gear and weathered face looked like he'd been out in the field for weeks. Robert Shelburne in his upscale gear and cultivated tan looked ready for a photo shoot for *Outside Magazine*. As for me, I was comfortable in aged boots and a worn backpack, unweathered enough to take notice of Robert's stylish look, acutely aware of the messages we sent with the gear we chose.

Like bandanas.

Walter was now studying the bandana in the dirt. "That's his?"

"I'd lay money on it," Robert said.

"Meaning what?" I asked. "He flagged the trail?"

"No need. I know the way."

"Yeah, but..."

"He gets clumsy. He probably dropped it."

"And the color?"

Robert cocked his head.

"Silver," I said, "unless you'd call it light gray."

"Silver," he agreed. "That's his color."

"So do you read anything into that?"

"Beyond the color identifying it as his bandana?"

"Yeah," I said, "beyond that."

"I've already told you what the color signifies."

He had, yesterday in our lab. "Tell me again." Now that we're in his territory. "What does it signify about his state of mind?"

"The state of his mind," Robert said, "is often chaotic."

Walter cleared his throat. "And yet functional enough. Else we wouldn't be here tracking him."

We fell silent, gazing down at the bandana. There was no way to tell if it had been dropped days ago, or an hour ago. The ground was thin-soiled, thick with fallen pine needles. There were no footprints to be examined and identified.

Robert picked up the bandana and stashed it in the cargo pocket of his hiking pants.

We moved on, continuing our ascent, stringing out along the narrow path, Robert resuming his impatient pace again, Walter soon lagging, me claiming the middle, keeping track of my companions. I tracked Walter by the sound of his heavy breathing. For the briefest moment the thought floated, *he's getting slower in the field*. And then the thought floated away. I tracked Robert by the red of his backpack, which stood out from the green of the brush. I wondered if he was brooding on the color silver.

That odd smell came again—something loamy and rotting, it seemed, beneath the trees beyond the brush.

I thought, not for the first time today, this is not my turf.

Ten minutes later the trail jacked hard left and then like a gift the trail and I escaped the besieging woods.

We'd achieved the upper slope and it was paved by a field of bedrock. Rubbed raw by ancient fingers of ice, this field was not going to give us an easy traverse. The rock was too steep for us to take a high line, and I saw no ducked trail marking, no little pyramid of stones to point the way.

Robert quickly found his traverse, charging ahead.

I followed.

Bare-bone bedrock would normally lift my heart but not here, not now, not pinned to the rock face with a thirty-pound pack on my back and that bandana on my mind.

I looked behind me and saw Walter, just beginning the traverse. He was slower in the field, yes, but sure-footed. Not young, but surely not old.

I returned my focus to the path ahead and judged the bedrock—by its silky golden sheen and crinkly foliation—to be phyllite, a rock one metamorphic step beyond slate, not the rock we were hunting but perhaps a close neighbor.

Ahead, Robert had reached a hackly break in the bedrock where a ladder of switchbacks ascended the wall.

Chapter 1

Shadows moved across the rock. I looked up. I didn't much like the bruised clouds darkening the sky. The weather report had forecasted a chance of showers, and we were prepared for the possibility of a full-blown storm. In the mountains of the Sierra Nevada range, bad weather was not out of the question, especially in September's dying days.

By the time I reached the switchbacks, the breeze had begun to bite.

Two switchbacks up, as I was mulling the idea of digging a poncho out of my backpack to have at the ready should the skies open up, there came a clattering sound like rain—no, like hail hitting a sidewalk—and Robert up above shouted, "*Look out!*" I flinched. Rock fragments shotgunned down onto the bedrock trail. A slaty sharp-edged piece impaled itself in the tongue of my right boot. It stung my foot. I was glad it missed my head.

Walter, still below on the traverse, called, "Cassie, what happened?"

"Dislodged talus," I answered, "it's okay."

But it wasn't. Robert Shelburne in his haste was courting recklessness. I called up to him, "Be more careful."

He called down, "It wasn't me."

"What?"

"It came from that ledge, up above."

I tipped my head way back. Several switchbacks above Robert there was a ledge, slightly overhanging the trail. You don't get talus unless it's been wasted out of a rock face and that meant this bedrock sheet we were climbing continued above the ledge. The ledge was a false ridge, with a debris field hanging on its lip just waiting to be dislodged.

Robert called down, "Probably a ground squirrel."

Or a hiker, I thought. Random, or not.

Down on the bedrock trail, the three of us waited, but no more talus rained down.

My foot throbbed. I bent to extract the rock fragment. It had torn the leather skin of my boot tongue and bruised the top of my foot.

Hiker slips in the talus, carelessly scattering it, and over the ledge it goes. More likely, it was Robert's squirrel, although those were a good number of big rock frags for one small squirrel. Could have been a bear. I once encountered a shifty California black bear patrolling a ridge, waiting for hikers to arrive and shuck their packs and open the trail mix. I respected bears--I'd kept the trail mix in my pack and the bear and I each pursued our own paths.

"Let's *move*," Robert yelled down at us.

I straightened up.

If we hadn't been following his rogue route, hunting an erratic man, I might have written off the falling stones. Unfortunately, mistrust came with the job. If I had been, say, an apple farmer taking the day off to enjoy a hike in the woods, I wouldn't have given the incident another thought. But I'd spent enough years with Walter encountering the darker side of *Homo sapiens* and I did not always reach for the innocent explanation.

It was certainly conceivable that it was the owner of the dropped bandana who had dislodged the talus. And now he'd found himself a vantage point to watch for us. Be sure we were coming? If so, why not just announce himself? I answered my own question--that chaotic mind. In any case, if it was a man and not a bear, I hoped he'd dislodged that talus by accident.

If not... What the hell, Henry Shelburne?

2

GAIL HAWKINS WATCHED the three hikers on the rocky slope down below.

And then she stepped back from the pile of rotten rock. She could still see them, the after-image of them, strung out on the trail. She still could hear them, the echo of them, shouting. *Look out look out*. And then...a *squirrel*? Seriously? She laughed, silently. She had their measure, now. They needed to believe that.

Although she felt no need for haste, she abandoned the ledge and climbed up to the ridge. From here, hidden in the trees, she could track them without being seen. They could look up but all they would see was a glimpse of brown, and call it a tree trunk. The moment they looked up, she'd vanish, deeper into the trees. Maybe *up* a tree. She laughed, silently. That's where she'd be, perched at the very crown of the tallest tree. And she'd keep watch, her golden eyes missing nothing.

Now, they were nearing the top of the rocky slope. Soon they'd reach their own trees, and then it would be trees all the way to the summit.

Now, she waited.

She'd learned to wait, when she learned how to hunt.

And she'd been born to hunt.

When Gail Hawkins was a child, a terrible storm had come, and the wind knocked out power in the crummy old house and blew down the old oak, and the oak crashed into the roof and opened her bedroom to the dark sky. She had bitten her hand to keep from screaming. Her parents rushed in, her dad with a flickering flashlight and her mom with the emergency candle in the mason jar. They set the lights on her dresser and sat on her bed, sandwiching her, telling her it was going to be all right. Telling her she was brave, for not crying. In the flickering lights of the dying flashlight and the candle, they didn't see the blood on her hand, where she'd bitten one knuckle to the bone. Her mother was cupping her chin, tipping her head so that she could see herself in the dresser mirror. "Look at you, Abigail!" her mother said. "Your hair is a waterfall of gold!" Gail had looked. Her mother was right. Her hair looked different. In daylight, her hair was the color of sticks, and like sticks it didn't want to bend into braids, so she let it run wild and pretended she was a porcupine. But *now*, in the mirror, her hair was the color of the inside of the candle flame. Her mother hugged her and said, "You're my brave golden girl."

After that, she asked her parents to call her Gail, not Abigail. They said yes! It was that easy--she could change her name to fit her nature.

Golden Gail.

After that, she had her dad move the dresser so that the light coming in from the window made the mirror glow. She learned to angle her head so that her hair, sometimes, was a waterfall of gold.

After that, she learned to hunt. One day she found something in the gravel in the backyard--it was a pebble flecked with gold! She was thrilled, but she wasn't surprised. She was Gail with a hard-G, golden Gail. She showed the pebble to her parents. They smiled. She went looking for more and she found the color again and again, and her parents smiled and said, "Of course, we live in gold country!"

That warmed her to the deep.

She took her collection of pebbles to school and showed the teacher. The teacher grabbed one and rubbed it with a key, and there was a smell like rotten eggs. "Gold has no odor," the teacher said. "That's pyrite. That's fool's gold."

That stung Gail to the deep.

After that, she vowed never to be fooled again.

She read library books. She went online. She learned about her heritage. She learned where gold lived. This really was gold country. She'd inhaled its mountain dust, and that dust came from rock that covered the land that hid the gold. She breathed the air that whispered, gold. She claimed the name that shouted, gold.

When she looked in the mirror at her brown eyes she learned how to angle her head to pick up the light, and then her eye color turned amber. Nearly gold.

As she grew older, her hair darkened and even the light in the mirror didn't work. So she bought Revlon ColorSilk and streaked a length of hair at the nape of her neck, a vein of the pure true color. It was hidden under the brown hair. It was just for her. It was not for anyone at school to see, to say, that's not your true color, that's fool's gold.

She would never be fooled again. She would find the real thing.

As she grew even older, she trained for the hunt, and she grew fast and strong. She didn't tire.

When she was old enough to go into the wilderness on her own, she backpacked for days--and then weeks!--deep into the flanks of the gold country. And there she found the gold that was put there by the water, waiting for her. It was in flakes and rice-grained bits, which filled a small vial and looked pretty in the light.

It was everything.

And then it was not enough.

She wanted the real prize. She needed to find the source.

She changed her hunt. She studied more. She roamed the mountains. She went to old mines. She followed the legends. Once she found a chunk of ore the size of her fist with a fingernail of gold in its heart. It lay in a stream bed. She tried for years to find the source. She failed, but that only fed the need.

She'd been fooled once, climbing a promising ledge, the sunlight hitting rock, a flash of gold, and she'd reached to take hold, too fast, careless, slicing the back of her arm on the rock's sharp edge. Even as pain surged and blood ran, she'd recognized the rock as pyrite. She'd gotten her first aid kit and tended to the cut. Later, when she removed the bandage, she found a hard grain of pyrite under the skin. Later, a doctor told her it was encapsulated, and it would do no harm.

She knew better. It was a fool's mark. She wore it as a warning.

And she kept hunting.

Now, here she was. Opportunity had knocked. Knocked? Opportunity crashed into her like an oak falling in the wind. And she was so ready. The people she hunted were going to lead her to a prize like no other.

She watched her targets come up the mountain. They were still on the rocky part. So slow. She could run that path. She was fit, she'd trained herself. She could dash off right now and run down there, running them into the ground. Hurry them up.

But of course she wouldn't.

Now was the time to watch. Now was the time for stillness.

Chapter 2

She breathed in and out, sucking mountain air. Centering herself.

Observing.

She already knew things about them. What she didn't know, she could find online.

In the lead: male, 34, Robert Shelburne. Fit enough, but she could overtake him.

Second: the female, age 28, Cassie Oldfield. Fit enough, but jumpy. No contest.

Third in line, the straggler: male, age 59, Walter Shaws, fit for his age, but slow. So easily taken down.

She watched them, from her precipice. Female, 37, name Gail Hawkins and proud of it, fitter than any of them.

And where was Henry Shelburne? She'd seen the bandana on the trail. She'd seen Robert and Cassie and Walter huddle around it. When she'd seen Robert pick it up and put it in his pocket, she'd nodded. It was Henry's, all right.

She looked away, into the thick trees of the summit. If anybody was in those woods, she couldn't tell. She didn't like that. She needed to find a new vantage point, up high, where she could watch, silent and hidden.

She needed to know more about her targets. Out in the wild, there was always something new to learn.

She watched, and waited.

Like a hawk.

3

THE SHELBURNE CASE had begun on the other side of the Sierra Nevada range.

It was late morning on Monday and I was at my workbench finishing a report--stolen Lexus, thief's muddy prints led to the location--thinking about lunch, in truth, when Robert Shelburne appeared at our lab.

Normally, our business didn't come from droppers-by. Most of our work came from law-enforcement referrals and defense-attorney requests. Still, we had a Sierra Geoforensics sign over the door and a working website and someone looking for our kind of expertise could find us easily enough.

Our home base was the mountain sports town of Mammoth Lakes, on the steep eastern face of the Sierra, across the crest from the gentler western side with its gold-rush towns.

We ran a two-person lab situated on Mammoth's main drag. It used to be a real estate office--Walter bought the building in part for its huge street-view window. He liked the idea of watching the world go by, as he put it.

This time, the passer-by paused at our door, opened it, and strode into our lab. He gave it the once-over, tossing us a smile and an inquiry. "Good morning, my name is Robert Shelburne and I'm in need of some help. I drove three hundred and fifty miles this morning from San Jose to your delightful town. Left before dawn. Nice drive. Might I steal fifteen minutes of your time?"

Walter rose from his workbench, let a moment pass, then said, "That depends on what you intend to do with them."

"I intend to convince you to take my case." Shelburne extended his hand. "I hope arriving in person demonstrates its urgency, Mr. Shaws."

"Normally, prospective clients phone first to request an appointment." Nevertheless, Walter accepted the extended hand--politeness bred in his bones.

And then Shelburne crossed the room to me. "And you'll be Ms. Oldfield."

Clearly, the man had done at least some of his homework. I rose from my workbench and stuck out my hand. We shook. He held onto my hand a moment longer than introductions required. Not a flirtation. It was more of an assessment, I thought, giving us each the chance to take the measure of the other. His handshake was firm, his eye contact was direct. Professional.

That should have impressed me. It nearly did.

It certainly gave me the time to assess him.

He had the air, and look, of a man who took charge. For a man who'd just driven a boatload of miles, he looked remarkably fresh. He had a strong face with a bladed nose and black brows that cambered like bird wings. His green eyes were narrow. His face was all angles. He looked to be in his mid-thirties. His black hair was slicked back and feathered at the neck. He wore a multi-pocketed khaki jacket over black hiking pants. Power grooming, mountain style. He carried a stylish and very large leather satchel.

I thought, this guy is accustomed to success.

He released my hand and moved to our big map table, raising his satchel. "If I may?"

Walter gave a brusque nod.

I moved a little closer.

Shelburne set the satchel on the table and removed a box. The box was metal, the size of a lunch box, scratched and dinged. "My brother went missing," he said. "Because of this."

Walter said, "A missing persons case, you should..."

Shelburne held up a hand and opened his palm. "Please, it's a bit complicated. I feared if I phoned you for an appointment, you'd have told me to contact the police."

"We would have. I'm telling you the same, now."

"Before you show me the door, how about that fifteen minutes? I think you'll be interested."

Walter eyed the scratched lunch box on the table. "Very well, Mr. Shelburne, you have our attention. For another ten minutes."

Shelburne flashed a surprisingly nervous smile. He laid a hand on the box. Fingered the latch. Snapped it open. Lifted the lid.

Inside was a chunk of rock with a reddish-brown hue, rough and lumpy, a gravel of pebbles and small cobbles cemented together. Unlovely.

Shelburne's eyes were on us, not the rock. "You understand what that is?"

Pretty much.

Walter grunted.

I knew that grunt. Walter was interested.

I was wary.

Walter got his hand lens and bent over the specimen, giving it a close inspection. He said nothing. He kept his nose to the rock for an inordinate amount of time.

Chapter 3

I shifted. I could have done a full mineralogical and chemical analysis in the time he was taking to do this hand-lens study. Was he going to take until lunchtime? I could have gone into our mini-kitchen and eaten my lunch, in that time frame—turkey sandwich, nectarine, decadent brownie, the whole nine yards. Geological epochs have passed in less time. I glanced at Shelburne.

Robert Shelburne waited, perfectly still.

My stomach growled. I said, finally, "And so?"

Walter straightened and passed me the lens.

I put my own nose to the lunch box, playing the twenty-power magnifier across the rough face of the rock. Right off the bat I could say that this was a conglomerate that consisted of well-rounded rock fragments, primarily quartz and diorite, cemented in a matrix of sandy clay. There were a few angular black pebbles, potentially of more interest, but my focus skipped to the sparse freckling of another color--a deep golden yellow. These tiny grains were flattened, irregular, their surface pitted, so unobtrusive that when I set aside the hand lens they were nearly invisible to my naked eye. I snatched up the lens again, looking again, and now the grains stood out in sharp relief because I understood that I was looking at pure gold. Perhaps only a few dollars' worth but striking enough to silence my stomach and make my pulse leap.

And then I noticed a lumpy spot near the bottom of the specimen and shifted my angle of view and saw a small inclusion in the lump, about the size of a melon seed. More gold. Coarse gold. By definition, big enough to be called a nugget.

I tore my attention from the ore and found Walter looking at me. His blue eyes had gone brighter, bluer.

When I was kid—summer job in Walter's lab doing scutwork—he had tried to hook me on his hobby, puttering around with the geology of precious ores. He claimed to be in it for the history, prowling old mining sites, bringing back chunks of quartz-studded rock not unlike this one. By the time I came aboard officially after grad school, and then became junior partner, he had largely put aside the hobby.

But now Robert Shelburne walks into our lab with a gold-flecked nugget-bearing rock and sets it in front of Walter, like catnip.

Walter cleared his throat. "Mr. Shelburne, this ore specimen is connected to your brother?"

"That's right. And now, as I said, Henry has gone missing."

There was a brief catch in my chest. I'd had a little brother named Henry. I took in a long breath. No doubt the world was well-populated with little brothers named Henry.

Walter asked, "In what sense is your brother's disappearance connected with this specimen?"

"Everything in Henry's life is connected with this."

"Oh?"

"Let me give you a backgrounder on our family." Shelburne paused, as if selecting, and rejecting, family details. He continued, "Henry and I grew up in a small town in the gold country foothills. Our mother died of cancer, leaving us to our father's care, and he cared above all for one thing. Chasing gold. He was an auto mechanic during the week but he lived for the weekends. As soon as Henry and I were old enough, Dad would drag us along, following the veins, panning the rivers. Henry went for it big-time. He still does. He's not comfortable living in the present. He's a throwback to the nineteenth century, to gold-rush times."

"And you?" Walter asked.

"I took a different path. I'm a venture capitalist. I help companies get a start. I suppose you could say my gold country is Silicon Valley—although I'd never put it that way to my brother. Gold country is *gold* country for Henry, pure and

Chapter 3

simple. And this," Shelburne tapped the rock, "is what sent Henry into the wilds yesterday. And what brought me to you."

"Why us?" Walter asked.

"Well, *you* specifically. I found you online."

"Our website."

"Yes, and I found a couple of articles you'd written on the subject of gold."

"Those were published decades ago."

"Everything lives on, on the internet."

"Mr. Shelburne, I must clarify that I am not a mining geologist."

"But you have the expertise."

After a long moment Walter said, "Let me give *you* a backgrounder. Did you ever watch a television program called *Dogtown*?"

"Sure, when I was a kid. One of those old shows you can stream online."

"It lives on," Walter said, voice brittle.

"Why do you ask?"

"My mother was script supervisor. My father was production manager."

"No shit?"

"No shit," Walter confirmed. "When I was a boy I haunted the set, which was a false-front mining camp. For me, it was faux-gritty enough to pretend it was real. There was a consultant, a mining geologist, and one day he took me aside and scraped the gold paint off a 'nugget' and explained how that quartz pebble could be associated with real gold. And then I no longer had to pretend. I *knew* how to make the false real—become a geologist. Much later, when I was in graduate school, my thesis adviser was asked to consult with the FBI about a murder, in which sand was found in the pant cuffs of the victim. I came along. Two things hooked me. One, pinpointing the site was an absorbing challenge. Two, the victim's son sent us a thank-you note--our help nailed a suspect, and that mattered to the man who'd lost his father.

Shelburne smiled. "For my purposes, you're just the man for the job."

"Mr. Shelburne," Walter said, "this has been interesting but I repeat, you should contact the police about your missing brother."

Shelburne gave a small laugh, shaking his head. "What if I told you the police are familiar with me and Henry?" He added, "To be accurate, the county sheriff."

Walter's eyebrows lifted. "I would say you had better explain."

"Our father died..." Shelburne paused, as if to give us the opportunity to offer condolences.

Walter took it. "I'm sorry to hear that."

"Thank you. He was a bastard but he was our dad."

"Why was the sheriff called in?"

"Dad drowned. Gold country river. Hiker found the body. Sheriff's deputy investigated. Name of Vicky Bleeker. Determined that it was an accidental death."

"What happened?"

"Dad hit his head on a rock, in the river. The body was near the shore, shielded in part by overhanging trees. Which was why it had been there a day before being noticed. Deputy Bleeker notified me--when she was at the scene. She found Dad's ID in his wallet, which was in his backpack. I was listed as emergency contact. It was arranged that she'd notify me when the body was recovered and transported to the medical examiner. It was arranged that I would then come to identify the body--that was the next day. Henry ended up coming as well. He insisted. The room was cold and sterile--just like in the movies. My father's body was on a table, under a sheet. The attendant uncovered it enough to reveal the face." Shelburne took in a deep breath. "Animals had been at the body, and... A little too Wild Kingdom for me, I'm afraid. So Henry stepped in and did the ID. I owe him, for that."

I thought, holy shit.

Walter took that in. "Again, condolences." He let a moment pass. "Is your father's death connected to your brother's disappearance?"

"In some sense. It certainly upset Henry."

"Then let's get Deputy Bleeker on the phone."

Shelburne glanced at the big clock on the wall.

"Forget the time limit."

"Thank you. But let me first tell you why *you're* the one to find Henry."

I spoke. "Hang on."

Shelburne turned to me.

I said, "First tell *us* about Henry."

Walter glanced at me, giving me the long look.

I gave my partner a nod and focused on Shelburne. "You said this piece of ore is what sent Henry into the wild. He found it, and..."

"No," Shelburne said, "our grandfather found it, but it only surfaced after Dad died."

"When was that?"

"Three weeks ago. I got the call from the deputy and drove up to Yuba City, to Henry's place. He still lives in the old hometown. We drove to the medical examiner. Afterward, Henry wanted to go to Dad's place, which was originally our grandfather's place. It was on the other side of town. Dad kept the key in one of those fake rocks. We stayed the night. Got nostalgic. Went up to the attic and sorted through old family stuff, going back to Granddaddy's day. And we're wading through decades of accumulated junk, and Henry suddenly produces a letter from the old man himself. I mean, Henry saved *everything*, family photos and letters and whatnot, but this one turned out to be the jackpot. Turns out Granddad had given this letter to Henry years ago, before he died, with instructions not to open it until after our father's death. Seems Granddaddy distrusted just about everybody--paranoia runs in the Shelburne family--and he really distrusted his son, our father. But he had to leave his damned rock to *somebody* so he picked the most antisocial guy in the family. Henry. He knew Henry would do precisely as instructed, wait to open the letter. Henry follows the so-called code of the West, honor and all that. So he brought this letter he'd been saving when we went to the morgue, and then to Dad's house. The time finally came to open it. So, Henry and I are in the attic and he finally opens the letter, which says look under the floorboard under the giant chifforobe, and so we haul that monster out of the way and open the loose floorboard and there sits this ugly customer. Henry understood it right away."

"To be clear," I said, "you found the ore specimen three weeks ago, but it wasn't until recently that the rock sent Henry off searching?"

"Right. Yesterday I got a message from Henry's landlord saying Henry had disappeared. He rents a room in a big house, real old-timey place, several tenants. Landlord wouldn't have been concerned about Henry's absence--he went off on his wanderings all the time--but this time he phoned and said he might have left the faucet running in his room. Landlord looked, faucet was off, but there was a note that said *call Robert*, with my phone number. I drove up there. I figured I knew where he'd gone--off hunting the source of Granddaddy's ore."

I still wasn't getting it. "But he left the specimen behind?"

"Not entirely. He left *this half* behind." Shelburne indicated the rock in the lunch box. "It was on his table, along with a microscope and tools and a lot of rock dust. He'd split the rock.

Hammer and chisel, bam bam bam. He took half, left me half. Very melodramatic. That's Henry."

"And you're certain he went looking for the source?"

"Pretty damn much."

"He'd know how to do that?"

"My brother is something of an amateur geologist—if you'll pardon the expression. All those years tramping around the gold country, he's schooled himself in the kind of things he needs to know. Doesn't take a rocket scientist to figure he's gone hunting. Figuring *where* does take a geologist. At least, for me."

I said, "We don't do treasure hunts."

"How about to save a life?"

I folded my arms. "Is there a life in danger?"

"Henry's note could be read as suicidal."

"You just said he was hunting the source of the rock."

"That's right."

"Doesn't sound like somebody who intends to kill himself."

"It does, and it doesn't. I don't know. Look, I spent the night at his place trying to decide what to do. Early this morning I decided to do what my brother clearly wanted. So I drove up here and came to see you two. To ask you to take the case."

Walter asked, "Did you bring Henry's note?"

"I did." Shelburne took a folded paper from his jacket pocket and passed it to Walter.

Walter opened the paper and read. "This does not say suicide." He passed it to me.

I read. It was two short lines. Shaky writing. *I need help, call Robert*, with the phone number. And below that, a postscript: *rogue route*. I returned the paper to Robert Shelburne. "Yeah, this doesn't sound suicidal. Does sound cryptic. Rogue route?"

Shelburne waved a hand. "It's a route we Shelburnes sometimes took, hunting gold. The key is that Henry wants my help. He *never* asks me for help."

"Only now he does. Why didn't he just phone you?"

"We're...in different worlds. We don't communicate well. This," Shelburne held up the note, "is his way."

"Calling the landlord is a roundabout way to get the note to you."

"Not just the note. There were three other items. First, the split rock. Second, his laptop, open to that link to the articles Mr. Shaws wrote. And from there he found your website--he had a window open to that, as well."

Walter frowned. "The path you said that *you* followed to find us."

"That's right. Henry set the path. He knew I'd need expert help."

"You mean, he intended you to engage us in order to find him?"

"That's what I mean."

"And to find him," I put in, "you're supposed to follow this *rogue route*?"

Shelburne nodded. "Tradition, I guess. But it only takes me so far. Beyond that, I need you two."

I did not feel flattered.

Walter asked, "And the third item that he left for you?"

Shelburne took another, smaller metal lunch box from his satchel. He opened it and withdrew a plastic dish and set it on the table beside the ore sample. He withdrew a small vial, unscrewed the cap, upended the vial, and let the contents slide into the dish.

I thought, *whoa*.

Silvery drops found one another and congealed into a puddle.

I wanted to stick my finger in it. I wanted to scoop it up and roll it around in my palm. I'd done something of the sort in college chemistry lab, although it was officially discouraged.

Chapter 3

"*Mercury,*" Walter said. "This is part of your brother's message?"

Shelburne turned over the small lunchbox. Crudely etched into the bottom was *Property of Henry Shelburne*. "He collected the stuff, as a kid. I didn't know he still had this, until I found it sitting on the table beside the microscope."

"Still, that does not say suicide."

"I fear it might. I know my brother." Shelburne's eyes seemed to take on a metallic glow. "We're a pair. We're like gold and mercury—numbers seventy-nine and eighty on the periodic table of the elements. Side by side, brothers and fundamental opposites. But when they come into contact, they mix."

I said, "Please put the mercury away, Mr. Shelburne."

"It's not toxic, in the elemental state."

I said, "It oxidizes upon exposure to air. In its vapor phase, it's very toxic."

"Not quickly. In a small overheated room, yes."

"Nevertheless, please put it away."

"Certainly." He took a large eyedropper from the lunchbox. He suctioned up the puddle and expelled it into the vial. He screwed the cap back on, tight. He returned the vial and the dish and the dropper to the small box.

Two metal lunch boxes, side by side.

"Gold and mercury," Shelburne said. "One precious. One poison."

4
———

WALTER SAID, "Tell us why your brother might be suicidal."

"Let me introduce him first." Shelburne took yet one more object from his satchel. It was a padded envelope. He removed a photograph and laid it on the table beside the lunch boxes.

The photo was an eight-by-ten studio portrait--black and white with a faux burnt border, clearly meant to evoke an Old West vibe. The subject sat in a saloon chair with a rough planked wall as backdrop.

The subject was a very young man. Slender as a quill. Left thigh tied to a low-slung holster holding a six-shooter, hands resting on thighs, fingers loose, ready to outdraw you. He wore a high-collared white shirt, too short in the sleeves, his thin wrists sticking out, looking breakable. Over the shirt, he wore a pickaxe bolo tie and a vest with shiny stripes in silver and black and a folded silver bandana tucked into the vest pocket. He wore baggy woolen pants and cracked leather boots. He stared somberly at the camera. He was a smooth-faced wet-combed teenager whose only marks of experience were two sculpted lines beneath his eyes, as if he were squinting at the far horizon.

"That photo was taken ten years ago," Shelburne said. "I have nothing more recent."

The subject in the photo had light brown hair, same color that my little brother Henry had. My Henry was reed-thin, too. Thin-blooded. He'd worn a red cowboy hat just about every waking moment, at least during that last year. If my Henry had lived into his teens, he might have gone to a studio to have an Old West photo taken. He would have tried for a squint like that.

"Something wrong?" Shelburne said.

I looked up. Both Shelburne and Walter were watching me. Walter, with curbed concern. Shelburne, puzzled. I blinked. Eyes dry, no tears. What, then? Maybe I'm just that readable. I considered shrugging off Shelburne's question but that would have made this too consequential, something that couldn't be spoken. I said, "I'm just reminded of my own brother. Another Henry. He died very young. End of story."

"Another Henry," Shelburne repeated, softly. "I'm sorry."

"Thank you." I returned my attention to the photo, looking this time at the tooled leather belt holding up Henry Shelburne's woolen pants. A big silver buckle anchored the belt.

Robert Shelburne noticed me noticing. "Dad gave him the belt."

Something was written on the buckle, in thin curlicue lettering. I took up my hand lens.

Shelburne added, "It says *quicksilver*. Dad gave him the nickname, too."

I put down the lens.

"Quicksilver is what miners called liquid mercury, back in the day. For the color and the volatility." Shelburne gave a sad smile. "Henry liked to play with the stuff."

"Yeah, who doesn't?" I glanced at the lunch box containing the vial of mercury. "Not very smart, though."

"No, he wasn't. He knows better now but it's too late. Maybe that's why he left his mercury kit along with the note."

Walter said, "Are you saying he intends to poison himself?"

"He already has. But next... I don't know what he intends. His mind is at times chaotic." Shelburne touched his temple with his forefinger. "Even as a kid, he was uncontainable. Quicksilver was the right name for him—mercurial as hell when he didn't get his way. And he never did, with our father. Whatever he did to impress Dad turned into a flop. And then he'd regroup and try again."

I glanced again at the photo, at Henry's cool-guy squint. I wondered if he practiced it in front of a mirror before posing for the camera. Quicksilver: bright and shiny, squint-worthy, but difficult to contain. I turned to Robert Shelburne. "And you?"

"The opposite. In fact, I'd say Dad was always trying to impress *me*."

"I mean, did you have a nickname?"

"Oh. Yes. Henry gave it to me." Shelburne shrugged. "Golden Boy."

"And now," I asked Shelburne, "your father dies and that sets Henry off? Is that what you think?"

"I *know* he was deeply depressed, afterward. Of course, depression is one of the many symptoms of mercury poisoning. And that's on top of Dad poisoning. Dad spoon-feeds him the family legacy, berates him, Dad dies, Henry opens the letter and then finds the legacy rock. All of a sudden Henry's the man. The mission, which he chooses to accept, is to find the source of the rock."

"Might he not succeed?"

"What if he doesn't? The final flop. Can't even impress a dead man."

My heart squeezed.

"Either way, he sees himself as executor of the legacy."

"Meaning, find the gold?"

"Not just that."

"Then what?"

"Finding what our father was after, for most of his adult life."

"Not gold?"

"Gold, sure. But in the context of something more fundamental."

Walter, at my side, stirred.

"I'm going to have to go in-depth here. Another backgrounder. Our grandfather—known as the great bullshitter—claimed to have found a hidden ore deposit, from whence this rock presumably came. And turns out he hid it under the floorboard, as I said, and left the letter for Henry. But there was another letter—the old man was big on writing letters and setting the family to play his games. This was a 'clue' letter, flowery, vague as hell, teasing. Full of boasts. My father ended up in possession of *that* letter. And he signed on big-time. Keep in mind, this became the family legend."

"There's no need to warn me about legends," Walter said.

Shelburne tipped his head. "So my dad started looking for this deposit, dragging Henry and me along, preaching the letter. When we weren't out hunting, Dad was feeding us the bullshit along with our breakfast cereal. Fast-forward twenty years. Dad dies. Henry opens *his* letter from Granddaddy, we find the rock, and we get the bullshit clue letter out of Dad's files." Shelburne eyed us. "Maybe not bullshit, after all. You geologists will know, right? Is this rock from the... Well, you have a look and tell *me*."

Shelburne took the ore specimen out of the lunch box. He walked over to Walter's workbench and placed it there.

Walter followed.

"Like I said, Henry split the original chunk of ore and left me this half. And let me tell you, when I saw the fresh-cut face it was damned dramatic."

The fresh-cut face didn't show on Walter's workbench because Shelburne had placed the rock cut-face down.

"Go ahead," Shelburne said. "See for yourself."

Walter turned the rock over. He sucked in his breath.

I might have made a noise, myself. The cut face was blue, the blue of glacial ice.

Walter spoke. "I never expected to see this. It's rarely seen, today."

"That's right," Shelburne said. "At least that's what Dad always said. The blue is buried."

I turned to Shelburne. "It's chemistry. Your rock, where the old surface shows, has been exposed to oxygen and so the iron minerals in the matrix have changed to an oxide. That's why the color is reddish. But there, on the fresh face, which by definition hasn't been exposed for long, the iron is not oxidized. That's why it's blue."

Walter said, to me, "It's not the chemistry I was remarking upon, Cassie. It's the legend."

I replied, "You're becoming as elliptical as Mr. Shelburne."

"I'm just gobsmacked. This is, quite possibly, an ore sample from the deep blue lead."

Shelburne said, "Looks like I found the right guy."

"The blue lead." I searched my memory. "Isn't that…"

"Extraordinary," Walter said. "Mr. Shelburne has walked into our lab with a rock that every geologist who harbors an interest in the story of gold dreams of seeing. The blue. The deep blue gold-bearing gravels. The blue lead."

Shelburne nodded. "That why you wrote those two articles? On the geology of the blue."

"I wrote them at a time when I was hobbying."

"Well, my brother found them."

"When?" I asked.

"I assume after we found the rock under the chifforobe. I assume he went searching online, as only Henry could obsessively search."

I glanced at my partner. "You never told me about the articles."

"I didn't think you'd be interested."

That stung. He was right. I said, "I am, now."

"Legend has it," he said, to me, "that long ago there was one special river channel, different from all others, where the gold-bearing gravels were deposited. The miners followed that path and they called it the 'lead' because they thought it would lead them to their heart's desire."

"Isn't that where legends normally lead?"

Walter smiled. "Of course, the *reality* is that there were many channels, many tributaries. But down deep in those channels, down in the gut, the legend is true because the gravel of the lower stratum is a striking blue color and it's there where the gold ran rich."

"You're talking about the ancient river channels."

Shelburne said, "The lost rivers of California."

"They're not lost," I said. "They're simply hidden by subsequent geologic events. Eruptions. Uplift. Erosion."

Shelburne turned to Walter. "She doesn't have much romance in her soul, does she?"

I flinched. Don't I?

5

"Speaking of romance," I said, to Shelburne, "what about you? The blue lead and the gold in the rock? Your eyes lit up."

He lifted his palms. "You got me."

"I do?"

"We're all products of our childhood. Those lessons run deep. You do what you can with them when you grow up. Take them to heart, rebel, whatever. But you don't erase them. I found my niche in the business world but sure, I still have an eye for gold."

"Then why didn't you join Henry in the hunt?"

"He didn't invite me."

"But he's inviting you now."

"Yes, the clues. That's the way Henry communicates. His memory is damaged so he plays these little games. They started as a mnemonic, a way to remind himself of things. Remind others. And it became ingrained. The way I read the clues he left behind this time, he wants me to follow him, help him."

"Help him find the gold?"

"Help him if he doesn't."

"Or do both?"

Shelburne abruptly unzipped his jacket. Underneath, he wore a slim green T-shirt with a Club One Fitness logo. He lifted the shirt. For a bizarre moment I thought he was showing off his gym-toned abs, and then I noticed the belt holding up his hiking pants. It was a tooled leather belt with a big silver buckle.

I couldn't read the curlicue lettering without coming closer but I knew what it said. *Quicksilver*.

"Henry left the belt behind, as well. I'll be wearing it until I find him."

I thought, very effective. If Shelburne had practiced this pitch in front of a mirror he could not have performed it more convincingly. Isn't that what venture capitalists prized?

Shelburne let his shirt drop. "Henry's a wounded soul. Please help me find him."

And then I felt unduly suspicious and very small. I glanced at Walter.

He lifted his eyebrows.

Decision time. Technically, because I was junior partner, Walter had the final say in taking a case. In practice, we usually decided jointly. This time, clearly, he was seeking my input. Were we going to sign on to find Henry Shelburne? If so, I needed to proceed with the understanding that this case could dredge up the past. Two Henrys, the one already resonating with the other. Funny thing, much as my brother's death took up residence in my heart, it had readied eleven-year-old me for the promise of Walter's lab, where something could be *done* about calamities and bad shit. If I'd taken a safer path—an apple farmer, like my uncle—would that have been easier? No expectation of dealing with past calamity. Just a never-ending supply of applesauce in the cupboard.

Walter cleared his throat.

I would have preferred if Robert Shelburne's brother's name had been, say, George. But it wasn't. I met Walter's look.

He said, to Shelburne, "Before we go any further, we'll want to speak with Deputy Bleeker."

6

DEPUTY VICKY BLEEKER suggested we consult via Zoom because she had something to show us.

Her face, boxed onscreen, was overly bright and shiny, floodlit by a fluorescent ceiling panel. She wore a tan shirt with pointy pocket flaps, and a black tie. Her sleeve patch was black and gold. Her gold badge was a five-point star on a black background. Her hair was dark brown, pulled back in a bun so tight it looked like it must hurt. She had a wide mouth that tightened into severity when she wasn't speaking.

The wall behind her was beige, its only decoration a huge topographic map of the county.

The topo map impressed me.

Deputy Bleeker--*Vicky* as she told us to call her--impressed me with her intense focus on the matter of the Shelburne case. Shelburne had explained how his brother asked for his help, leaving the ore sample and the website opened to Sierra Geoforensics and the links to Walter's blue-lead papers. Walter had explained how Shelburne showed up at our lab and made his case to us, requesting our help. Deputy Bleeker took that in. Then, rather than jump ahead to the item she wished to show us, she began with the call, three weeks ago, that had summoned her and a hastily assembled response team to the South Yuba River, where a body had been found.

Walter asked, "Who called in the discovery?"

"A hiker," she said, "female, anonymous. Our front desk took the call. Hiker said she'd seen a disfigured body in the river. She gave the coordinates and hung up."

"Disfigured by animals, I understand."

"Possum."

I'd once surprised a possum eating the remains of a squirrel in my backyard. It had turned on me and hissed, its long scaly tail whipping. I must have flinched, now, at the memory.

Vicky looked at me, mouth compressed into that severe line. Then she said, "Possums do a job. Clean up."

"Right," I agreed. They do. Still.

Shelburne, I saw, had momentarily bowed his head.

"Vicky," Walter said, "what can you tell us about the scene?"

"The victim, Cameron Shelburne, was found facedown in the water near the river bank. My responders recovered the body. I worked the scene on the river bank, where he'd left his gear."

"Had he drowned?"

"Yes. Precipitated by a skull fracture that knocked him unconscious. Possibly he lost his footing, wading, and hit his head on a rock. Fell facedown. The water was shallow but it doesn't take much, facedown."

"What was he doing in the water?"

"Panning for gold, it looked like."

"You found the pan?"

"We did. It was not far from him, bumping up against the river bank. Green, plastic--that's what modern prospectors use, not your old-fashioned iron pan. It's lightweight. So your hands don't get so tired."

Chapter 6

Walter smiled. "You're knowledgable, Vicky."

I thought, sounds like you might have done some panning yourself, Vicky. Well, her territory was the gold country.

"It's common knowledge," the deputy said.

Walter nodded. "And your theory would be that Cameron Shelburne was panning for gold when he lost his footing?"

"It would."

Made sense, I thought. Perch on a flattish boulder in the river, squat down, swish your pan around. The boulder is slick, you lose your balance. Or, you're *in* the water on the riverbed, standing on those hopefully gold-bearing gravels, and it's cold and your legs cramp. I asked, "What was he wearing?"

She said, "Sun hat with a chin strap, long-sleeve shirt and pants--quick-dry nylon--and river shoes. The ones with mesh tops and grippy rubber soles."

Sounded like my field gear, around rivers. So, he was either on the boulder, or wading on the riverbed. I asked, "What other gear was found?"

"Backpack. Opened at the top. A nylon parka was stuffed in, like he'd removed it, didn't need it any longer."

"Was it a hot day?'

"Weather records put it in the eighties."

"Was the water cold?"

"It'd be warmer in the shallows. But yes, cold water."

True. Still, you're bending over the pan, swishing it around, with the hot sun on your back. I tried to make something more of the scene, and failed.

Walter cleared his throat. "Vicky, you have something to show us? Part of his gear?"

"Yes. A water bottle." She folded her arms and angled her head to direct her gaze at the box with Robert Shelburne's face. "I'd like you to ID it, if you can."

He shrugged. "Sure."

"Hang on," I said. "Vicky, was the bottle with his gear? Is there some reason to think it wasn't his?"

The deputy shifted her gaze to me. "The bottle was not with his gear. Or on his person. It was found just downstream from where he, and his gear, were found. It was uncapped, partially filled with river water, with a bubble at the bottom so that it floated upside down. A buckle clip was attached to the cap end. I assume that weight had tipped it. It got caught in some trash. Plastic bags and beer cans and fishing line and whatnot. People treat the river like a dump." Her folded arms tightened. "Anyway, the bottle was found about a week ago by one of our responders, who lives in the general vicinity of the Yuba, who was out for a hike." Vicky shifted her attention to Shelburne. "Silvia was on the response team. That's why she thought of your father, when she found the bottle--she thought it might have belonged to him."

Shelburne gave a nod.

I thought that over. "Was there a water bottle found with his pack?"

"Yes. One, Nalgene, thirty-two ounces, wide-mouth, stowed in the right-hand mesh pocket of his pack. The left-hand pocket was empty."

"Could be where he normally stored a second. I mean, people usually bring two bottles. So, makes sense that the bottle your responder found was his?"

"Yes. This is why I wanted to get an identification from Robert. We have the belongings of Cameron Shelburne in evidence lockup, including the clothing removed by the medical examiner, and I'd like to close out the case and dispose of the belongings. Including the bottle, if it belonged to Cameron Shelburne."

"I thought the case was closed. Determined accidental death?"

"Yes. But we've been holding the belongings in order to get written authorization from next of kin, in regard to the disposal. Once the post-mortem report was completed, I emailed Robert, who said he did not want the belongings. To be thorough, I emailed Henry, who did not respond. I decided to give it another week, given Henry's understandable state of mind. When I'd met him at the morgue, he exhibited extreme distress." She added, "Robert was more controlled." She shrugged. "People have different reactions to trauma. My job isn't to judge."

Seemed to me she was a little judgy, right now. I thought, comes with the job.

Robert Shelburne said, "My brother and I are as unlike as oil and water."

As mercury and gold, I thought.

"Vicky," Walter said, "might we see this unidentified water bottle?"

"Yes." She bent, dropping out of camera view, and then reappeared, holding up a water bottle. It was a Nalgene, thirty-two ounces, wide-mouth, same make and dimensions as the one stowed in the backpack. Standard choice for those engaged in outdoor sports. I supposed gold panning qualified. The hanging buckle clip she'd mentioned was attached: carabiner at one end--to hook onto a belt or pack strap or whatever--and a webbed buckle attached to the carabiner, and attached to the other end of the buckle was a rubber ring which fastened under the collar of the bottle. I could understand how the bottle got upended in the river--the clip was heavy enough to tip it.

"Robert?" Vicky prodded. "You recognize that?"

He had been looking closely, leaning slightly forward, crowding our already crowded group around Walter's desktop. He said, "The bottle? Sure, he's used that kind. The buckle clip? I don't recall. Keep in mind, it's been a good long while since I was out packing and camping with my father."

The deputy regarded him. "I'm going to take that as a possible ID, especially given the location it was found. Especially given the empty mesh pocket of his pack. It was a hot day. You don't go out on the Yuba on a hot day without water. I'd carry two bottles."

I said, "So he would have clipped it to, say, his belt when he was panning in the river. But he had to have unclipped it, given that it floated away. So he unclipped, drank--drained the bottle--and then what? Lost his balance, let go of the bottle, took a fall."

"I suppose," Shelburne said.

"What about the pan? It was bumped up against the river bank. Did he just let go of the pan, when he was unclipping the water bottle? Or maybe he set it on a boulder, and it slipped off, into the water."

Shelburne turned to me. "Your point?"

I wished I had one. "I'm just trying to understand the scene."

Vicky said, "I put it together the same way. So, Robert, can we ID this bottle?"

"Yes, right, fine," Shelburne said. "We'll call it his. If you're asking, do I want it? No. Henry? I'll speak for him. No. In fact, I'll take responsibility and decline, on behalf of my brother, for the entire collection of my father's belongings. We don't want them. Henry has his own gear. Henry doesn't need a dead man's gear. As you took note, my brother was upset about his death."

She nodded. "As you say." The bottle disappeared. "Now, what is your plan? And what do you need from me?"

"My plan is to find my brother. We're checking in with you at Walter's request."

She folded her arms again, fingers anchoring on the sleeves of her tan shirt, wrinkling the fabric.

"And of course," Shelburne added, "I welcome any suggestions you have, in the matter of finding Henry."

"Is he vulnerable?"

Chapter 6

"Yes, and no. He suffers the effect of mercury poisoning--as you saw, when you met him. But he's been on his own for years-- much of that time tramping around the wild--and I suspect he's adapted."

She glanced over her shoulder at the big topo map on the wall. "If I need to arrange a full search and rescue, I'll need time. And resources."

"I'm not requesting that," Shelburne said. "At least, at the moment. Right now, I have the resource I need to find my brother." He glanced at Walter. "At least, I hope I do."

Walter said, "*I* would need to know that we can call on Vicky if a full SAR mission seems warranted."

She unfolded her arms. "You have a satellite phone?"

"We do."

"As do I," Robert added.

She said, "It's not always possible to get a signal in those canyons. Message your location, when you can. That is, Walter, if you are signing on with Robert? Given your relevant expertise, with the rock specimen and the blue lead?"

"You're familiar with the lead?"

"Of course. This is gold country. It's almost a legend. Can't say I knew much about it, though, until Robert just explained why he wanted to hire *you*. So, Walter, are you signing on?"

Shelburne watched us.

Walter and I exchanged a glance.

And looking at Walter put me in position to look over his shoulder, at the lab's far wall, where a poster hung. It's from the Disney flick *Alice in Wonderland*, the part where Alice is tumbling down the rabbit hole. Walter likes the message: you follow the evidence wherever it takes you, down the rabbit hole if you must.

That's where Henry the wounded soul had evidently gone.

I'd never been a fan of Alice, or her topsy-turvy world. And right now I was, in particular, not a fan of that whacked-out character she meets, the Mad Hatter. Back in Chem 101 I'd learned about the effects of mercury—and in a textbook sidebar, the reason the hatter went mad. Back in the day, hat-makers used mercury in the process of curing animal pelts to make hats. Day in, day out, breathing in the vapors. It affected speech, coordination. It led to mental instability. Hallucinations. Dementia.

Mad as a hatter.

And now we were gearing up to go hunting for Henry Shelburne who, according to his brother, suffered the effects of mercury poisoning. Who left behind his vial of mercury as a fare-thee-well.

Who was reminding me of my own little brother, who suffered the effects of a genetic disorder. Who died while I was looking out the window.

Henry Shelburne and Henry Oldfield, each of them damaged goods.

So yes, I'm on board with taking this case. Let's find the Henry who is still in need of help.

I said, to Walter, to Shelburne, to Vicky, "Yup."

Walter nodded. "As my partner indicated."

7

"Mr. Shelburne," Walter said, "before we proceed we'll require your signature on a contract. And a retainer."

Shelburne flashed a grateful smile and took out his checkbook. Walter went to the file where we keep our brochures and reports and contracts. They sat together at the map table.

When they'd concluded the paperwork, Walter moved to our mini-kitchen to start a fresh brew of coffee--this being a ritual he likes to indulge, if the client is willing—his version of breaking bread together, a symbolic sharing of the basics in life, establishing trust.

Shelburne packed away the photograph and the mercury kit. Exhibits no longer required.

I turned to the blue-faced rock.

Striking as it was, the blue face was not going to get us where we needed to go.

There was a better clue cemented in the rock. A crackerjack

clue. I assumed Henry the amateur geologist had noticed it, as well. Why else grab his microscope?

I grabbed mine.

Mine—well, Walter's and mine—was a bulk-specimen stereoscopic scope. It had an articulated arm that could lift and reach and twist and accommodate a thick object like this chunk of ore. It looked vaguely prehistoric. I'd wager it cost more than Henry's.

I placed the rock on the stage and focused in on the angular dark pebble.

The digital camera built into the scope sent the view to the attached monitor.

Under magnification, the pebble showed its structure, a mosaic of tiny interlocking grains that made the rock tough, that shouted its name.

Hornfels—very very cool.

Even cooler was the exquisite crystal with a black Maltese cross piercing its heart.

Walter brought me a mug of coffee and paused to admire the magnified pebble. He lifted his hand. We high-fived. He said, "I believe I'll start with the maps and see if that hornfels can lead us to its parent." He headed to our map cabinet.

Shelburne took his place, brew in hand. "Parent?"

"The source," I said. "The jackpot."

"Now you're speaking my language."

I resumed my own. "That pebble is chiastolite hornfels, which..."

"What does that mean?"

"Chiastolite from the Greek *khiastos*, meaning a cross. Hornfels from the German, meaning horn rock, because it's flinty and sharp-edged."

"The names aside—what does it mean for our search?"

Chapter 7

I took a sip of steaming coffee, a celebration in honor of the coolness of geologic names.

Shelburne drummed his fingers on his coffee mug.

I said, "It narrows the neighborhood. Notice that the edges of that pebble are still angular. That means it was not transported far from its source. If a stream had carried it far, pounding it against other rocks, wearing it down, the edges would be rounded. But they're angular and that tells us the source was a nearby hornfels zone."

"How do we find that?"

"Hornfels is very site specific—it's not all over the place."

Shelburne glanced at Walter at the map cabinet. "Meaning look at a map?"

"To begin. But hornfels zones can be small and not always mapped."

"So we could be shit-out-of-luck?"

"Not necessarily. We can look for the birthplace. Hornfels gets born when a dike of hot magma intrudes the rock already in place—call that the parent rock. The dike cooks the parent rock, metamorphosing it. And then the magma cools and hardens into igneous rock."

"You have a name for that one?"

"Most likely diorite."

"Meaning some definition from the Greek?"

"Meaning we have diorite pebbles in the ore specimen. So that's one signpost we'll look for."

Shelburne nodded. "And what about the cross?"

"That's a gift. That tells us the nature of the parent rock. The chiastolite is a carbon inclusion, which suggests that the parent rock contained organic matter which became the carbon. So that parent rock is likely a carbonaceous slate that got cooked into chiastolite hornfels when the magma intruded."

"Could Henry have figured that out?"

"You said he's an amateur geologist."

"He's also a romantic. He'd follow that cross and call himself a crusader."

"We'll follow the clues and call ourselves detectives. And if we keep our eyes open, and read the geology, we'll find our way to a dike of diorite that is sheathed by a ring of hornfels--and that 'horn rock' will be studded by chiastolite crosses." I lifted my coffee mug, a toast. "Here's to romance. Geology gets downright sexy."

Shelburne grinned. "You put on a good dog-and-pony show."

"It's not..."

"It's a compliment."

I shrugged. It was really more of a petrology-and-geochemistry show, but never mind.

Walter called out, from the table beside the map cabinet, "Come on over and let's see where we are."

Shelburne and I joined my partner.

Walter was hunched, hands pinning a map to the table. It was a geologic map of the gold country, with symbols showing the major rock units. Walter's crosshatched hands were weathered, symbols themselves of his years in the field reading the rock.

"This is the Mother Lode," he said. "It's roughly three hundred square miles. If we narrow that to likely hornfels neighborhoods, we're looking at many dozens of square miles."

"I can do better than that," Shelburne said.

Walter looked up, from map to client.

"I can narrow it down to about twenty square miles." Shelburne ran his finger across a slice of the gold belt. "That's where my father searched, following the clue letter. That's where he dragged Henry and me searching. What you need to do is figure out *where* in that neighborhood this rock came from. That's where Henry will be searching."

"Then we'll want a larger-scale map." Walter moved to the map cabinet. "Meanwhile, help yourself to more coffee, Robert. We have donuts, as well."

The coffee ceremony had expanded, I saw. Donuts. First-name basis. Walter had just welcomed Robert Shelburne onto the team.

Shelburne smiled. "You have any glazed?"

Walter and I spent the remainder of the day completing paperwork for a current case, shuffling appointments, and doing a deeper analysis of Henry Shelburne's ore specimen.

Meanwhile, Robert Shelburne did some errands and booked himself a motel room for the night.

We planned to leave first thing next morning.

Walter texted our timing and the coordinates for our route to Deputy Bleeker.

Around six, Robert--we were all on a first-name basis, now--brought in take-out from the Thai restaurant in town. Good choice.

Walter and I worked another couple of hours, then called it a night. Catch a good sleep before tomorrow's trek.

At home, packing my backpack, I remembered to add river shoes.

I packed two Nalgene bottles, one in each of the pack's mesh pockets. I already had a couple of carabiners in my gadget kit--handy for clipping things like flashlights and water filters to a tree branch. I'd never used a carabiner buckle clip. Well, I'd never done gold panning, didn't intend to, but I could see a buckle clip coming in handy to keep the water bottle at the ready, under the hot sun. Actually, it might be useful in other situations. I made a mental note to pick one up next time I was at REI.

Later, in bed, trying to get to sleep, my mind kept drifting to Henry Shelburne. Out in the wild, waiting for his brother. Looking like the Henry in the photo because I could not conjure up an alternative. Squint-eyed, on some mission.

In need of finding, or not.

Either way, we'd signed on to find him.

8

Next morning, we left at dawn, taking Robert's upscale Land Rover.

We drove a hundred and fifty miles on the high-desert highway that flanked the steep eastern side of the Sierra Nevada range, and then crossed the spine of the Sierra to the lush western flank, deep into gold country, deep into the heart of the Mother Lode.

I rode in front, chatting on and off with Robert, probing, trying to find out what a venture capitalist in Silicon Valley actually did. He was blunt: scout talent, kick off startup companies, have fun, make money. No philanthropy? I asked. He laughed. Not into opera or struggling soccer clubs. He did give a sizeable donation to a food bank every year. It made him feel good. He liked feeling good about himself. I thought, what you see is what you get, with Robert Shelburne.

In turn, I told him about a few cases we'd worked. Help solve crimes. Bring justice, for the victims. I began to feel a little sanctimonious. I added, and have fun. Reading the rocks and solving the puzzles is downright fun.

He threw me a conspiratorial wink.

Walter, in the back seat, didn't add much to the conversation. He was re-reading Waldemar Lindgren's *Tertiary Gravels of the Sierra Nevada of California*--meaning, the gold-bearing gravels. The book was a classic. An original copy would fetch a price in the hundreds. Walter had a hardcover on his shelf, dating back to his hobbying days. He'd downloaded the ebook to his tablet for this trip.

He read in pixels for online research, taking part in forums, sharing docs with colleagues, and such. But he preferred to read books on paper—poetry, biographies, and mysteries, from the current crop all the way back to Sherlock Holmes because, he liked to point out, Sherlock was the first forensic geologist, albeit fictional.

This morning, as we waited in the cold outside the lab for Robert to pick us up, I'd teased my partner. "The bible of the deep blue lead in *pixels*?"

He'd replied, drily, "The font can be enlarged."

For the past couple of years, Walter has been making snarky comments about the tests of aging.

Now, as I rode upfront in the Land Rover, I could not help glancing into the side-view mirror, spying on Walter in the back seat. Hair grayer than when I'd last paid attention?

Funny thing: Walter had looked old to me when I first met him. I was eleven and he was in his early forties. To a kid, that was old. Over the following years as I worked in the lab—part-time after school and full-time in the summers—the only aging I paid attention to was my own, particularly when I crashed into my teens. Then, during my college years, I would come home for the summers and grace the lab with my learning, spouting textbook tidbits like they were insights. During that stretch, I didn't notice either of us aging. I was too busy proving myself. By the time I'd completed grad school and took my book-learning back into the field, what I noticed was the authenticity of Walter's skills.

Old? He'd perhaps grown a bit vain, fretting over his graying hair and creasing face.

I turned from the mirror and directed my attention to the scenery.

The Mother Lode was mostly unknown to me. Not my country. It was pretty enough, and I never met mountains I didn't love, but I was a stranger here.

The road worsened. Ungraded, now.

In the back seat, Walter was still deep in Lindgren.

I'd downloaded Lindgren, as well, given the nature of our mission, trying to up my game.

Lindgren, I thought, could not have predicted the can of worms he was opening with his guideposts to gold.

9

ROBERT SHELBURNE PARKED the Land Rover on a nearly hidden fire road.

There were no other vehicles in sight. I asked, "Is this where Henry would have parked?"

"He doesn't drive. He walks, takes the bus, and would you believe it sometimes takes an Uber. Here, though, I'd guess he hitched."

We got out, geared up, Robert locked the door, and then he led us to a nearly hidden path heading up the mountain.

Walter eyed it. "Not much of a trailhead."

"Not much," Robert agreed.

"Who cut the path?"

"Originally? I don't know."

"Not your father?"

"No. He just claimed it, and then dragged Henry and me along, marking it with the Shelburne family footprints, year after year, making it our own, blazing it with his ego."

"Did he know that you and your brother called it the rogue route?"

"I think he overheard us, at some point. I think he liked it."

Chapter 9

I regarded the narrow path in front of us. Back at the lab yesterday, when Robert showed us the route on the map, there was no indicator, no trailhead, no goat path marked--there, on paper, it did not exist. This morning, as Robert plunged us into the gold country canyon, navigating narrow roads, I'd followed along with the Google Earth map open on my phone. There was at best the hint of a path, here and there, barely visible beneath the canopy of trees and bushes. Now, in the field, up close and personal, it looked to be more of a suggestion than a way up the mountain.

Walter got the satellite phone and messaged our position to Vicky.

Robert Shelburne flashed us a smile and said he'd take the lead.

And so we embarked upon the Shelburne family route, signless at the head, steep at the get-go, infested by brush, scented by that odd vegetative smell. Fifteen minutes into our climb we came upon the silver bandana littering the ground. Thirty minutes into our climb we got hit by falling talus.

What the hell, Henry?

We might have debated the question but Robert pushed onward, upward, and it was a shorter pitch to the top than to turn around and traverse back across the rock field.

I picked up my pace.

Walter picked up his.

Nothing more fell from the ledge above and in the course of my climb I began again to entertain the theory of the squirrel or the bear.

I soon caught up with Robert, hiking so close I had the leisure to examine his red backpack. I distracted myself with the question of his pack. It was an Arcteryx Altra, one I admired and would not afford. Made sense, I supposed, that he had a state-of-the-art pack because the backpack he would have used as a kid being dragged along by his father would not fit him now, as a grown man. I also took note that the floating-top lid of the Arcteryx was stained and one water-bottle pocket had been patched with Gore-tex fabric repair tape.

I shifted my assessment down to his boots. Asolos, top of the line. Creased at the toe break, slightly worn around the edges of the Vibram soles. Broken in.

I wondered where and when he'd done his backpacking.

In another five minutes we topped the climb, which leveled onto the narrow ledge.

Nobody was there waiting.

It was a false ridge, because the slope rose another couple hundred feet into woods again, up to the true ridge, sky-silhouetted above. A couple of yards westerly, beneath the slaty cliff, a rotten patch spilled talus onto our ledge and fanned out to the rim.

We stood rooted.

Looking. Listening. All of us winded. Catching our breath.

"Let's take a break," Robert said.

We shucked our packs and sank to the rock. It was chilly. We retrieved parkas. We grabbed our water bottles and drank. The water was sweet cold eastern Sierra water, bottles filled from taps because the sweet cold Sierra rivers and lakes had to be considered contaminated with a parasite called Giardia, because some people had crappy wilderness manners. I took another drink of purified water. It had chilled during our hike. The rock beneath my butt was stone cold. There was not enough sun to warm the phyllite--even its golden sheen was dulled in this gray light. I shivered. I drew up my knees, hugging them.

Walter got out the trail mix. I freed one hand, opened my palm, and he filled it. I nibbled like a squirrel.

Walter passed the mix to Robert.

Chapter 9

The breeze that had been coming and going now came stronger, more consistent.

I sniffed for the odd odor but smelled nothing other than salty peanuts and sweet dried pineapple.

Robert stirred. "Whenever you're ready."

Walter said, "I'm content to rest here another moment."

I studied my partner. Face still slightly flushed, even in the growing chill. Hair mussed and, yeah, mostly gray. He still wore his sunglasses. His eyebrows—gray flecked with brown like feldspar in granite—bushed above the rims of his shades. He caught my scrutiny and lifted his brows.

I said, "Yeah, feels good to sit." The rock was warming beneath my butt.

I watched Robert return his water bottle to the side pocket of his pack. That, and the bottle in the other pocket, were thirty-two-ounce titanium ultralights. Major cool factor. I didn't know the price but figured if I had to ask, I wouldn't want to pay it.

Robert was a gear-head with expensive tastes. Still, you had to know what you needed in the field before you laid out good money. And if you were going to lay out good money you'd want to get plentiful use of your gear.

I asked, "Been up here recently?"

"*Here*? Not since I was a kid."

"But you still do some backpacking?" I indicated his grown-up pack.

"I took a trip with Henry a few years ago, one of our attempts to re-connect. Had to buy new gear."

I nodded. "Did you and Henry do any gold hunting on your trip?"

He flashed a grin. "It's not possible to be in the gold country with my brother and not take a passing glance at a piece of promising quartz."

"What about now? You find Henry. Henry finds the source of that ore specimen he left you? You'll take a glance?"

"I don't know. Let's see." Robert opened his pack and took out the chunk of ore and held it cupped in his hands. The blue face was hidden. The melon-seed nugget was just visible above the fleshy part of his palm. Otherwise, in the dull light, the rock looked dull. There was no sparkle of mica, or of the microscopic gold flakes. Nevertheless, Walter and I leaned in, the way you'd lean in on a cold day when somebody lights a fire.

Robert smiled. "Wicked alluring, isn't it?"

I had to admit that it was.

Walter tore his attention from the ore, back to Robert. "You didn't answer. What if Henry finds the source of this specimen? What if there is gold?"

Robert put the rock away. "My interest lies in finding Henry."

And Henry's interest? I studied the talus spilling across the ledge. It told me nothing. Talus won't hold a footprint. There was no way to tell what, or who, had kicked those rock fragments over the edge.

Easy to do, though.

I said, "Is there a chance it was Henry up here, in the talus?"

"How can I rule out a *chance*?"

"If it *was* him up here, then why?"

"You're asking me to guess."

"You're his brother."

"All right, my best guess. Watching for me. Make sure I followed his note. Make sure I'm coming."

"Not just you--us too."

"Yes, of course. He'd assume I followed his laptop clue and got the help I'd need."

"Why not just show himself now? Here we are. We could all go on a treasure hunt."

Robert gave me a long look. "Same reason he didn't just

phone me and tell me where to meet up. He wants me to follow him. Find him. Maybe it's just, me proving I'll make the effort to help him."

"Okay," I said.

Robert suddenly pushed to his feet. He walked over to the talus pile and picked up a nasty-edged rock fragment. He angled his wrist and flung it, like you'd skip a rock. It sailed out from the ridge, a good distance, then arced down. Then he found another spot and scuffed his foot, dislodging a small pile of rotten rock. The stuff skittered, some of it skittering over the edge. It did not arc.

Nobody had *thrown* rocks down upon us. So, accidental.

Robert turned to us. "My call? A squirrel or two."

Or, I thought, a random hiker scuffing his feet.

"We good?"

Walter and I exchanged a look. A nod.

We're good.

10

Gail Hawkins had found a new lookout to watch them down below on the ledge. They did what she'd expected, sat and rested and drank and ate. Recovering from their climb.

She could not hear what they talked about, but she hoped it was how to find what they were looking for.

When Robert took the rock out of his pack, she was electrified.

She trained her binoculars on it. The binoculars were high-power Celestron, the best. She had excellent vision but even her golden eyes couldn't pick up the fine detail. Through the high-power lenses, she was *there*. She focused in on the rock in Robert's hands. She had an A-1 closeup of a nugget. Even Cassie, sitting right next to Robert, didn't get that close a look.

Gail was privileged.

When Robert put the rock away, and they started talking again, Gail's mind wandered to her first taste of real gold.

When she was twelve she went on a school trip to Sutter Creek, where gold was first found in California, a legendary place. But now it was tarted up for tourists. There was a sluice where the kids could pan for gold. There was a fake miner dressed in old-time clothes and he salted gold flakes into the watery sand in the trough. But it didn't matter how fake the setup was. The gold flakes were real. Scooping sand out of the water and swishing it around in her pan was real. She was a natural. She quickly got the hang of swishing out the sand she didn't care about, leaving behind the tiny golden specks. All the sounds around her went away—the other kids' chatter, the miner talking and talking, the teacher and chaperones asking where to get lunch. All she could hear was her heartbeat. All she could see was the gold. She put a finger into the pan and a tiny flake stuck to her fingertip. She put her fingertip to her nose, and sniffed. There was no smell. She put the flake on her tongue. There was no taste.

The kid beside her at the sluice looked at her like she was crazy.

"The gold is pure," she told him. "It's not fool's gold."

"You're a fool," he said and stuck out his tongue.

She looked at him. He was background, he didn't matter. He was like all the other kids here, and the teacher, and the chaperones, all of them Level-4 people. She had categories for people, so she'd know who mattered, and who didn't, so she wouldn't waste time. The fake miner was Level-4, too, but right now he was watching her closely. He'd seen her tasting the gold. She swallowed the flake on her tongue. She picked out another from her gold pan and put it in her mouth. If he did anything about it, if he spoke to her, he would become a Level-3 and she would have to do something about him. Apologize. Or tell him she was sick and gold made her well. Or, tell him her parents were lawyers and would sue him for harassment. But the miner just gave her a grin and turned away, so he remained Level-4.

And now her focus snapped back to the ledge. Robert was standing, and Cassie and Walter were staring at him. Gail wondered if something happened that she missed while she was wandering in the past. She scolded herself. Robert and Cassie and Walter were Level-2s, and Level-2s *mattered*.

Robert went to the pile of talus and picked up a piece and threw it over the edge. It was a good throw. The rock shard flew far, then dropped. And then Robert kicked the pile of talus, and some of those shards skipped over the edge and fell straight down onto the bedrock trail below.

Gail nodded in appreciation. Good show, Robert.

And now Robert said, a *squirrel*. Or *two* squirrels--enough little feet to kick enough rock shards over the edge. To make it believable.

Gail laughed, silently.

Robert, she thought, was good. Didn't hurt that he looked like a movie actor, one of those sidekicks who was good-looking, and a little snaky at the same time.

She had his number.

11

We busied ourselves closing up packs, shouldering them, fastening hip belts.

Robert set off in the lead.

Walter and I fell in.

We followed our ledge to the far end of the bedrock and then plunged into ponderosa pines and oaks and red-limbed madrone. A boy could play hide and seek in those woods. I wondered if Henry Shelburne had played that innocent game when his father took the family on his rogue route.

As we hiked, Robert Shelburne surveyed the woods, and then he shouted his brother's name. He slid me a look, and shrugged. "On the off-chance."

But there was only silence, nobody playing hide and seek.

Our wooded trail climbed gently, in a wide arc, eventually giving out onto the true ridge, a broad forested crest.

Here, we intersected a marked trail, the Ridge Trail. We'd studied and inked the map of this territory back in the lab.

Out in the field, I got my bearings.

This was the divide between the canyons of the Middle and the South Yuba Rivers, muscular waterways flowing east-west, coming down from the High Sierra. The rivers were transected by north-south metamorphic belts shot through, here and there, with igneous dikes.

Robert said, "We had a name for this, when my dad took us hunting gold--the Trail of Trial and Error."

We were in the twenty-square-mile neighborhood that the Shelburne family had marked, by trial and error, one generation after the other.

We were following the path of a huge Tertiary channel cut by the ancestral Yuba River.

The deep blue lead.

It was now deeply buried, for the most part.

I tried to see it through Henry's eyes, the amateur geologist, the squint-eyed teenager in the tricked-up Old West photo, and before that, the kid fed legends with his breakfast cereal.

So how did Dad Shelburne tell the tale?

I gave it a shot.

Once upon a time, Henry, a great river came from a distant land, carrying a peculiar quartz that it ripped from bedrock veins along its journey, veins gorged with gold—and here, I figured, Henry can't contain himself and interrupts to say *nuggets*? And Dad Shelburne says put a cork in it, kid, and listen--at least that's the way my dad would have told it, if my Henry had interrupted. And Henry Shelburne puts a cork in it and his dad continues. The long-ago quartz-carrying river was so strong and mighty that it carved a deep channel and laid down its load. And then volcanoes erupted—boom boom boom—sound effects, Henry, keep your attention on what comes next—and the lava buried the ancient river. *Oh no*, Henry says, the river is gone, all that gold gone. Dad snorts. Be a little man, kid, the gold's not gone. Listen up: a new age comes and the land rises like a trapdoor opening and lifts the old river channel up high. And Henry lifts his chin and looks up. No no, Dad says, you can't *see* it yet, not until new rivers are born. Here's where the tale cuts to the chase: the new rivers cut deep new canyons in the lost land, down through the lava deposits, and they slice open parts of the old river channel and lay bare the auriferous gravels. How about that, kid? *Auriferous* means gold-bearing, a little prospecting lesson for you, wouldn't hurt you to start learning this stuff if you want in on the family legend. Now finish your cereal before the school bus comes.

That's the way I imagined Henry learned it.

Who says there's no romance in my soul?

The story of the ancient rivers played out up and down the Mother Lode, producing many gold-bearing channels, but this channel of the ancient Yuba was the biggest, the richest, the most legendary.

Once upon a time.

I'd been doing quite a bit of reading.

Now, all that remained visible of this ancient channel and its tributaries were interrupted fragments that cropped out here and there, most of them already found and laid bare by the miners. Still, the blue lead was said to crop out in all kinds of unthought-of places, on the ridge tops or the gouged flanks that ran down to the river bottoms.

Back in the lab at the map table Robert Shelburne had shown us the tributary his grandfather explored, the Shelburne family's own deep blue lead.

We'd drawn bullseyes on the map, targets along the Shelburne blue lead where the geology indicated a possible contact zone between the slate and the diorite. It was a coin toss where to begin on the route because there were targets at either end and in between.

But Henry had told Robert where to begin, this time--the rogue route.

And so far, for us, it was certainly the trail of trial and error.

Out here, in the field, we were following the Shelburne offshoot that intersected the main channel and then went its own way.

Once upon a time, Henry my little crusader, your grandfather found a gold-specked chunk of ore with black carbon crosses in its heart.

Somewhere along this route.

We traveled more slowly now, eyeing the geology.

The chill breeze accompanied us, bringing the ozone odor of impending rain.

The ground underfoot was hard andesite breccia, the cemented remains of the lava flows that had buried the ancient rivers. We found a hard spine of oxide-stained quartz blading out of the ground, sign of an ancient channel buried somewhere nearby.

We picked up pieces of diorite float, rock fragments that had weathered off their parent and traveled by water or wind or gravity.

We followed the float to a place where a stream had cut back and exposed layers of weathered slate. We found a hornfels zone but the hornfels was innocent of Maltese crosses.

We looked for signs of Henry.

We listened. A breeze fingered through the pines and oaks that cloaked the trail, ruffling, whispering. Nothing more.

We marked off the target on our map and continued the hunt.

The trail dipped down a little gully, an eroded funnel of decomposed rock. Down at the bottom, vegetation overtook us. There were thickets of sugar and digger pine, and tangles of manzanita and toyon and other bushes I could not identify.

And, again, there was that odd scent.

There was a rustling sound.

I nearly called out Henry's name. A ground squirrel

appeared, and disappeared. I was glad to have held my tongue. I didn't try to silence the voice in my head. *Come out come out wherever you are.* I'd played hide and seek with my Henry, usually bored out of my mind because I considered myself too old for such games, and because Henry was too young to hide well. And because my mom and dad and my older brother and I all told Henry at least once a day to be careful, and so I always mixed worry in with the boredom. Usually, I'd pretend not to be able to find him. I'd finally yell, *come out come out wherever you are*. And you'd think he'd won the lottery.

Our trail wound back up the contour and we achieved a higher ridge top without incident.

It was still wooded up here, hardly a view worth achieving, but then again my mountains of choice were the abrupt eastern Sierras where a summit was not easily achieved but once achieved, it would slay you with the view.

We paused. We'd reached a fork in our trail. The Shelburne family offshoot tangled with other offshoots of the main blue lead and there were two paths to take us where we needed to go.

Walter said, "Which way?"

"The fastest way," Robert said, taking the high path.

I fell in.

Walter, behind me, muttered something.

Wanted to avoid this, I thought he'd said.

I turned.

He waved me onward.

The trail began to descend and in another fifteen minutes we found ourselves funneled onto a narrow path that traversed a steep slope. We were yet again closed in by the woods. It was easy going, gentle hiking, but I figured I knew what lay ahead.

We penetrated a scented grove of cedar and Doug fir and a thicket of manzanita, in which anyone might have hidden, and then we came upon a wide gully that exposed a pitch of cross-bedded gravelly sandstone, upon which my boots slipped, shotgunning gravel. Easy to do.

Be more careful.

The trail twisted out of the woods.

The trail bent sharply and took us to a precipice that gave a view of what lay below.

I halted. Slayed.

I'd seen it mapped—on paper an elliptic of dotted pale pink against a field of green. But the map was utterly two-dimensional. Here, it was 3D in your face.

Walter knew it by experience. He'd been here before, decades ago. Why hadn't he warned me? Why hadn't he said, *you're going to have to brace yourself*?

Because a warning was not enough.

There were no words for what I saw down below. I simply had no words.

12

Finally, words did come to mind.

Catastrophic event.

Those are the words geologists use for earthquakes, eruptions, hurricanes, floods.

There had freaking well been a catastrophic event here only you couldn't lay it at the feet of mother nature.

Walter asked Robert, "Is this the way your father took you?"

"Yes. It's in my grandfather's clue letter. It's a bloody monument. It's mining on the grand scale. It's what the great bullshitter called *the void*."

Walter grunted. "It's what's left after removing a mountain."

I stared into the monumental hole. "How much did they take out?"

"Four million bucks in gold," Robert said.

"I meant, how much of the mountain?"

"Forty million cubic yards."

Walter said, "You know your numbers."

Robert shrugged. "I'm a numbers guy."

I tried to corral the great pit with numbers. "How big is it?"

"Mile long, half-mile wide," he said. "I learned this shit in my teens. Hydraulic mining. How they did it. The miners had to get down through six hundred feet of compacted gravel to reach the holy grail. They built forty miles of canals to bring enough water to feed the cannons. Eight cannons, twenty-four hours per day, firing sixteen thousand gallons of water per minute to ream out the mountain. The project had a ridiculous name, though. I'd never greenlight a project with that name. They called it the *diggins*. No third *g*. Just the folksy *diggins*."

Of course they did, I thought. They would not have called it a catastrophic event.

Walter had picked up a chunk of andesite breccia and was examining it like it was the Rosetta Stone.

Out of the corner of my eye, I caught movement on the cliff tops on the opposite rim. I turned to fully look. Nothing. Maybe a hiker, now absorbed by the trees.

"In the end," Walter said, "it was mined to extinction." He tossed the chunk of andesite into the void.

I watched the rock fall into the abyss where a mountain had been. The great pit was shadowed now, clouds moving overhead, shapes moving down below. The wind picked up. For a moment I thought I glimpsed something other than a shadow moving down there but maybe it was just the wind moving the vegetation. I caught that odd odor again, carried on the wind.

Walter said, "What did Henry make of it?"

"A big playground," Robert answered. "Fantasyland."

Fantasyland. I could not stop looking. And what was empty, nothing—a void—became strangely beautiful. Where the mountain had been washed away, the ancient gravel beds were exposed in the cut cliff walls, layered like a summer cake in yellow and red and white and orange, eroded here and there into spires and fluted hoodoos. It had a fantastical monstrous beauty.

Walter said, "So it's likely Henry came this way, this time?"

"Beyond likely."

"And from here..."

Robert jerked a thumb. "Down there."

Shadows flickered, down there.

I said, "Hey guys, I think there's somebody down there right now."

"*Henry!*" Robert Shelburne's shout echoed.

All of a sudden thunder sounded, in the distance, but there was no other reply.

"I just caught a glimpse," I said. "Could have been a pack."

"Backpack?" Robert asked.

"Could be."

"We're not the only hikers in the area."

"*If* it was a pack," I added. "It was moving in that willow jungle down there."

Walter asked, "Could it have been an animal?"

"It was brown." Brown deer, brown bear. Too big for a squirrel. "Could have been."

"*Henry!*" Robert shouted again.

No answer. No discernible movement.

Come out come out wherever you are.

Walter got the sat phone and messaged Vicky our updated position.

And then we began our descent into the pit on another of Robert Shelburne's unmapped trails. Hardly a trail at all but it was the most direct way down.

The soil was too sandy to hold footprints. If there were any recent scuff marks, Robert, in front, was scuffing them into oblivion.

We descended single file, Robert then me then Walter.

Now and then, when I could safely take my eyes off the treacherous trail, I scanned the landscape below. Nothing. The lower we got, the more limited the long view became.

I shifted my focus to the near view, right under my nose. The trail was so narrow I kept brushing against cliff walls and acquired a coating of dirt. The walls told the story, without the romance. Volcanic andesite breccia capped layers of Eocene river gravels, which were interbedded with sand and clay.

Robert said, over his shoulder, "My dad called these bastard gravels."

Walter, behind me, said, "All the way down. And then the pay gravel is buried."

Yeah, I got it. No holy grail awaiting us down there, because the basal blue lead, laid down upon bedrock, was now buried beneath the tailings and landslides in the bottom of the pit. Any blue gravel that happened to crop out would have been oxidized into reddish rusty rock.

Would have been mined to extinction.

The Shelburne family offshoot, according to the map, zigzagged through this neighborhood.

What I did see, once again, was a flash of something brown, off in the far side of the pit. And then, deer-like, it bolted. And then Robert shouted *Henry* and a clap of thunder came in reply and the wind picked up and a few fat raindrops fell.

And then ceased.

We continued down the trail.

Like Alice hiking down into the rabbit hole.

13

Five hundred feet down, we bottomed out.

If I had not known a mountain once stood here I would not have known this was a manufactured landscape.

The hosed-out world of the pit was now jungly, bristling with pines and alders and willows and brush that crisscrossed in a maze that could screen an army of hikers.

The soil was gravelly. I looked for, and did not see, footprints.

We crossed a little stream—runoff, I presumed, from the upcanyon watershed. The stream wandered into a thicket of brush.

I wondered if there was a trail down here. I had no idea which way to go.

Robert did. As ever, he took the lead and we followed and damned if he didn't discover the path.

We passed through a tunnel of pines and emerged into a small clearing where old mining equipment was on display. My attention caught on the huge lengths of rusted pipe, jumbled like pick-up sticks. I stopped and stared. A man could hide inside that pipe.

Robert saw me looking. "He hates enclosed spaces."

My Henry would have been in there.

"Not hiding in the water cannon, either."

Beyond the pipes was a giant rusted cannon that looked like something out of a Civil War textbook. I still had to wrap my head around the idea that it had shot water, not iron balls.

"Let's go," Robert said.

Walter held up a hand. "Shouldn't we have a look at the sluice?" He indicated the long wooden open-top box set upon a frame.

Robert shrugged. "It's a sluice."

"I presume your brother sent us this way for a reason."

"*Yes.* The rogue route. The fucking trail of trial and error."

I thought, *whoa*. What's up?

Walter voiced it. "Is there a problem?"

Robert shrugged. "Just...nothing more to say."

"It gives *me* a problem," Walter said. "The dirty secret of the gold rush."

"Yes. So let's go."

"In a moment. I don't know what your brother intended, sending us *here*--certainly we're not going to find the blue lead down *here*, and clearly he wouldn't need a geologist to know that. Nor do you, I assume, so..."

"This is a waypoint," Robert interrupted. "On the *off-chance*," Robert glanced at me, "that Henry is tracking us, we're going his way. Ideally, we'll find him along his way. If not, along the way maybe you geologists will spot that source of hornfels you're after. If not, we'll arrive at the end of the rogue route and from there, you can lead me because I'd have no *clue* where to go. Here, though, it's just the old family stomping grounds, it's tradition, so let's just..."

Walter interrupted, "Give me a damn moment here."

Chapter 13

Robert closed his mouth.

I stared at my partner.

"It would be a crime," Walter continued, "to look away. I visited this *diggins* once, long ago, up at the rim. Looking down into the pit, understanding what happened--it's what put me off hobbying with gold. And I didn't care to venture beyond the rim, down here. Now I'm here. I'm going to see, up close, what I was unwilling to look at back then. And so tell me, Robert, what shit you learned in your teens." Walter jerked a thumb at the sluice. "Tell me about *this*."

Robert recovered himself. "Fine. Clearly, you know what they did here, but fine. The miners ran a slurry of water and gravel through the sluice. The riffles trapped the heavy grains of gold. The lighter stuff, they trapped with mercury. The metals mix into an amalgam, making the small stuff easier to capture."

"How much?" Walter asked.

"You mean..."

"You're a numbers guy. Tell me."

"Fine. You got it--the miners used ten pounds of mercury for every foot of sluice. That's eighty thousand pounds a year. Thirty percent of it washed away. Poof! I'd never greenlight a project with that level of waste."

I thought, that's a lot of mercury. I thought, Robert's got a lot of numbers at the ready. Who remembers precise numbers like that? Especially when you learned this stuff as a kid. If it were me, I'd just say the miners put a shitload more mercury into the ground than they took out in gold.

Rober shrugged. "Not *Dogtown*, hey Walter?"

Walter didn't answer. He was staring up at the rim, where the summit of the absent mountain would be.

I felt I ought to say something to my partner. Yeah, you got hoodwinked by a Hollywood facade and the reality is your grown-up hobby has a real dark history, but I understand you can be captivated by something and yet appalled when you look closely. I understand why you wanted to avoid this place.

But I decided to say nothing. Walter had said it all.

I turned to Robert. "So, your father brought you boys here. He tell you the numbers?"

"Not at first. We were kids. We didn't care about numbers." Robert pulled his titanium water bottle from the side pocket of his pack. He toasted the sluice. "Dad just let us play here. He brought vials of mercury and a baggie of gold dust. And a bottle of water. The gold was the prize. The mercury the waste." Robert opened the bottle and drank.

I wondered if Dad put it that way to his sons. *Robert, you're the prize. Henry, you're waste.*

I drifted over to the sluice box. I glimpsed something inside, caught between riffles. Something silvery. I thought, if that's a drop of mercury in there right now, then Henry Shelburne AKA Quicksilver was playing some damn stupid game.

I moved in for a closer look. It had disappeared. I blinked. Glint of sunlight on a nail head or something. Now you see it, now you don't. Sunlight's playing hide and seek.

Walter said, voice steady, "Shall we move on?"

I looked at him. He gave me a nod.

I started to move. In the process, my field of view altered a smidge, enough to get a fresh look into the sluice box, to see that the *something silvery* that had caught my eye wasn't a nail head. It was a dime.

I said, "Somebody dropped a dime."

Robert was suddenly beside me, hands braced on the rough rim of the sluice box. Strong hands. Manicured. City-boy hands on rough wood. Fingers flexed. Knuckles white.

Walter joined us. "Somebody dropped a number of dimes."

I looked further. Dimes were scattered throughout the sluice box. They had a fine coating of dust. How long must a dime lay in a sluice box in a dusty pit before acquiring at least a freckling of dust? Hours? Days? These dimes were coated.

Robert picked up a coin.

I said, "Henry?"

Robert spun, scanning the trees around the clearing. "Give me a minute," he said, his voice hoarse. He jammed his water bottle into the backpack pocket and shoved off.

Walter and I stood flatfooted. A minute to do *what*?

"We don't want to lose him," Walter said.

Hell no, we sure didn't want to do that, not down here in this jungle.

We plunged back into the maze where Robert had disappeared.

But we had already fallen behind. Although I could hear him rustling through the vegetation up ahead, I could not see him. I had no means of judging distance, no map to consult, because quite clearly the way through the maze altered season by season as the underbrush crept this way and that. I shouted, "*Wait!*" and Robert somewhere up ahead muttered something in reply but it did not matter because his voice was the clue and so I followed the bushwhacked path to the left instead of to the right. I heard Walter behind me, the rock hammer and trenching tool tied to his pack rattling like coins in a pocket. Like dropped dimes. Only they weren't dropped, right? They were placed, scattered throughout the sluice box so as not to be missed. *Henry* placed them. Who else? And spooked his brother in the bargain.

And now as I crashed through the woods my sense of smell kicked in. My nose stung. There was that odd odor, much stronger now than when I'd first sniffed it hiking up the ego-blazed trail into the Shelburne family neighborhood. It was a medicinal smell. It was like bitter greens I'd once boiled to oblivion. It had an undercurrent of rotting sweet fruit. I turned to Walter and said "What's that stink?" but he was too far back to hear me or too short of breath to reply.

I shouted ahead, for Robert, "*Wait.*"

There was no reply.

We good?

14

Finally, I broke free of the willow jungle.

When Walter emerged, the two of us plunged onward, wading hip-deep into cattails.

And then I saw Robert, on the far side of a stinking pond red with iron-rich silt. He was wading through a field of brush, peering into a thicket of pines beyond.

I shouted.

He stiffened. Turned. Lifted a hand to us.

We skirted the pond and joined him.

I expelled the words. "What. The. Hell?"

"I thought...." He passed a hand across his eyes. "Thought I might find Henry."

"But you didn't?"

"No."

"But the dimes said he came this way?"

"I think so."

Walter said, "Call for him."

"Haven't I been?" Robert lifted his palms. "Fine, I'll shout my fool head off. *Henry! Henry!*"

There was no reply.

Robert glanced up. Around.

I followed suit, looking up to the rim of the pit. There were a dozen viewpoints. More. I looked around us. Jungle. Woods.

Walter said, "And if he's watching?"

Robert flashed a grim smile. "Then shit, Henry." He shouted to the sky, "*You want the dog-and-pony show?*"

There was no reply.

Walter said, thinly, "Why don't you give *us* the dog-and-pony show?"

Robert gazed beyond us, as if still looking for Henry, but no, it seemed to me he was looking inward, not outward. And then he refocused on us. "Why not?"

I wondered why he had to think it over.

Walter folded his arms.

Robert gave a nod. "All right, here you go. It starts with a dime. Did you ever hear the expression *you're on my dime*? Dad loved that expression. He wasn't talking allowance, he was talking *I own you*." Robert unbuckled his hip belt. "So of course Henry and I would challenge each other to do outrageous shit, betting a dime on it. In particular, there was the time I flicked the dime into the sluice box, making a particular outrageous bet."

"In what sense outrageous?" Walter asked.

Robert slipped his pack off one shoulder and slid it around to access the stash pocket. He retrieved something. Then he shouldered the pack.

"What's in your hand?"

He displayed a box of matches.

"Good *grief* man," Walter said, "you're standing in mountain misery."

I looked at the brush, which was some kind of ground cover, low-lying ferns. My nose stung. It had not stopped stinging since

Chapter 14

I'd crashed through the maze. Now I realized I'd found the source of the odd odor. It came from the ferns.

"That's the point," Robert said. "The thing about mountain misery is this time of year the leaves are coated with resin. Flammable as hell."

I said, "Are you out of your mind?"

"Far from it. There's a pond behind you. But it won't be necessary. If I may?"

Walter gave a brusque nod.

"Here's how it works. You've got two boys pretty much brought up in the wild. Daring each other to do the outrageous. You've got a father who leaves them alone with dangerous toys. Some dads give their boys boxing gloves to pound out the rivalry. Ours gave us all this. So we made bets. Always a dime." He paused and made a slow survey of the jungle, of the rim. Then his focus snapped back to us. "Let's pretend Henry is standing here with me in the misery. We're facing each other. Use your imagination."

I didn't need to. Henry was parked in my mind.

"Here's how it was played," Robert said. "We flipped the dime to see who went first. I chose heads. The dime landed heads-up. I went first." Robert lit a match. He watched it burn down. When the flame neared his fingers he blew it out. He snapped the matchstick in half and put it in his pocket. He took another match from the box. "Henry's turn." Robert lit the second match. "I'm playing Henry here, of course." Robert watched the match burn down. Blew it out. Snapped it, pocketed it.

I watched, uneasy. If Henry was somewhere around here watching, what was he thinking?

Robert took out a third match. "My turn again." He lit the match. "Mind you, we went through a lot of matches before we got up the nerve to finish the game. But I'm going to fast-forward to the last turn. My turn." He watched the match burn down. Before the flame could lick his skin he opened his fingers and let the match drop. It fell onto a netting of fern. There was a tiny explosion, and then a tiny flame licked along the adjacent ferns in a delicate dance. Oily black smoke curled up.

Reflexively, I reached for my water bottle.

Before I could unscrew the cap, Robert stomped out the tiny conflagration.

When the fire was fully extinguished, I said, "Just to be sure I've got this straight—which one of you tried to set the forest on fire?"

"I did. Henry flinched. Blew out his match."

The smell of rotting overcooked ferns turned my stomach. I felt a bit like Alice navigating her inside-out world. Henry Shelburne was supposed to be the mercurial kid, the one who didn't understand limits, but now Robert Shelburne was demonstrating the reverse.

Robert waded out of the mountain misery. His boots and pant cuffs were streaked with pitchy black resin. "By the way, the game wasn't *playing with fire*. It was *reclaiming the gold*."

Walter leaned in. "What do you mean?"

"Right around here was a remainder of the sluiceway system. Henry and I found it, nearly overgrown with mountain misery. The sluice was full of sediment, and the sediment was laced with amalgam." He glanced at me. "The gold-mercury mix."

I remembered. Bonded like brothers.

"You went after the gold," Walter said.

"We went after the gold," Robert agreed. "We bled off the mercury with fire."

"*You vaporized the mercury?*"

"We vaporized the mercury."

Walter shook his head.

I said, "You've got to be kidding."

Chapter 14

"We stayed upwind. No harm done."

"No *harm*? Does your brother not have mercury poisoning?"

Robert shot me a hard look. "No harm that day."

"Meaning?"

"Meaning no harm *that* day but I put an idea in my brother's head. He took it from there. He kept messing around with mercury, on his own. Burning old riffle blocks impregnated with amalgam. Panning slugs of amalgam from the rivers and then cooking them over an open fire to separate out the gold. And Henry thought he could keep dancing away from the vapor. More like dancing with the devil."

I said, chilled, "And your father?"

"He didn't know. Until it was too late."

"*He* set you boys playing that sluice game, to start."

"This isn't about him. It's about me, Cassie." Robert expelled a long breath. "Henry left the dimes for *me*." He shouted once again, to the sky. "*I get it, Bro.*"

"So what does he want?"

"I don't know. An apology, maybe. An admission of guilt."

Walter said, "Is there a chance he wants revenge? To harm you?"

"He's had years to nurse that grudge. He could have sent me a bucket of dimes a hundred times over."

"Then why now?"

"My best guess? This is a culmination, of a lifetime of failures. Dad dies. Henry opens the letter, finds the rock. Now he has a fresh shot—a last shot—at finding the legacy. He can't prove himself to Dad. Dad's dead. So he'll show me. Quicksilver will do what Golden Boy didn't. And to do that, Quicksilver needs Golden Boy to bring the geologists who can help find the source of that rock."

"Let's be clear about something, Robert. We signed on to

help you find your brother. There is no treasure hunt, afterward."

"You've been tracking the blue lead ever since we started on the Shelburne family offshoot. You'll need to track it further, to find Henry."

"To find *Henry*."

Robert studied him. "And then you walk away, no problem? You wouldn't want to follow that lead to its end?"

Walter didn't answer.

"All's good," Robert said. "You get me to Henry and I'll take it from there."

"Still," I said, "you're dealing with that chaotic mind."

Robert took a moment. "Let me ask you something. You told me your brother died. How did that happen?"

"How is that relevant?"

"If you'd rather not..."

I said, "He had hemophilia—a blood-clotting disorder. He fell and hit his head. Bled into the brain."

"I'm very sorry."

"So was I. How is this relevant?"

"What if you'd been able to catch him when he fell? What if you'd been there?"

"I *was* there."

Walter put a hand on my arm.

I added, "I wasn't paying attention."

Robert said, "What if you could go back in time, and pay attention?"

"What a damn fool question."

"Maybe so. But I don't want to be asking myself that damn fool question some day."

15

GAIL HAWKINS SAT on an iron-stained boulder, Celestron binoculars hanging around her neck, boots planted firmly on the ground, Weatherby balanced across her knees. She was in a brushy area on the rim of the pit, with good coverage, but also with a good view down below.

She was worried.

She had watched Robert lead the geologists to the old mining display. She'd watched Robert run off, into the brush. She'd watched Walter and Cassie rush to follow him. She'd watched as he appeared near the red pond, as he'd tramped into the mountain misery, and stopped there.

She'd watched Walter and Cassie find him.

She couldn't hear what they said but she could read their body language.

They were confused.

She'd raised her binocs for a closeup of their faces.

They were worried.

She couldn't hear what they talked about, but all of a sudden Robert looked up and shouted *Henry Henry*.

She'd ducked, reflexively.

And then she straightened, because Robert wasn't looking in the direction of her stakeout. He was looking at another spot on the rim. She took a moment to look in that direction, too, but she had no clear field of view through the trees and the brush.

She waited. They waited, down below. There was no reply to Robert's shout.

He'd been on the lookout for his brother from the time he found the bandana.

She'd kept an eye out, too. Her hawk's eye. She'd seen no sign of Henry. She hadn't seen *anyone*, so far, during her quest, aside from her three targets.

But what worried her was what came next, the dog-and-pony show.

She knew what a bullshit dog-and-pony show was, it was a sales performance, to wow you. But she had never seen something like Robert's show, with the matches. When he dropped the match, and she'd smelled the burn, the sweet mountain-misery burn, she had smelled her own burn, her need flaming. And she wondered what Robert was *doing*.

The wrong thing.

Walter and Cassie looked like they thought so, too.

And then Robert had shouted again, looking up at the rim. "*I get it, Bro.*"

What did he *mean*?

Nothing good.

All of a sudden her muscles screamed. Her nerves sang.

That's when she'd unslung her pack and set it on the ground and withdrew the Weatherby from its case and set it across her knees.

The familiarity of it settled her.

The Weatherby extended her fitness.

She had come to master the rifle back when she began to

train herself, going into the wild to learn the land, to learn herself.

Her parents had worried about her, out in the wild, alone. She'd refused to stop. So they gave her the rifle. They taught her how to hunt deer and rabbit and wild pig. And soon she was able to take down an animal on the run, with one shot. Never for fun. Only for food. Only so that she could stay in the wild of the gold country for days, for weeks, fit for the real hunt.

It was then that she fully claimed her family name, *Hawkins*. She'd grown up with it, ignorant of its meaning. Thoughtless. It was just a name. Even when she claimed her name as *Gail*, she'd gone no further. Finally, she'd understood she'd been born for this. She was a Hawkins, who hunted. Who learned to be still and watchful as a hawk. Who could watch for hours, and then explode into action when it was time.

So she hunted. And she succeeded.

She found the flakes and nuggets, and twice a veined rock, but never the real prize. When she grew away from her home and her parents, when she was on her own, year after year, when she found a job and then another job and then a better one, she still made the time to hunt.

And then opportunity knocked.

And now, here she was.

She knew what Walter and Cassie could do. What *Walter* could do.

She knew what Robert knew. What he had. She'd *watched* him--an hour ago?--take that chunk of ore out of his pack and hold it in his hands, reverential, like he knew where it could lead.

But now, having *watched* him throw a match into the mountain misery, she wondered if he was on the wrong track, if his thing with Henry was leading him astray.

As they all talked and talked down there, in the pit, almost as if they'd forgotten what they were hunting, she grew worried.

She raised the Weatherby. The blued steel was cold in her hands. Her hands trembled a moment, until she gained herself.

She scanned the rim of the pit, watching for Henry.

Observe.

Be still.

She was Gail Hawkins.

Be a hawk. On the hunt.

Protect her assets.

16

We set off.

We rounded the pond, giving the cattails and the spongy soil a wide berth, circling to the far side of the great pit, passing the crumbling mouth of a dark tunnel. The little stream we'd crossed earlier appeared here, braiding with another little stream, ferrying muck and sediment into the tunnel.

I peered inside. No light. The sound of flowing water. A blast of cold air. I shivered.

"No," Robert said, "he won't be in there."

He doesn't like enclosed spaces. I got it. He was claustrophobic, among his other impairments.

Robert led us around the tunnel and out of the giant mining pit and over the lip down into the canyon below.

"We're still on the trail of trial and error," he said. "The fastest way down to our next target."

He took us by way of the bouldery outflow of the tunnel, the escape route of sludge and debris once washed out of the sluiceway and into the drainage tunnel, where the pit once and still disgorged its waste, where the father taught the boys to pan the tailings for pickings. Robert Shelburne shouted *Henry* and we listened for a moment to the hiss of water streaming out of the tunnel and boiling over the boulders as it picked up speed on the downslope.

The debris stream fed into a larger creek that cut a channel into the side of the canyon.

The canyon steepened.

Waterfalls muscled down over boulders.

The trail veered close to the tumbling creek and I thought, easy to lose your footing here.

Robert nimbly navigated the trail like he'd done it a thousand times before.

We dropped until our trail bottomed out onto an oak-studded ledge overlooking a wide rocky river.

The river ran like a boulevard through a high-rise canyon.

I looked downriver, to the west, and then I looked upriver, to the east. We were in the southern district of the Shelburne neighborhood.

Walter said, "Which way would Henry have gone?"

Robert said, "I'm sure he's been all over this river canyon but which way now? I don't know. From here, the trail goes east and west. From here, we follow the river. At least according to my grandfather's letter, as interpreted by my father. The trail meets the waterway, at the southern grapes."

"Grapes?"

"Early explorers found wild grapes growing along the banks and named the river for them. They spoke Spanish. Grapes in Spanish is *uvas*. My grandfather spoke Spanish. My father got a Spanish-English dictionary. Voila, the Yuba River. South fork."

"So from here," I said, "Henry might go either direction."

Robert nodded.

"So. Which way?"

He said, "Which way would you go?"

17

WHICH WAY WOULD I GO?

Up above us, at the canyon rim, was the spot where I'd thought I saw movement. A flash of brown. Bear, deer, backpack, tent being taken down, who knew. As I looked again, now, as I squinted and stared, I saw nothing but the native trees and brush and rock.

So the brown thing had moved on.

There were a thousand places to disappear along the canyon rims, on the canyon slopes.

Down here, we three stood out like dimes in a sluice box.

I shook off the image. So if there was a hiker, no surprise. We did not have this canyon and this river to ourselves.

Alternatively, what I'd glimpsed up above could have been the passing shadow of a cloud, a storm in the offing. I got the sat phone and checked the River Forecast Center and learned that all flood-forecast points were below critical stages. Normal.

Robert repeated, "Which way?"

I refocused on him, taking a moment, and then I said, "I'm sorry but, which way leads to the place where your father drowned?"

"You're asking if that's the direction Henry would have taken."

"Yes. Sorry."

"No need. It's a valid question. Deputy Bleeker gave us the coordinates for the site. We already knew it. We've been there many times, with my father. Cameron's last time there...well, we could envision it. And we dealt with it." He shrugged. "So I thought. Maybe Henry wanted another visit."

Robert was, I thought, being scrupulously matter-of-fact about the location of his father's death. About the sorrow of his father's death. He was being, I thought, Robert Shelburne venture capitalist of Silicon Valley. In control. Or, at least, reaching for control. I gave him a sympathetic nod.

He said, "Let's focus on what we *do* know. Henry left his laptop open to your website. He wants *you*, to lead me to him. There's only one reason I can think of, for that. The blue lead. Your expertise. Not just Walter's background--your skills too, Cassie. That hornfels lesson was skillful."

And now, I thought, he's selling again. No need. We're on board. I said, "Thank you."

"So," he continued, "the site of my father's drowning is upriver, from here. If that coincides with the direction your geology indicates, then it coincides."

Okay then. I turned to the geology. We had studied the geologic maps back at the lab. Now, out in the field, it was decision time.

Which way?

The Shelburne family blue lead offshoot splintered at the river. There were mapped outcrops west, and east. So the question became, in which direction lay the contact metamorphic zone with the chiastolite hornfels? Because that was the landmark Henry Shelburne would have sought.

I spread my hands, east and west. "Okay, in either direction we have a pluton invading metamorphic rock. A pluton is a large body of igneous rock that can cook the country rock to hornfels."

"Good, fine," Robert said. "So which one do we want?"

"Thing is, we're not necessarily looking for a large mapped pluton."

Walter nodded. "Could be a small and unmapped igneous dike."

"So," Robert said, "you're guessing at this point?"

I said, "Don't knock guessing. A good onageristic estimate can be useful." I added, "An onager is a wild ass."

Robert found a smile.

Walter said, "I like the mapped unit upriver."

As did I. That rock unit was known to have been intruded by numerous small igneous dikes. I said, "I tend to agree."

"Then let's go." Robert turned. "Upriver."

To start, that meant *above* the river. The river was a good sixty feet below us.

I paused to read a wooden interpretive sign staked into the ground. Once, the river had been level with the ground we now stood upon. And then debris had washed down from the mining pit above, elevating the bed of the river. And then, over time, the flowing water had carved out its bed anew, leaving behind compacted-gravel benches like the one beneath our feet.

We set off, at the mercy of the topography. It was a roller-coaster of a trail that took our breath away. It paralleled the river, but the rugged rock of the canyon walls forced the route to climb, traversing the descending ridges and knife-gullied canyons. Now and again the trail dipped down to steep rock benches to skirt the river but there was no way down to the gravel banks, save a dicey scramble.

We pushed on.

Finally, the trail jacked hard right and we switchbacked down to the river's rocky bench.

"What do you think?" Walter asked me.

I took in the lay of the land. The river bank was paved in cobbles and pebbles, armored with boulders. A gravelly sandbar extended halfway across the water. "I think it's prime."

Walter turned to Robert. "We'll stop here and do some sampling. We need to establish a baseline. This appears to be a natural catch basin for anything coming downriver--sediment, debris, minerals. Including, perhaps, float from a metamorphic contact upriver."

"A catch basin," Robert repeated. "That's what makes this a prime spot to pan for gold."

It took me a moment. And then I envisioned a green plastic pan bumping against the river bank.

Walter got it, as well. He shot Robert a sympathetic look. "This is the place?"

"Yes. This is *the* place my father liked to do his gold panning. This is the place he took me and Henry, countless times, to chase dreams. This is the place he died." Robert added, voice tightly controlled, "Doing his panning."

"Our condolences," Walter said.

"No need. Cassie asked about it--here we are." He shrugged. "It coincides with our route."

I said, "Not easy access."

"Deputy Bleeker and her crew parked at a developed campground, a couple miles to the south. From there, they hiked in. So she told me." He added, "Not the way we came, today."

Would have been easier, I thought, Vicky's way. But Henry clearly wasn't interested in easy.

Robert dropped his pack and took a seat on a boulder. "I'll leave you to it."

Walter and I turned to our work. We shed backpacks and

Chapter 17

took out field kits. Walter claimed the rocky bank and I headed out on the gravel bar to sample the geology mid-river.

I found a promising spot, a submerged bedrock hump that bridged the water and slowed its flow. A group of boulders gathered, forming deep crevices, a natural hydraulic trap on the river bottom where material coming downstream was likely to get lodged.

Cameron Shelburne might have come out on this gravel bar to access a place like that.

I knelt to do my own sampling of the riverbed.

The water was low. I wondered how much of a rainstorm was needed to saturate the watershed feeding this river. Right now, shafts of late afternoon sunlight glassed the surface. Where clouds shadowed, the river turned inky. A rainbow trout nosed the bottom, the fish multicolored as the gravel. I scanned the riverbed, noting how the rocks and sand acted as riffles, thinking geologically speaking this was an eminently likely site to find grains of gold. Nuggets, even. Nuggets by definition were water-worn pieces of gold, set free from the veins in which they formed. Taken hither thither and yon by downflowing watercourses, and then dropped. Gold was heavy. Water needed a brute-force flow to suspend gold and move it along, and the moment the water slowed, the heaviest grains and nuggets bailed out and settled into pockets and crevices.

Good place to put your green pan in the water, scoop up some of that gravel, swish it around and hope for the right grains to settle out, something to make your back-bending work worth the trouble

I peered into a large crack. Looking, I abruptly realized, for the telltale metallic flash. I shifted position and *did* see a flash but it was silver—muscovite mica. Still, my mouth had gone a little dry. I moved on to the next crevice, the next little hollow. The gravel here was mostly buried under silt and sand that had settled out of the river flow. I bent lower and plunged my hands into the water, wetting my sleeves, running my fingers through the sandy bed, unearthing grains of quartz and chert and mica and serpentine and every other freaking mineral that lived in this micro-niche, but no gold.

Hold on. What are you looking for again? You're looking for float. Diorite. Hornfels. *That's* what should make your mouth go dry.

Not gold.

I glanced at Walter, who was examining a specimen under his hand lens, and then I glanced at Robert, who was still parked on his boulder, staring into the distance.

They were paying me no attention.

It struck me then--bending over to reach down into the water, down to the sand--what an awkward positioning this was. I thought of Cameron Shelburne, squatting here on the bar--or wading out in the shallows to do his panning. He had to have done, at some point, because he ended up facedown in the water. Hit his head on a rock, knocked himself unconscious. I spotted a number of nasty candidates out in the river, some boulders smooth, some sharp-edged. And how does he lose his balance? Any number of ways, I guessed, but given that he lost hold of his water bottle, I envisioned the scene that Vicky had explained over Zoom. He uses that clever buckle clip to attach the bottle to his belt, but when he wants to take a drink, he has to unclip it. It's hot in the sun, he tips his head back to drink. Drinks it dry. And gets dizzy, or slips on an unstable rock. Loses his balance. Loses the bottle.

Maybe. But something bothered me about that scenario. Why clip the bottle to his belt, in the first place? Why not set it on the gravel bar and wade over when he wants a drink? I mean, he's gold panning. He's squatting in the water with the bottle hanging from his belt, and that bottle is going to bump into the pan he's swishing around. At the least, bump into his thigh. Distracting. It would just get in the way.

My mouth was still dry. My own water bottle was in my pack, which sat on the river bank.

I shrugged. We all do things our own way.

I turned my attention back to my own job here. There was a little pool and riffle pocket down there where, in my professional opinion, something worth examination might be lodged. Upon closer examination, I noticed a ledge. It was recessed, in shadow, and the riffling water was silty, but nevertheless I could make out the shape of a cobble in there. Hard to tell the texture and color but it was worth a closer look.

I reached.

My fingers closed on the cobble.

I yelped.

I'm not afraid of snakes but for a moment I thought this must be the hump of a coiled water snake, clammy and cold. But if it was a snake it would have moved, would have recoiled from my touch, would have slunk out from the crevice and swam away or, worse, wrapped itself onto my hand and given me a bite. This was no snake. This did not recoil. It simply pushed my fingers aside.

Walter was suddenly beside me. "Cassie?"

I let go of the thing and sat back on my haunches. My heart was pounding.

Robert sprinted across the gravel bar to flank me on the other side. "What is it?"

It was a moment before I could speak. "Something's down there."

18

Walter and Robert looked at the water, and then looked to me.

I said, "I don't know. But I touched it."

Neither of them made a move to put a hand in the water.

I cast about, to explain my reaction. "It felt...soft. It fit in my hand. About the size of my fist. It made me think..." The image rose, coming from some primitive zone in a dark corner of my mind, no doubt planted long ago by one of those stupid horror movies I watched as a kid. "Made me think of a heart."

Robert went white.

I bent back to the water, leaning further, angling for a better view of the ledge down there, and now I got a straight-on look and saw the thing for what it was. It sat cupped on its ledge in the crevice. I understood my earlier confusion. It was indeed rounded as a river cobble, but not solid. It was big as a heart and it quivered slightly, fanned by the riffling water.

"*Cassie*," Walter said, "what the devil is down there?"

I straightened. "Mercury." A quivering heart of elemental mercury.

Robert sucked in a deep breath.

"Well that's not surprising," Walter said.

"It sure surprised me."

Walter said, with an edge, "Millions of pounds were lost from the sluices. You'll find it in the soils, and waterways. You'll certainly find droplets in catch basins like this."

"Not droplets." I cupped my hands, to demonstrate the size. A heart.

His eyebrows lifted.

"Look," Robert said, "you get enough droplets caught in a hotspot, they coalesce. I've heard of guys finding puddles big as pillows. When my dad brought us here panning, we sucked up mercury with a turkey baster. It's all the hell over the place."

Big as pillows? A heart was big enough for me. I said, "You know a lot about it."

He shrugged. "Like I told you, Dad marched me and Henry upriver and downriver."

"But not recently."

"Last time I panned for gold I was twelve years old." He retreated across the gravel bar.

Robert took up his old station on the river bank boulder.

Walter moved to sample upstream of the gravel bar.

I finished collecting riverbed sand and sediment and minerals, hoping the mess contained float from a metamorphic contact that would tell us we were heading in the right direction.

There were no flashes of pure yellow within the multicolored collection from the river bottom.

I scrupulously avoided the riffle pocket with the ledge that contained the aggregation of mercury. It had, at first, given me a fright. And then a sense of, well, wonder--that this stuff still persisted, littering the waterways. And then there was a childish part of me that wanted to grab the silver heart again and roll it around in my hands. Dig my fingers into it like it was Play-Dough.

Instead, I left it alone.

I stashed my samples in specimen dishes and secured them in my field kit, then started back across the gravel bar, intent on that water bottle in the pocket of my pack.

That's when Walter shouted, from upstream. "*Here*! Come here!"

19

I sprinted the rest of the way across the gravel bar to the rocky bank.

Robert was already sprinting along the bank.

We joined Walter and looked where he was looking, down into the river.

The water was clearer here than at the gravel bar. It ran over bedrock and it ran fast and everything on the riverbed was glaringly visible. A metal bottle lay on the bottom. It was cylindrical with a screw-cap top lying alongside. The bottle was open. It was rusted. It was about the size of an extra-large water bottle but you wouldn't want to drink from it. A word came to mind: *flask*. In my reading last night in preparation for this job, I'd come across that word. Heavy iron flasks were needed to hold heavy liquid mercury. Each flask held seventy-six pounds of quicksilver.

A few of those pounds were scattered downstream from this submerged flask, carried by the fast-moving flow, a silvery trail. It didn't take much of a leap to assume that some of the stuff had been carried still farther, reaching the catch basin. And there, some of it found its way to the hidden ledge, where droplets liked to coalesce, where some of it formed a silver heart.

Robert Shelburne muttered, "You idiot, Henry."

I said, "Henry. You sure?"

"Who else?" Robert's face was grim.

Walter spoke. "I suppose one could find flasks abandoned in old mines."

I went cold. Flasks, plural.

"Is that likely?" Walter asked Robert. "And if so, how would he transport it? The weight."

"Likely, sure. Transport? My best guess, he's got a heavy-cargo backpack. Our father used one on outings, hauling all sorts of gear to make camp for a couple of weeks. He was a handy guy."

"Henry has your father's pack?"

"Could. Or, he could buy one online."

"Does he have any idea what he's done?"

Robert shrugged. "I've asked that question most of our lives."

Walter snapped, "I mean *here*. Now."

"You mean..."

"Damn it, man, I mean *methylation*. Do *you* understand?"

Robert snapped, "Do *I*? I'm the numbers guy, the guy who learned all this shit. As I said. Up at the pit. Down here, this shit in the river?" He indicated the globules. "Storms churn up the river all the time, and that riles the mercury-laden sediments, flouring the inorganic mercury into little tiny bits that bacteria can convert into the nasty form. *Methylation*. And that gets into the food chain."

I glanced at the river.

"I wouldn't eat the fish." He gave a tight smile. "In fact, you can take that advisory all the way downriver to the San Francisco Bay." He added, "In fact, you can take it to a lot of the state's water transport system. So, this here?" He indicated the globules. "A drop in the bucket."

Walter said, "Henry's drop."

"Yes. Hence, you *idiot* Henry."

"Then he doesn't understand?"

"Sure he understands. At some level. That chaotic mind." Robert added, stiffly, "Are we done?"

"Methylated mercury is a neurotoxin. Your brother suffers from exposure. So no, I don't believe we're done."

"Then let's *get* done. Look, please, let's just move on. Let's find him."

Walter regarded him a long moment, and then nodded.

"Robert," I said, "one more thing. What's the flask for? Why leave it *here*? Can't be coincidental that your brother leaves it here, pretty much where your father died."

"That's my brother. He makes some kind of bizarre memorial."

"That what you think this is?"

Robert gave a tight smile. "I think it's preferable to what I thought you'd found, when you shouted."

"What did you think I'd found?"

"For a moment, a piece of my father."

20

Gail Hawkins looked down at the site where Cameron Shelburne had died.

From up here, near the canyon rim, her hawk's eye saw all.

She watched them on the river bank.

Robert dropped his pack beside a boulder and then sank down to sit.

Walter and Cassie chose another boulder to lean their packs against. They opened their packs and took out small tote bags, rugged-looking. Their geology gear, she expected.

Then they split up.

Walter moved along the river bank, eyes on the ground, stopping sometimes to kneel and examine something more closely.

Cassie went out onto the gravel bar.

Suddenly, Gail heard something behind her. She scrambled to her feet and spun around. There was nothing in sight, but she couldn't see far through the thick brush and trees. She withdrew the Weatherby from its case, and readied it. She stood frozen, listening. There came the scratch scratch of a small animal, scurrying along. Nothing more. She shifted, scanning this ledge where she'd taken up position. Nothing.

She blew out a long breath. She was weary, and if she was being honest, finding this hunt a challenge. It had been a challenge ever since Robert and Cassie and Walter had hiked down to the river. She'd had to find viewpoints along the canyon that rimmed the river, trying to keep them in sight. Once they'd reached the river and chosen their route, it was easier for her--they were confined down there by the steep canyon walls. Still, the terrain of her own route was rugged and she lost sight of them more often than she'd liked. But she was a hunter and this was her territory, and she always found them.

Finally, they'd made their stop at the wide spot in the river.

She'd been damned glad to stop, as well.

Now, assured that there was nobody in the brush behind her, or near her, she turned and took her seat on the flat rock, laying the Weatherby across her knees. And she resumed her watch.

Observing.

Down below, Robert hadn't moved from his boulder.

Walter still poked along the river bank.

Cassie, out on the gravel bar, was kneeling, leaning over to reach down into the water, her shirtsleeves rolled up, her bare arms submerged to the elbows. And then she sat back, bringing up something in one hand. Gail shifted slightly and got a better angle. She used the Celestron binoculars now, zooming in on Cassie's hands. One hand was cupped, full of pebbles. Gail watched Cassie pick through them, so intent, like she was looking for grains of gold.

Better not be.

Keep your eye on the job, Cassie.

You're not some weekend prospector.

Like Cameron Shelburne, pathetic old man, ended his life *still* panning the waters for placer gold, flakes and grains weathered out of rock and carried by the water--and he never found the source, the Mother Lode. Ended up drinking the river, becoming food for the animals.

Gail's attention shifted to Walter. Still combing the river bank.

As for Robert, he hadn't moved from the boulder. Thinking about his father, she guessed. Don't spend time worrying about the dead, she urged him. Worry about the living.

Gail was still focused on Robert, trying to get in his head, when Cassie yelped.

Gail jerked.

Robert and Walter went running onto the gravel bar. They sandwiched Cassie.

Gail couldn't hear what they said but she could read their body language. Cassie found something in the water that spooked her. When she cupped her hands to show them, Gail understood what she'd found. Gail gave a little shudder. She'd found the stuff herself, back in her panning days. She could picture the silver droplet in her pan. She'd found a stick and tried to coax the droplet out, rolling it up the sloped side, but it had a mind of its own and got away, rolling back down into the pebbles and the sand in the bottom of the pan, and she chased it with the stick but it moved like it was alive, a silver bug with no eyes and no feelers, escaping her. She'd cursed it. She wasn't going to let it win. She used her forefinger next time. Touched it. Pushed it up the side of the pan, unprepared for the heaviness. It was heavy for a tiny bug. Slippery. It got away. She trapped it again, this time pinching with her thumb and finger, and it dented, collapsed, squeezing out, draping her thumb. Cold. Clammy. She'd recoiled. She'd flung the contents of the pan, all of it, back into the river. If there'd been a gold grain in there, and the mercury touched it, that base metal would have broken the lattice bonds of the gold--the noble metal--and latched on to form an alloy. She'd read about that, in her learning days. She hadn't wanted to experience it, see a precious golden grain tainted. Instead, she herself had been tainted. Now, her hawk's eye fixed on Cassie and she felt a brief kinship. Those who touch it.

As the others returned to their previous pursuits--Robert keeping watch on the boulder, Walter combing the bank, now upriver--Cassie too settled back to her work.

Good girl, Gail thought. She nodded in approval.

Now, she took her own advice, stay on the job, and the job included watching her back. She stood and moved along her little ledge, slowly, looking for sign. Looking for footprints, for a flash of color deep in the bushes. She heard nothing, not even the scratch of squirrel feet on rock.

And then Walter shouted.

Once again, she moved to her viewpoint, scanning the area until she found Walter on the bank upriver from Cassie and Robert.

They rushed to join him, and the three of them lined up like an audience, leaning to look into the water.

She needed to see, too.

There was no place she could move to for a better angle, and so she waited until *they* moved, and then she focused her Celestron on the water, and saw what rested on the riverbed.

How could that be?

Robert and Walter and Cassie were asking the same thing, it looked like--arguing, it looked like--big body language, but voices not loud enough for Gail to hear.

Still, there was one word she *knew* they had to be throwing back and forth.

Same word that sat in her mouth like cold slippery mercury.

Henry.

21

Walter messaged Vicky, explaining where we were, what we'd found, requesting a hazardous material cleanup. He got a terse reply: you want to proceed?

We had already discussed it. Whether the flask Henry left was a memorial to Cameron Shelburne, or a rebuke to Robert, once we found Henry it would become Robert's business. He'd take it from there.

Now, Robert lifted his palms to us and said, "Please."

We're proceeding, Walter replied to Vicky. We'll keep you informed.

We packed up.

We set off, following the narrow trail upriver to a place where the water ran free of catch-pools, and because we were low on potable water we decided to stop. We got our bottles and filtering kits. Shelburne's pricey model and our bargain squeeze-bag filter both did the job, straining out gut-sickening bugs like Giardia. Either model should in theory filter out microscopic mercury. I would have paid for a filter that put that in writing.

Resupplied, we moved on.

The trail again left the river and began to climb. As I

plodded uphill I scanned the cliff tops, thinking that if I were Henry Shelburne and I'd been leaving messages for my brother I'd sure want to see his reaction. There were a hundred places to view that site from the cliff tops. But that would take time, to transport the flask, to scout the viewpoints. And it was the question of time that bugged me. Robert Shelburne said his brother left two days ago. If we assumed that Henry was now shadowing us, then had he abandoned the search for the source of the rock? Or had he already found it? Amateur geologist—two days in the field if you leave aside travel time from his place to the wild—bam bam bam and he goes straight to the source? I supposed that was possible. This was, after all, his territory.

Or perhaps he'd been in the area longer. Perhaps he was long gone from the South Yuba, leaving us to our own devices.

My fickle mind now lurched to the father. Having seen the patch of river where Cameron Shelburne slipped on a rock and hit his head and drowned, I wondered again about his buckle-clipped water bottle. I reached behind me to touch the top of my Nalgene, in its mesh pouch. No question that it would be easier access if my bottle were clipped to the front strap of my pack, or the hip belt. But items dangling from a pack were an annoyance. They could catch on brush, on a narrow trail. They would bump and bounce as I walked. I'd whack them with arm swings. And if I were panning for gold in the river--with a gravel bar beside me like a coffee table--a buckle-clipped water bottle was unnecessary. Just set it on the damned ground.

The trail roughened and I abandoned water-bottle logistics and paid attention to the ground beneath my feet.

Our route now traversed a gashed canyon gully and we detoured down a spur trail to the river's gravel bank in order to do some sampling. Small cobbles of quartz and chert chinked underfoot. Of more interest was the fractured bedrock near the river's edge, which was emplaced with jade-green serpentine. I'd found serpentine pebbles in the catch-pool just downriver--float, I assumed, from the parent rock here.

Walter pointed out the rock face, to Robert. "That's serpentine. Its soils are associated with gold."

Robert looked. "That green rock? Never knew I should care."

"Good heavens man, it's the state rock of California."

"There's a state rock?"

I said, "The state mineral is gold. More to the point?"

He shrugged.

We moved on, up and over another spiny ridge. Then back down to the river bank, monitoring the cliff tops, watching the sky. At some point, it looked like we were going to get wet. How far could we get before we had to find a high spot to make camp, before the rain or the night came?

The clouds answered, coalescing to form a seamless roof.

Hurry up.

And then, down another spur trail, at a little pool and riffle system, Walter picked up a large pebble and took out his magnifier. He studied the pebble under the twenty-power lens for a good minute, and then he passed the lens and the pebble to me. I had a look. It was black, fine-grained, with the luster of mica and a hackly fracture. It was hard, flinty. I went low-tech, taking a steel nail from my kit and dragging it across the surface of the pebble. It did not scratch. Its shape was subangular, the edges rounded by transport down the river.

I nodded and passed it back to Walter because he carried the high-tech tool.

He already had it out of his pack. The handheld XRF spectrometer looked like a hair dryer but shot like a gun, firing X-rays at the target, exciting the atoms to display their elemental ID. He laid the pebble on the ground. He put the snout of the XRF to the rock and read the results on the display screen. "Chemically speaking," he said, "woo-hoo."

I said, to Robert, "He means that's a probable match to our hornfels."

Robert picked up the pebble, turning it over and over. "There's no cross."

"That could be a question of random chiastolite distribution in the parent rock."

Walter said, "She means, we keep going."

Thunder sounded, echoing down the canyon.

We pushed on. We did not have to go far. Ten minutes later, following the bouldery river bank, we hit the mother lode.

The first angular black pebble I picked up was studded with tiny white crystals that were themselves intruded by black carbonaceous inclusions disposed in the form of a cross. My mouth went dry. Here it was. We'd seen its like in the lab, looking at the angular black chiastolite hornfels embedded in the ore sample. We'd done the geology. We'd set out to find its brother in the field. We'd hypothesized where to find it. And find it we did. Here it was, a little stone in the river. Sweeter than gold.

I passed it to Walter. He eyeballed it and his face creased into a smile and then he brought out the XRF to confirm. He said, "Woo-hoo, to the max."

I said, to Robert, "We've found the neighborhood."

"So where to now? Wild-ass guess time?"

Walter turned from the river and looked up the offshoot side canyon.

I followed suit. It was a narrow canyon showing abrupt walls polished to a glacial sheen, so steep as not to be haired over with vegetation. I moved to examine the near wall, a slab of intertonguing slates and cherts and meta-sandstones. Here was the rock formation we'd been aiming for, the Shoo Fly Formation. I did not know the provenance of that name. Rock units were usually named after a patch of the local geography and I guessed some hapless geographer had been swatting flies when he named this unit. I took a moment to celebrate the coolness of geological names, to ease the tensions of the hunt.

A thin creek fed out of Shoo Fly Canyon—as I decided to name it—meeting the South Yuba River.

A confluence of two waterways.

We were in the neighborhood and now the question became, which way to go?

The float could have come down the Yuba from a source farther up the main canyon, or it could have come down the thin creek from a source up Shoo Fly Canyon. Or perhaps—however unlikely and undesirable—it could have come from both waterways, in which case an onageristic estimate was not out of the question.

Walter and I sampled a dozen yards farther up the South Yuba and then a dozen yards up Shoo Fly Creek. We struck out on the Yuba. We struck cross-studded float on the side-canyon creek.

Life just got simpler.

Walter got the sat phone to message Vicky, but there was no signal. Robert tried his, shook his head. I looked up. Narrow canyon here, not a lot of sky to catch a passing satellite. Well, at some point we'd no doubt come to a spot with better coverage.

We headed up Shoo Fly Canyon.

We began to find a new and interesting addition to the float, salt-and-pepper colored diorite.

Robert shouted, "*Henry!*"

I thought, he's expecting a reply. I nearly did, myself. We were getting closer. We all sensed it. We were closing in on the contact zone between the slate and a diorite dike, birthplace of chiastolite hornfels. We were in range of the address and the question would then become, is Henry living there right now?

We moved slowly because there was no trail, no path, just a

rock-hopping contour up the creek. We stopped twice to sample because there were two skinnier side canyons that fed creeklets down into Shoo Fly creek and we did not want to miss a turnoff.

More problematic, the slate-gray sky was darkening by the yard.

And then it began to rain.

We dug out ponchos and covered our heads and our packs with urethane-coated nylon. The clouds heaved and the rain hardened. We pussyfooted, now, slipping on wet rock and clay soil turned to slickenside. And then we were no longer searching for float, we were hunting a flat spot to anchor and wait out the rain. If need be, to set up tents. We checked out a couple of hollows in the canyon wall--hints of an alcove--which might accommodate two skinny people without gear, at best. And then Robert said, there's old mining tunnels in these canyons, and so we kept going, and within five minutes we indeed came upon the black mouth of a tunnel.

I gave Robert a thumbs-up.

He returned a weary smile.

The tunnel cut into a sturdy stretch of the rockwall and, peeking inside, we saw that it was a straight-shot gullet, empty and dry.

Walter retrieved the mini-G gas detector from my pack and went into the tunnel. He came out and nodded.

We moved in.

We shucked our packs and dripping ponchos and huddled near the mouth and watched the flux of rain and then, shit, sheet lightning smeared the rock of the gorge.

The Shoo Fly Formation lit up like Christmas.

22

Thunder followed the lightning, as it does.

Thunder echoed up and down the gorge like rocks kicked over a ridge.

Thunder got right in the tunnel with us, a long-period rumble that I felt in my bones.

I wondered where Henry sheltered—since he didn't like enclosed spaces.

We sat shivering until the thunder stopped and then in hurried consultation we chose to wait until the storm passed, or night came.

An hour later, night came.

Thunder and lightning were sporadic now but the rain did not falter.

We unrolled our pads and sleeping bags on the hard rock floor. We removed our boots and rubbed our feet and put on clean socks and campsite sandals. Walter switched on our LED lantern and Robert unpacked his stove. Robert offered to heat the water, to reconstitute the freeze-dried glop that would pass as dinner. Walter rummaged in his pack to find dinner packets, offering to share our Chili Mac.

Chapter 22

I sat, weary, with nothing to do until the water was hot, glad enough to let others get things going. I watched Robert use a Piezo igniter to light his fancy canister stove. Or, I watched him try. He pressed the button on the back of the igniter but it didn't produce a spark. He tried again. And again. He sat back, and caught my eye. I shrugged. It happens. He returned his attention to the igniter. Again, it failed. He stared at the little gadget in his hand as if he didn't accept this failure. I was about to remind him that he carried matches--unless he'd used them all, in the mountain-misery show--but the look on his face stopped me. In the castoff light from the LED lantern, Robert's angular features softened. He looked almost boyish. He looked, I thought, a little lost. I was taken aback. Surely Robert Shelburne hotshot maker of deals was accustomed to glitches. The man certainly knew gear. This gear, the igniter, was a backpacking standard, not particularly high-tech. He shook it, as if it were unwilling to do its job. He pressed the button again. Nothing. His hand shook. I straightened, in alarm, thinking something's wrong with him. His water filter didn't do the job. He's been sickened with Giardia. Or something worse. His face was pale. He just stared at the spent igniter.

I said, "Hey, I've got matches."

He sucked in a long breath and then, slowly, sat back on his heels, and looked at me. "I didn't understand how tired I am."

We all were. "No problem."

Walter was watching us now. He said, to Robert, "We'll use our stove."

Robert glanced at the igniter in his hand. "Damn thing."

I said, "I've had one fail." I hadn't, actually. The lie was unnecessary, and useless. Robert just looked away. I thought, he's beyond tired. Maybe it's events catching up to him. He's haunted by his father's horrific death. Haunted by his brother's damaged life, admitting to his own role in Henry Shelburne's chaotic path. And then his low-tech piece of gear fails him. Reduced to the simplest of needs, he can't cope. I said, "We'll find him, Robert."

He gave a weak smile.

I dug the matches out of my pack and held them out. Our fingers brushed as he took them. I thought, for a moment, he was going to grip my hand. I thought, sure, I'll give you a hand.

Walter interrupted. "I've *got* it. Cassie, you find cups and utensils. Robert, you relax. Well, first, you want to pass me your water bottle? I'm a little low."

Robert and I sank away from one another, and turned to the tasks that Walter ordered.

And then all was quiet, but for the hiss of the little gas flame on Walter's stove.

Nothing to do but wait for the water to boil.

I rubbed a hand across my eyes. I could drop to sleep right here. I was certainly drifting. I stared at the lantern light flashing off Robert's water bottle, sparking the titanium, silvery as mercury in clear river water.

Ten minutes later we were eating the glop that passed as Chili Mac.

The rain hardened and lightning and thunder returned, as if they'd taken a break and were now refreshed.

Deeply and thoroughly fatigued, we moved to our sleeping bags.

Walter switched off the lantern.

I stripped down to a long-sleeve T-shirt and pulled on silk long underwear, suitably modest. I slipped into my Crocs, grabbed my poncho and ventured just outside the tunnel to pee. No need for a flashlight. Lightning lit my way.

Walter and Robert followed suit.

Chilled, I wormed into my sleeping bag and shivered until body heat flared and my thoughts fuzzed.

Chapter 22

Next thing I knew I was back at the bedrock hump across the Yuba watching lightning bolts duel. Rain like needles. Me, sodden. Benumbed on the gravel bar. Electricity in the air. The taste of ozone. Me, thinking I'm sticking up like a sore thumb on this flat river. And then a lightning bolt the size of Nevada strikes the water, spears down to the bed of the river and snatches up on its sharp point a silver heart. It quivers in front of me. I put out my finger to touch it. Who can resist?

Sometime later I thought I heard bees.

I woke.

Snug in my sleeping bag, water sampling on my mind.

After-image of that lightning bolt, removing that mercury heart from the river.

Not the way it's done.

Hydrology 101 back in college, learning how it's done. Sampling water for contaminants. I'd collected samples from a boat, from shore, and then directly, wading, careful to reach upstream as far as possible from where my shuffling feet had agitated the sediment. I thought now of Cameron Shelburne wading in the Yuba, panning for gold, losing his water bottle-- that scenario had bugged me, why buckle-clip the bottle to your belt and then wrestle it free and open it, all the while holding onto your big plastic gold pan? Maybe he didn't. What if he'd put aside the pan and turned his attention to the state of the water? Just unclip his bottle from his belt and submerge it and glug glug glug he's got a sample. It's called a grab sample. I learned that. Only I freaking well did it following the protocol, using an approved container. I didn't use my damned Nalgene water bottle.

So why would Cameron Shelburne use his?

He wouldn't. He wasn't sampling the river water.

He was panning for gold.

I shook off the dream and sat up.

It was dawn. The early light was silvered, foggy.

Just enough light to make out Robert's hunched form at the mouth of the tunnel, up there watching the day break. Humming to himself.

It sounded like bees.

I wetted my lips. My mouth was cottony, tasting of ozone. I cleared my throat, to ask Robert if his father had ever tried to scoop up mercury droplets from the riverbed.

I said, "Hey."

Robert didn't hear me. Probably could not hear me over the drum roll of Walter snoring.

I shivered. I pulled the sleeping bag up to my neck. I noticed that Robert was cold, as well. He'd put on a wool cap, yanked down over his ears. He wore a puffy parka, one I hadn't yet seen. A down parka was not recommended in the rain. Rain had stopped, though, thank you very much.

If my backpack was in reach I'd drag it close and dig out my own warm vest, not down but well insulated.

Walter turned over, muffling his snores.

Thoroughly chilled, fully awake now, I cast aside my muddled dream scenario.

I cleared my throat. "Good morning."

Robert turned. Just dipped a shoulder and angled his head. Acknowledgment. A listening man. In profile, backlit, he looked like he'd been sketched—an artist's quick strokes framed the man. But, I now noticed, the artist got the nose wrong. It should be stronger, bladed.

I went very cold.

It wasn't Robert Shelburne.

23

Two things, in quick succession:

I said *shit* and Walter stirred.

I stared at the place where Robert had set up his gear, close to the tunnel entrance, and saw that his gear was gone.

The figure at the mouth of the tunnel did not move an inch. Shoulder still dipped. Head still angled.

Holy holy shit.

I tried to exit my sleeping bag, entangling myself, making struggling noises.

Walter slowly sat up. He looked at me, head cocked.

I nodded toward the entrance.

Walter turned to look.

The figure, unmoving, carved there by the artist for all eternity, watched us in turn. "How do you do?" he said. And then when we did not respond, "I do poorly."

His voice was soft, reserved. Frugal.

Time passed. Seconds most likely. Possibly a full minute. The light outside intensified, as if an hour had passed and full morning had bloomed. It was a trick of radiating sunlight, tearing a hole in the fog. A matter of seconds.

I said, "Henry?"

He said, "Yes."

Walter spoke. "Henry Shelburne."

I thought perhaps Walter's use of the surname was for my benefit, as if Walter thought I had just awakened, myself, and was in that exit-mode from the dream world where reality is conditional, as if I had another Henry in mind, one only accessed in memory.

"We have five minutes," the figure said. Henry Shelburne said, in his soft parsimonious voice. He shifted slightly, crooking his left leg so that he could more fully look at us. "I can't come in."

Walter turned on the lantern.

Henry Shelburne was still backlit by the dawn light outside, and now also front-lit by the cool LED glow of the lantern. I could see that his cap was Sherpa-style, with earflaps. I could make out the color of the cap and parka: brown.

It was a disappearing-phantom-in-the-woods brown.

I could just make out his features. He looked remarkably like the wet-combed teenager from the Old West photograph that Robert had showed us. But, in this light, the marks of the years would not be apparent. What was apparent was his left hand gripping his thigh.

In the photo, I recalled, in which Henry sat in the saloon chair, his left thigh had been strapped to a holster. No holster, now. No fake six-shooter. Just faded jeans encasing that thigh. Jeans, down parka, wool hat. Muddied hiking boots. Henry Shelburne looked like any other hiker on a foggy mountain morning.

Chapter 23

I tried to wrap my mind around this new Henry, the real deal, not the fragile teenager in the photo.

Walter said, "How do you do, son. My name is Walter Shaws and my associate here is Cassie Oldfield. We're geologists in the employ of your brother, who has been searching for you. Who is extremely concerned about your welfare. But I expect you know all that."

Henry Shelburne's hand tightened on his thigh.

"I'm sorry to hear that you're doing poorly," Walter said. "How can we help?"

"You helped," Henry said.

"I assume you mean in the sense of leading your brother here."

"Yes, I mean that." Henry angled his head toward the canyon outside. "That was resourceful, Robert."

I looked beyond Henry but if Robert Shelburne was out there, he was masked in the fog. Henry's thought processes were...off. Chaotic, as Robert had said. Still, the word *resourceful*. The phrasing. Henry Shelburne was well-spoken. I didn't know why that surprised me. A chaotic mind did not mean an ignorant mind.

I said, "What did you mean by we have five minutes?"

Henry lifted his left arm. His parka sleeve was too short. It rode up. He rotated his arm and looked at his wrist, as if demonstrating the concept of telling time. There was no wristwatch on his wrist. His wrist was still stick-thin.

Chaotic, confused? Or just making a point? I asked, "What happens in five minutes?"

His left hand began to tremble. The tremor traveled up his arm.

Neurological effect, I assumed, of mercury poisoning. Yeah, he was doing poorly.

He caught me staring and jerked his hand back down to clutch his thigh. He said, "We need to travel."

"Travel where?"

"You, go home. I go back."

"Back where?"

"Where Robert is waiting."

I asked, "Where is Robert waiting?"

"Up ahead."

"Why doesn't he come back in here and tell us that himself?"

"He wrote you a note." With his right hand, his steady hand, Henry fished in the pocket of his parka and produced a small notebook. "I carry this," he said. "To keep track of things." He opened it and tore off a sheet of paper, then placed it on the ground beside him. He picked up a small rock and set it on on top, anchoring the paper.

I couldn't make out what the writing on the paper said, from where I anchored, in my sleeping bag. "What does it say?"

"It says what I told you."

I repeated, "He could have told us that face-to-face. Why didn't he?"

"He wants you to see I am doing well."

Walter said, "You just told us you're doing poorly."

Henry Shelburne put his hands to his head. His fingers splayed across his temples. "I know you followed me. You followed the black rock... The black rock. I lost the words." He closed his eyes. "It's in the microscope, Henry. Look, Henry. And there's a cross. What *is* that called? Look it up Henry. It's a black rock and there's a white crystal with a black cross. The cross is beautiful, it's like a sign to show the way..."

Like a crusade, I thought.

"...it's called a ...what *is* that?" He drummed his fingers on his temples. "Look it up Henry, it's..."

"It's called chiastolite," I said. "Henry."

His fingers stilled. He opened his eyes and stared at me. "Yes, it is."

Walter said, "And the black rock is called hornfels."

Henry slammed his hands down onto the ground and twisted his body to face Walter full-on. "I almost *had* it."

"Take it easy," Walter said.

Very slowly, Henry Shelburne pushed himself backward, pushing down on the ground to lever his body up, uncoiling with surprising control, given the tremors in his left hand when he'd unloosed it. He stood now at the mouth of the tunnel and he shoved his hands into his parka pockets and gave a little nod in our direction, into the tunnel, a nod that I read to say *I'm outta there*. I'm free.

And then I thought, watch yourself. Don't read things into Henry Shelburne.

Don't act as if you know him.

24

By the time Walter and I managed to extract ourselves from our sleeping bags and scuttle up to the tunnel entrance, there was nothing to see outside but the fog-tricked walls of Shoo Fly Canyon.

There was only the note Henry had left for us.

I knocked the anchoring rock aside and picked up the note.

Walter moved closer, gaining a good view.

We read it together: *Connected with Henry. All good. Please return home. Will contact you when I return. TY.*

We stood shivering, me in my silkies and Walter in his thermals.

"Polite," I said. "Please and thank you."

Walter said, "The handwriting is unsteady."

"Assume they were standing outside. So Henry gives Robert the notebook. And Robert is holding it, and writing. Hard to write neatly."

"Or," Walter said, "that's Henry's writing."

Yeah. Tremors. Shaky hand.

"In which case..." Walter didn't finish his sentence.

Chapter 24

Yeah. I said, "You saw Robert's handwriting, on the contract, back at the lab."

Walter nodded. "It was just his signature. Something of a scrawl."

"Like a busy venture capitalist's sign-off."

We fell silent. I didn't know what to think. I didn't know what to do.

I said, finally, "Robert could have waked us, thanked us, told us to go home and the check will be in the mail." I raised the note. "I mean, why do it this way?"

"Walk it through," Walter said.

"Okay. Occam's razor--the simplest explanation. Henry... does things differently. So, he shows up, looks in the tunnel, and Robert is closest to the entrance. I know, Henry doesn't like enclosed spaces, but maybe he gathers his courage and tiptoes inside. Wakes his brother. Or, he stands at the entrance and softly calls to him."

"And we slept through that?"

"Evidently we did."

Walter considered. "And then Henry and Robert confer, outside. Out here. Robert agrees to doing things Henry's way. And Henry waits for us to wake so he can give us the note, tell us to go home."

"He didn't exactly *wait*. He was humming. That woke me up."

"Meanwhile," Walter continued, "Robert is waiting for him out here in the canyon. He's achieved his goal, reunited with his brother."

"And his brother's goal?"

Walter rubbed his chin. "This is where I get stuck. Henry is evidently in accord with Robert, with the gist of Robert's note. But Henry sent Robert to us, in the first place, with the ore specimen. With the links to our website. To my old articles..."

"Yeah, because you're the blue-lead guy."

Walter said, stiffly, "Yes."

"*Yes*, and you followed the lead, and its offshoots, getting us where we are. You did the job."

"Not entirely. There is the ore specimen. The Shelburne family legend."

"Okay. So the reunited brothers can now do their treasure hunt."

"That's fine with me, but I would like to hear directly from Robert that all is well." Walter gave me a look, his eyes sharp as quartz. "We signed on, Cassie."

Actually, I wasn't clear what page of the contract we were on. I knew the page that bothered me. That said we're bringing Robert to find his brother, who might, or might not, be suicidal. Having finally met the man, I had no idea. He was certainly doing poorly, whatever that meant. I was at a loss. In truth, I'd signed on, in a sad corner of my heart, to help Henry Shelburne because I was carrying a load of guilt about another Henry, and that was a damned useless reason to pursue *this* Henry, now. I had to wonder if we'd be walking into something we weren't prepared for. Still. Walter nailed it; we'd signed on. I said, "Fine. Let's go."

Once decided, we hurried--wrangling into clothing, packing our gear.

We took a moment to assess the spot where Robert had slept. His camp sandals were here. Everything else was gone. Presumably, he'd hurried, trying not to wake us. He'd grabbed what he needed and left.

It bugged me. He could have waked us. He could have waited until we awakened, and then explained that he was taking it from here, heading off with his brother. There was no compelling reason for him to sneak out, to leave the note with Henry. There was no compelling reason to have his brother tell us to head home. Robert Shelburne was nothing if not straight-up sure of himself. He said what he thought. He asked for what he wanted. If he wanted us to leave, why not straight-up say so? And yes yes, he was now doing things Henry's way. Playing Henry's games. Still. It bugged me.

When we found him, I'd ask.

We headed out of Shoo Fly Tunnel.

If we'd had satellite service in this deep canyon, we would have messaged Vicky Bleeker. We'd have to wait to find a better position.

If we'd had sat service I would have checked the forecast. Since we didn't, I relied on the sky, gray fog rather than dark clouds, the kind of foggy drippy aftermath of rainstorms in the Sierra that often say, all done for now.

For the briefest moment we paused. Which way had they gone? Upcanyon, or downcanyon? The most reasonable assumption was that they were heading for the site of the hornfels, and that—judging by the float we'd been following—was upcanyon.

We did as we were trained to do: follow the geology.

25

GAIL HAWKINS WOKE WITH A START. Voices. Out in the canyon. She reached for her Weatherby but her fingers grazed nylon. Then she realized. She was in her tent. She'd pitched her tent facing into the little alcove in the canyon wall, using that meager shelter to store her gear. Her wet poncho. Her pack. Her boots. Her rifle in its case.

She groaned. She was sore from yesterday's trek. She was tired. Groggy. Judging by the gray light seeping through the thin tent wall, it was early morning.

Her mouth was dry. She put up a hand and wiped the dew from the nylon ceiling and then licked the dew off her palm. Thirsty. She found her water bottle and took a long drink.

Better.

She stretched and unzipped the front of the tent

Voices.

She strained to hear.

Must be them.

They weren't far away. She knew this. She'd tracked them to their shelter yesterday.

Yesterday was almost a blur. Tracking them had been

exhausting. One thing stood out to Gail Hawkins: they'd left the canyon of the Yuba for this side canyon, and there could be only one reason. Cassie and Walter with their noses in the gravel had figured that the source of the ore was up this way.

Gail had felt flakes on her tongue, the pure noble metal that had no taste.

And then the lightning came, and the rain. She'd tracked them to the shelter they found, a tunnel, and then she'd backtracked and found a place just downcanyon, where she'd hear them if they came back this way. It was a stingy place, where the wall indented. There she'd set up her own shelter, crowding her tent into the shallow alcove.

She'd slept hard.

And then the voices woke her up.

Now, groggy, fighting to clear her head, she listened for the voices.

They had stopped. They had already left.

Fucking hell, Gail Hawkins had overslept.

She scrambled. She was already dressed, but for her outerwear and boots. She'd gone to sleep last night ready. It took her only moments to get out of the sleeping bag and stuff it in its sack, to roll up the foam pad. She shoved the sleep gear through the unzipped tent door, and then crawled out into the alcove.

In the gray light, she saw that something was wrong.

She spotted her pack and poncho, as she'd left it.

She did not see her boots.

She did not see the long padded case that held her Weatherby.

She went cold with an icy fury.

They did this. They had found her, asleep, and robbed her.

In her cold fury, in her mind's golden eye, she pictured them now. They'd be positioned on the cliff top, holding her Weatherby at the ready, waiting for her to come out and search for her stolen boots. Because without her boots, she would be hobbled in this rough sharp terrain. She would have to come out. And then they would shoot. She saw it, coldly, playing out.

And then she blinked. She saw clearly, now, that they had no reason to turn murderous. And they had shown no knowledge that they were being tracked.

It wasn't them.

Gail Hawkins stared at the empty places where her boots had sat, where her Weatherby had lain.

This was Henry's doing.

He had tracked her. Hadn't she sensed him? All along. And now he'd made his move. It would be Henry, not the others, up on the cliff with her Weatherby.

Henry was now a Level-1, the center of her world. She'd never had a Level-1, not even her parents. They had been her night and day, her protectors, her creators; they were Level-2, they mattered, until she went out on her own, fully, until she'd left them behind and they'd receded to a visiting duty that she'd performed, Level-3, until they'd passed on and became Level-0.

She'd always wondered what a Level-1 would be like. Now she knew. A Level-1 could stop you.

She was stranded.

Her fury flamed, flickering from cold to burning. Blinding.

Her hawk's sense told her, slow down. Center yourself.

She breathed in and out. Deeply. In and out.

She needed to watch, to observe. She needed to understand.

She saw herself, through Henry's eyes. In her tent, asleep, vulnerable. If he'd wanted to kill her, he could have done so. He came into her territory, stole her belongings. He could have done more. A knife through the tent wall. A shot through the tent wall.

But he didn't.

Chapter 25

She understood. He didn't want her dead. He wanted her hobbled, unable to continue her hunt.

That could not be.

She envisioned the chunk of ore in Robert's hand, as he'd displayed it to Cassie and Walter yesterday, sitting on that ledge. She could see it, close up, the way it looked in the lenses of her Celestron. She could see the golden grain, enlarged, the size of an eye, winking back at her.

She would follow.

She moved close to the mouth of the alcove, stooping to avoid the low roof, and studied the muddy ground. The bootprints were there, coming into the alcove, leaving the alcove, preserved in mud. And then they disappeared, because within a few yards the muddy ground turned rocky. She got her Celestron and scanned the open ground that flanked the tracks, as far as the tracks went. There was no sign of her boots. She scanned further, in the rocky area. No boots. He hadn't tossed them aside, for her to come fetch. He'd kept them. Maybe he was waiting for her to go out into the canyon, follow his trail, search for her boots. Waiting on the cliff top with her Weatherby.

She truly didn't think so but there was no reason to take the risk.

She would wait. She would give him enough time to move on--if he hadn't already moved on. That meant she would give Robert and Walter and Cassie time to move on. Not ideal. But she was a tracker. She would find them.

And she wasn't going to track them through the rocky gravelly terrain in her fucking *socks*.

She would use the waiting time.

She had learned a lot in her years in the wild, and one thing was how to make do.

She turned from the entrance and moved into the back of the little alcove. She unclipped her Spyderco knife from her belt.

She unrolled the sleeping mat. It was closed-cell foam, tough, not in the least cushy for sleeping. Gail Hawkins didn't need cushy. What she needed, now, was what she had right here.

She stood on the mat, crouched, and knifed a line around one foot, and then the other. Then she dropped to her knees and bent over the mat and, following the inscribed line, carved out a rectangle, two inches larger than her foot, all round. She repeated the process, carving a second rectangle. Then she got her first aid kit from the backpack and found the roll of kinesiology tape. She'd used it on strained ankles and knees, over the years. She had a new use for it, this time. It was beautiful material. Polyester, waterproof, breathable, stretchable, good adhesion. It came in several colors, including, she'd been pleased to learn, gold.

She sat and went to work.

She exchanged her dirty damp socks for clean dry socks.

She shod her right foot in the foam footpad, wrapping it again and again with kinesiology tape.

She shod her left foot.

She stood and took a few steps. Her footwear held.

She rolled the remainder of the foam sleeping pad and tied it to her pack. She stuffed her sleeping bag inside. She rolled the now-dry poncho and stuffed it. She broke down her tent and collapsed the poles and rolled it and stuffed it. She put on her parka.

She stared, for a moment, at her backpack, at the straps that should be holding her Weatherby. They would, again.

She took the time to eat two energy bars and drink more water.

And then she put on her pack and cinched the belt and moved to the mouth of the alcove. When she stepped outside, she didn't bother to scan the cliff tops, to search the gray mist. She stood tall.

Nothing happened. As she'd known.

Henry receded to a Level-3.

Robert and Walter and Cassie, somewhere ahead, were still Level-2.

They *mattered*.

She set out to find them.

26

Walter and I headed up Shoo Fly Canyon.

We traveled like thieves in the night, mindful of every truck-sized boulder that could hide a man. We scanned the cliff tops. We saw fog-wrapped trees that looked more human than arboreal.

It was not easy hiking.

We followed the creek, on the lookout for scat that would promise a deer trail or bear trail up ahead, but as with yesterday's hike up Shoo Fly, there was no trail, no path, just the boulders and gravel and the odd patch of fog-slicked clay soil.

Walter slipped on a wet rock, and cursed.

"You okay?"

"Could be worse."

All right then. We had a name for this trek. *It Could Be Worse*.

At a promising riffle in the creek, we stopped to sample. I ventured out on a wedge of slick boulders, courting balance, and was rewarded with two pieces of chiastolite hornfels float--a mineral pledge that we were on the right track.

Getting better.

The way grew rockier, spinier, and I jammed my right boot

into a crevice and ignited the talus-bruise from yesterday's hike. Weeks ago, it felt like. The top of my foot throbbed.

But it could be very much worse.

Farther along we came to an incursion into the northeast wall of Shoo Fly Canyon. It was a skinny side canyon, feeding a skinny creek down into our creek. We sampled another few dozen yards up Shoo Fly Creek and determined that the now-familiar hornfels float was no longer to be found. We retreated to the confluence with the side canyon and sampled up that way and we found our float again, same old same old salt-and-pepper diorite and cross-studded hornfels. We were too skittish to say much in the way of *woo-hoo*.

We simply nodded at one another and started the hike up Skinny Canyon.

Scanning the cliff tops. Gingerly navigating the rocky banks of the creek. Walking on eggs.

Same old same old.

Farther up Skinny Creek the float was more abundant, the edges of the hornfels sharper—barely rounded by transport. Not transported far, at all, from the source.

And then the canyon made a little bend and precipitously narrowed a dozen yards ahead where the rock walls closed in and formed a V notch.

My heartbeat ramped up. Up there was something new.

A thumb of rock stood at the notch, webbed to the right-hand wall.

We crept forward, carefully, thieves in the night.

We halted at the thumb. Waiting, listening. Straining to hear what, if anything, was occurring beyond that notch. Nothing, it seemed.

We had all the time in the world to take out our hand lenses and glass the thumb to identify the white and black minerals as the constituents of diorite. We turned our attention to the wall and took note that the familiar bands of cherts and meta-sandstones and gray-green slates had a new member, a lens of darker-gray slate flecked with black spots like an Appaloosa horse.

I considered the rocks.

If I were a young intrusive diorite dike and heated my way into the old Shoo Fly Formation, this is what I would look like. If I wanted to cook up some hornfels, this would be my neighborhood. If I wished to include Maltese crosses in my hornfels, I'd roast those carbonaceous spots in the slate.

If I was Henry Shelburne hunting the family legend, this is what I would see.

I shifted attention to my partner, who was still studying the display. I said, "What do you think?"

"Growing interested." He turned to me. "You?"

"I'd add a *very*."

He considered. "Yes. This deserves a *very*."

I smiled. There are still times in the field when I feel like a student, when I look for acknowledgment that I know my stuff. I didn't need it, here. I knew this stuff. Still, Walter's adoption of the *very* was nice.

Yeah but, there was a distance to go from very interested to nailing it. We'd found the general contact zone but not the hornfels itself. The jackpot, perhaps, was on the other side of the notch.

"Shall we?" Walter moved.

I said, "Wait."

He stopped.

"Do you smell something?"

It was a faint odor, drifting through the fog, drifting our way, so faint that it took Walter half a minute to acknowledge it.

"Mountain misery," he finally said.

"And smoke."

Chapter 26

We looked at one another.

Somebody on the other side was preparing to burn down the forest?

Walter got the sat phone, checked for a signal, and shook his head.

"All right," he said, "let's just nip through the notch and see what we can see. And then we can figure out what to do next."

A sketchy plan. But I did not have a better one.

I followed Walter through the notch.

27

WALTER and I stepped through the notch in the walls of Skinny Canyon, into a little valley that seemed almost lost in time.

Lost, that is, if you weren't looking for it.

Nevertheless, it was pretty enough to be called enchanted.

The valley extended several dozen yards before narrowing at the far end, and then canyoning upward again. It was lush, thatched with brush and trees, bisected by a creek—our own Skinny Creek—and caged by high walls.

And then I saw the fire, and the enchantment evaporated.

In a clearing in the middle of the valley was a rock ring holding timber tented over a brushy pile of kindling. The brush was brown, dried, but nevertheless I identified the crinkled ferny leaves as mountain misery. What else smelled like that?

My nose stung.

The timber smoked. The fire had almost gone out. Despite all logic, I ached to draw near. Add some of that dried kindling, help the fire along, and warm my feet.

Walter whispered, "See anybody?"

No. The fog was capricious, clearing the rock walls but

lingering in the trees. I whispered, "I think that's a tent back there in the trees."

We waited, watching.

After a time, Walter whispered, "Something else."

I turned to him. "What?"

He pointed. "It's hard to see, what with the fog and the bend in the southern rock wall, but there's a tunnel opening."

I turned. Peered. Saw it.

"This place," he said, "has already been mined."

Not lost, after all.

I said, "You thinking what I'm thinking? Abandoned mercury flasks?"

"It's not out of the question."

Just great. I expelled a breath and refocused on the tunnel. "Perhaps they're in the tunnel."

"Henry hates enclosed spaces," Walter replied.

"Maybe Robert's in the tunnel. Maybe that's why Henry brought him here."

We waited, watching for the Shelburne brothers.

While waiting, I looked over this valley with a treasure-hunter's eye. I could not deny that this place was as good a candidate as we had yet seen. The diorite thumb was webbed, on this side of the notch, to a full diorite hand that slapped against the southern wall, a wall shot through with spotted slate. There was no visible outcrop of hornfels but it surely had to present a face to the elements to erode off pieces of float. It was perhaps camouflaged in the brush, in the trees.

Equally to the point, these solid rock walls would hold an elevated ancient river channel intact for millennia. Indeed, I thought I could make out a high spur of gravel intersecting the rimrock of the southern wall.

Buried in that hillside, perhaps, was a stretch of the deep blue lead.

I wouldn't mind seeing that. Had I caught the itch, from Walter? Enchantment, after all. I whispered, "What'd you put in the Chili Mac last night?"

"What?"

"Never mind." I refocused. "Shall we take a closer look?"

He nodded. We inched forward and achieved a small knob of bald bedrock and got a new angle on Enchantment Valley, as I decided to name it, going with my first impression.

Walter nudged my arm.

I nodded. I saw him, saw Henry over there in the trees. Not certain how I'd missed him before. Perhaps, three yards back, our field of view had been obscured. More likely, it was due to the excellent nature of Henry's camouflage: brown cap, brown parka, jeans faded to the color of volcanic breccia. He sat cross-legged, left hand clutching his thigh. His right hand was not visible.

He was still as stone.

As were we, abruptly fossilized in place.

I thought he hadn't seen us, which was why I jumped when he called my name.

"Cassie." His fragile voice carried well enough across the little valley.

Walter whispered, "Answer him."

I called back, "Henry."

Like we were friends. He hadn't called either of us by name, back at Shoo Fly Tunnel. And now he did, using my first name, at that. Of course he knew our names—Walter had introduced us back at the tunnel—but the *use* of a name is a familiar thing. Like extending your hand for a shake. And I had now replied in kind. I watched. He did not lift his hand and I guessed that he couldn't without releasing the tremors, but he could have nodded, cementing the Cassie-Henry relationship. He did nothing. He sat rigid as the trunk of the tree at his back. The harder I stared, the more he seemed to blend in, like a deer in the woods. I knew this game. Hide and seek. I'd played this game with my brother, little Henry Oldfield, and the trick was to look but not see, let the quarry reveal himself when he was ready.

And then Henry Shelburne replied. "You found your way."

What?

I looked at Walter.

He put a finger to his lips. His gaze remained fixed on the scene down below.

I returned my attention to Henry. I had no idea how to pretend to understand this wounded soul. He did not think we'd follow? Didn't think we *could* have found our way, from our night's refuge, where he'd sandbagged us, to this lost valley? He'd *wanted* us to follow? Then why hadn't he said so, back at the tunnel? And what about Robert? Robert didn't want us to find our way here. Robert wanted us to go home--if that note could be believed.

Walter whispered, "We need to know where Robert is."

Yeah.

And then, as if conjured, Robert's voice sounded down there in Enchantment Valley.

"Hey Bro," Robert Shelburne's words rang out clearly. "No go."

I relaxed an inch. Robert was now on the scene. He must have been in the tunnel. He sounded fine, cheerful even.

Henry was speaking now, in reply to his brother, voice softened again. A murmur on the breeze.

"I'm *on board* with you," Robert answered, "but I don't know what I'm looking at in the mine. Look, I know you want to go it alone, just me and you, the family thing, but we're failing here. I'm not qualified. What I do is, I *hire* qualified people. In fact, I hired two of them--the ones you wanted. And we sent them home."

We? I thought.

Henry spoke, his voice again loud enough to carry. "They're here."

Silence, and then Robert's voice. "No shit?"

"Up there," Henry said.

I looked for, and did not see, Robert, and then Walter nudged my arm and pointed, and now I saw him, striding away from the tunnel opening in the southern rock wall. He didn't look up. He was heading for Henry. He spoke, to Henry, loud enough for us to hear, "Then I guess you'd better invite them down."

"I will." And then Henry untangled from his cross-legged sit, braced himself with one hand, got to his feet, and emerged from the cover of the trees into the full gray daylight. He tipped his chin. Looked straight at us. Called out, "You can come down." There was nothing fragile about that voice now.

There was a micro-moment during which Walter and I waited, me reconsidering our choice to follow the Shelburne brothers, Walter no doubt thinking along the same lines. But nothing had changed, really. The reasons we'd had when we started up Shoo Fly Canyon were still valid. And so were the questions. Why did Robert want us sent home? Why did Henry agree, when he was the one who had instructed Robert to hire us--when now he seemed to congratulate us for showing up?

Down below, the Shelburne brothers waited, chins tipped upward, watching us.

Walter said, "Shall we?"

I had no argument against it. Yeah. Let's get this done. I nodded.

Walter pushed up to stand and I followed suit and we came down off the knob to join the Shelburne brothers in Enchantment Valley.

And then Henry's right hand came out of his pocket.

28

It wasn't an Old West six-shooter in Henry's hand. It was a modern-day Glock, carried by cops at almost every crime scene I'd worked. Henry's Glock was matte black except for the slide, the metal there silvered where the finish had worn off, which left me thinking Henry Shelburne handled this gun a lot. Or maybe Henry 'Quicksilver' Shelburne had sanded the finish down to silver on purpose.

Henry pointed the weapon at his brother's boots, which were in the immediate neighborhood of Walter's and my boots.

Robert, Walter, and I stood in a lineup in front of the tunnel.

Henry spoke, to Walter. "I am hiring you."

Walter said, "We prefer not to work at gunpoint."

"It's just in case."

"In case of what?"

"*Just in case. Just in case.*"

Just in case, I figured, that Robert again tried to send Walter and me away. He had tried as we'd joined them--saying *you really aren't needed any longer*. He had stiffened in alarm when Henry said *yes they are*, and pulled the gun from his pocket.

Now, Walter said, gently, "Robert already hired us, to help

him find you. Here you are, reunited. And I think he's ready to leave. How about we all leave, together?"

Henry shook his head. "You found your way here."

That struck me. That's what he had said when he first spotted Walter and me up by the knob. Was this some kind of test? If we could follow the float up Shoo Fly, to the side canyon, to the notch, if we could decipher the diorite and the hornfels, we'd prove ourselves to this obsessed plagued man. I thought, shit.

Henry added his left hand to grip the gun, two-handing it, but his left hand shook and the gun oscillated.

Walter said, more gently, "Take it easy, son."

Henry steadied the gun. "A geologist needs to go in."

"Cassie will go," Walter said promptly.

"Does she know..."

"*Yes*," Walter said, "she knows everything there is to know about the auriferous channels. I taught her."

There was no universe in which I'd been trained for this. But I got it. Walter was going to stay outside with unstable Henry while I went on the treasure hunt. He thought he was protecting me. He always has. When I was a kid assisting in his lab and he took me to my first crime scene, he bought me a whistle in case we got separated. All these years later, he's still watching out. Vigilance is in his DNA. It's tattooed on his soul.

There's a man with a gun. And Walter is stepping up.

I stole a glance at Robert. He stood rigid, watching his brother. Unsure. I wished for him to find some leverage, take charge, lead Henry away from this standoff. But Robert wasn't at home here. Henry was. Robert looked like a guy who'd been sandbagged, taken off guard. His hair was mussed, no time to run a comb through it, groom it. He wore yesterday's clothing, the upscale khakis now dirt-streaked and wrinkled. Seemed he'd not had time to dig fresh clothes from his pack, when Henry extracted him from Shoo Fly Tunnel an hour or so ago. He'd had time only to grab his sleeping bag and pack and boots and follow Henry outside, where Henry had presumably given him time to pull on yesterday's clothing before sending him away, upcanyon, while Henry stayed behind to rouse Walter and me, to introduce himself.

And now Robert waited to see what his brother was going to do.

I refocused on Henry. He may have held the gun but he looked a little lost, as if he'd come out of hiding too soon. His face was more weathered than the teenager in the photo Robert had showed us, but the wool cap now cupping his head made him look young again. Still, he did not have teenage Henry's cool-guy squint. His eyes were reddened, blinking. Lack of sleep, trying to get a wet-wood fire going, who knew? His nose was pinkish, sunburned, peeling. I guessed the weather had been clear and sunny before we joined the hunt, although I wondered why an experienced outdoorsman like Henry Shelburne had not used sunscreen. His peeling nose—like the preposterous earflaps—made him look like a kid. I ignored that.

He was Robert Shelburne's kid brother, not mine.

Henry let go of the gun with his left hand and lifted it, gesturing at the tunnel.

I stared at his hand. The palm was pink, peeling, and I got a sick understanding that we weren't talking sunburn here. Shit, Henry, what have you been into?

Robert suddenly lunged.

Quick as a snake strike, Henry had both hands again on the Glock, had the gun aimed at his brother's head.

Robert raised his own hands. "Chill, Bro."

I said quickly, "I'm going in."

Henry pulled his arms into his chest, bracing his elbows, steadying his aim. "Thank you."

Cautiously, I answered, "You're welcome."

I felt sick. It was the weirdness that got to me, jumping from threat to good manners, as if this were normal, as if some neuron in Henry Shelburne's damaged brain had misfired.

But he held the gun and the threat remained.

Robert was in no position to fix this.

So now it became my show. I assumed I didn't need a gas detector, or Robert would not have emerged from the tunnel alive. I started for the tunnel. Henry stopped me. Told me to leave behind my pack. Told me to take only my tools. Told me to bring him a sample. I rummaged in my pack and got the field kit and belted it around my waist. As I rummaged in the pack again and pulled out the headlamp, Henry told me he'd started the generator, that the tunnel had lights.

I glanced inside. Yes, there was a glow, several yards inside. Good. I strapped on my headlamp. Better. I started once more for the tunnel.

As I passed into the mouth I heard Henry call to me, "Go all the way."

29

All the way *where*?

The tunnel was lighted, as Henry promised, bulbs strung along the rock ceiling overhead, but the lights didn't answer my question.

As far ahead as I could see, the tunnel ran straight.

Perhaps somewhere further ahead there were side branches, offshoots, whatever it was they were called in a mine, a term Walter would know. But Walter was outside facing a Glock and counting on me to return with some shiny thing to satisfy Henry. A nice nugget. Sure thing.

All I need do was go all the way, wherever that way led me.

I studied the rock as I passed. Bedrock walls, bedrock ceiling, bedrock floor, a sturdy incursion into the mountainside, a strong tunnel that needed no timbering, a tunnel with drill holes in the ceiling to ventilate, the only sort of tunnel I felt remotely comfortable traversing. When my eyes had fully adjusted and my nerves settled, I identified the bedrock as metamorphic slate.

As I moved I noticed that my leg muscles were working a little harder, and realized that the tunnel was angling upward. I assumed the tunnel-builders had done that on purpose so that any water that seeped in through the rock would drain out.

Good idea.

My body settled into a rhythm, releasing my mind to dwell on the question at hand.

How did Henry know where *all the way* led? He didn't like enclosed spaces. Presumably, not even lighted spaces, although he himself had switched on a generator that was located who knew where. He'd set the stage. And then sent Robert, and next me, in here.

And how would he know how far *I* went?

Quite clearly this tunnel was working its way into the hillside toward the buried river channel whose upper gravel reaches I had glimpsed on the ridge top. Clever, those miners. If you can't hose out a mountain to get to the gold, tunnel your way in. One way or another they'd found the way. One way or another those ancient Eocene river channels had condemned this countryside to an extreme makeover.

And that bugged me, because it should have bugged Henry.

Presumably, he wasn't looking for hosed-out mine pits or well-tunneled hills. Presumably, he was looking for a site lost since his grandfather's time, a site that nobody but *nobody* had since seen. Was he not disappointed to find that Enchantment Valley had already been mined? Walter was sure surprised. And Henry, I thought, should have been beyond disappointed. Should have been devastated.

Another failure for Quicksilver.

So why was he so anxious to have me go into this well-tunneled hill? If there was something legend-worthy in here, it would already have been found.

Poor Henry.

Henry with his peeling pink palms gripping the black and silver Glock.

Chapter 29

My sympathy evaporated.

Several hundred feet into the tunnel, the walls abruptly changed.

The bedrock was now overlain by gravel. It was mostly quartz and slate, cemented in clay and sand. I ran my fingers along the rough face.

I had entered the lost river channel.

There were pebbles and cobbles and even a few boulders—the well-rounded rocks of milky quartz that were legend in and of themselves, the defining characteristic of the blue lead, carried by long-ago rivers, carried to *this* place. Here was the legendary 'lost' river channel, right in my face.

I lost my bearings.

For a moment I forgot that I'd been sent in here. For a moment it seemed I'd chosen to come.

The tunnel drifted into a bend.

I halted and stared at the wall. Gravel sitting upon bedrock. Gravel the basal layer of the ancient channel. The basal layer being the deep blue lead.

Only, it wasn't blue.

It was reddish, the iron pyrite in the clay oxidized.

I fumbled open my field kit and grabbed the hammer and chisel and went to work on the cemented gravel, gouging my way through to the rock beneath.

And then I had to stop and stare.

It was virgin unoxidized blue.

It was blue as the wings of a jay.

Something like a fever took hold of me. Right here in front of my nose was the deep blue lead. I'd listened to Walter and Robert Shelburne rhapsodize about it, I'd read up on it myself, I'd contemplated the geology of it, but right now what made my pulse pound was the sheer reality of it, and I had to admit that I felt a thrill. If I had to name the feeling perhaps I'd call it romance.

Walter should see this.

And then I regained my senses. Legend-worthy to Walter, yes, but to Henry Shelburne? I recalled what Robert had told us, back at the lab, back when he was spinning the legend of the deep blue lead. He'd said Henry was hunting not only gold but something more fundamental. And since Henry had been hunting his entire adult life, could he not have already encountered the blue, somewhere, sometime? Hacked into some forgotten gravel outcrop? Maybe. As long as it wasn't buried in a mining tunnel. In any case, this patch of the blue lead was surely not the patch he sought.

To be certain, I switched on my headlamp and got my hand lens and had a twenty-power highlighted look. Nope, no visible gold. There was no visible treasure here. Perhaps there was microscopic gold somewhere within this seam but surely what was economically recoverable had already been recovered. There was certainly no diorite dike, no cross-studded hornfels sheath, no intrusion acting as a giant riffle, entrapping a secret pocket of gold.

The bedrock here was unviolated.

Nevertheless, I picked up the chunk of gravel ore I'd gouged out and put it in my field kit along with my tools. Better to return with something than nothing at all.

And perhaps there was something worth seeing around the tunnel bend.

Go all the way.

I wondered, again, if Henry knew where all the way led.

The tunnel was bending like a U, and there now appeared on the bedrock floor the broken remains of iron tracks. Of course. The miners had not hauled the gravel out in backpacks. They'd used rail cars.

Chapter 29

The tunnel now straightened into the second leg of the U. The tracks continued as far as I could see.

I continued, as well, following that deep blue lead.

Even oxidized, even rusty reddish brown, the rock held my attention.

And then I came upon a spot that was not oxidized, that someone had peeled away to show the bluejay color underneath. It looked like my work, on the other side of the U. I ran my finger along the gouged rock and my finger came away powdered in rock flour where the little excavation had been done. Recently. By Henry, maybe, his obsession swamping his claustrophobia? Or by Robert. Carried his own tools? Or provided by Henry. On the floor of the tunnel, directly below the gouge, were the bits and chunks that Robert had carved out. Detritus.

And then Robert had emerged from the mine tunnel telling his brother he'd found nothing.

Why?

Convince Henry that this place was a bust? Come back on his own some time, probe deeper into this blue lead, claim the family legacy for himself, the ultimate venture capitalist.

My stomach soured.

Whatever Robert was playing at, it was the wrong move. He hadn't counted on his brother pulling a gun.

I thought, don't make the same mistake.

I moved on.

Within a few dozen yards, the gravel receded. Within a couple dozen more yards, the walls were pure bedrock. And then up ahead I saw the faint glow of daylight.

Another exit.

Now what?

I thought it over. I found that I knew two things.

First, Henry had been camped in Enchantment Valley,

perhaps for a couple of days. Henry would have had time to crawl all over this place and would have found this second tunnel mouth. Which meant he already knew what was out there.

Second, what was out there could not be what he sought. What he sought *must* be in here, or so he must believe. Otherwise—again—why send his brother into the tunnel searching? Why send me?

I took in a deep tunnel breath. It tasted like stone.

Okay. I knew one more thing.

Third, I knew that Henry Shelburne was not going to shoot Walter, while they waited. There was no possible need. Walter was not hot-headed enough to go for the gun. Walter was Henry's insurance, guaranteeing my cooperation.

I exhaled, in a hiss.

I had not yet gone all the way.

It could not be more than a couple dozen yards to the exit.

30

I STEPPED out of the tunnel into silvery light. While I'd been underground the sun had begun to burn through the fog. The sky was now a thin pearl shell, ready to crack. Waiting for the pearly light to penetrate my skin, aching for warmth, I took in the lay of the land.

The tunnel opened onto another slim canyon, thickly vegetated. I stood on one side of the canyon. Opposite me, the wall rose to a high ridge. This canyon's slim floor angled downhill in a steep incline and put me in mind of an unrolling carpet.

Other than the works of nature, this place was all business.

The rail tracks exited the tunnel at the high end of the canyon. The tracks fed into the skeleton of a building that held the rusted guts of some sort of machinery. Walter would know the name, would know the mechanism, but I hazarded a guess that the cemented gravel had gotten crushed in there. Running downhill was a long ditch littered with boulders and cobbles and pebbles—a sluiceway, artery of the gold country. I could see its bones surviving here and there, stretches of wood planking forming the walls and huge riffle blocks crisscrossing along the bottom, stepping downhill in the gut of the sluice box. At the head of the sluice, just uphill from me, sagged a rusting metal tank. Quite clearly it was a water storage tank, water probably captured from the small creek that ran downhill along the sluiceway. Water to hose the crushed gravel down the sluice. To free the gold. I'd gotten the hang of sluicing.

It appeared that this slim canyon might feed into Enchantment Valley, which, if I had my bearings straight, was downhill from here.

I ventured farther outside to see what I could see.

Actually, to hear what I could hear because I now took note of the low humming sound. It came from a building of sorts, more a bunker nestled into the side of the hill, just left of the tunnel exit. I stepped over for a look. The door was ajar. The sound was louder. I peeked inside and the sound was louder still in there, along with the oily smell of machinery. Of course—the generator that handy Henry had got started. I assumed there was some cabling or something that went through some drill hole or something into the tunnel to light the overhead bulbs. There was one overhead bulb lit in the generator room itself. I assumed that Henry had gotten up the nerve to come exploring in here in the first place because light came in from outside. And he'd found the generator. Some miner, sometime, gave this place an upgrade and strung lights in the tunnel.

Much appreciated.

I now noticed another bunker, just uphill, to the right of the tunnel exit.

I moved up there for a look. The door was rust-patched iron, secured by a heavy iron latch with a heavy iron padlock.

The latch hung open and the padlock was unhooked.

How far was I supposed to proceed? All the way in there?

I went to the door and knocked, calling out *hello*, feeling monumentally foolish.

No answer. No surprise.

Chapter 30

There was nothing for it but to have a quick look inside. I grasped the iron handle and pulled the door open. Daylight streamed in but nevertheless it took a moment for my eyes to adjust, to penetrate the gloom inside. No need to step in. From the doorway, I could ID this room as a storage space. It was cluttered with equipment, stuff jammed in so tight that I could not tell the armature of one from the leg of another. Some stuff was quickly recognizable: shovels, a wheelbarrow, buckets. Other stuff Walter could name. All of it was in a state of rust and disrepair, dense with history. A maze of a pathway wound through the room.

And then my attention shifted to the shelves carved into the bedrock walls.

Half a dozen mercury flasks sat on one thick shelf.

I felt a sudden relief.

Only half a dozen. I had expected more. I had expected a shitload.

That is, if this was where Henry had obtained the flask he took to the river, where his father died.

So was this the place? The door latch was open, the padlock unlocked. He didn't like enclosed spaces but I'd already established that he'd entered the generator room and here, with the outside light streaming in, surely he could have brought himself the few steps necessary to heft one of those bottles off the shelf and into a heavy-load backpack.

And then transport it. And then at the river, open the flask and dump it.

Shit, Henry.

I envisioned his peeling nose, peeling palms, pink skin, some sort of rash. Contact dermatitis? Hyper-sensitive, surely, from a lifetime of messing around with mercury, dancing with the vapors.

I backed out of the doorway and shoved the damn door shut.

Henry Shelburne's mania was not my problem.

His Glock was my problem.

I turned my back on the bunker, spinning around to return to the others and give Henry what I'd found, a chunk of the deep blue freaking lead, and pray that satisfied him.

Rather than retrace my journey through the tunnel, I decided to go downhill and take what I judged to be a shortcut.

As I moved, something at the base of the opposite hillside caught my eye. It was a bald spot in the vegetation where black rock cropped out. In this pearly light I thought I detected a wink of mica and quartz. My heart jumped. This was it, right?

This was the door to the jackpot.

I charged across the little canyon, using the wooden riffle blocks as stepping stones in the ditch where the creek ran. At the other side, I put my hand lens to the outcrop. It took no time at all to identify the rock as flinty hornfels. It took a little more time to locate the squared crystal faces speckling the rock. In some faces the carbon inclusions were muddied, unfinished. In some faces the carbon formed crosses so distinct it looked like they'd been drawn with a pencil.

I took a moment to admire the perfection.

To savor the find.

It wasn't a dog-and-pony-show back in the lab. It was doing geology.

And that led here.

My congratulatory moment passed and I fingered a specimen, a flared Maltese cross that suggested obsession, crusade.

If I were Henry I would take a hammer and chisel and pop that talisman out.

But I wasn't Henry and I decided not to take the time or invest the effort to hack off a sample. If he'd explored this canyon, surely he found the outcrop. And if he had, I cursed him. He could have steered me here, to begin with. But I got it. I

Chapter 30

knew why he'd sent me into the tunnel. If he'd found the hornfels, he'd have filled in the rest of the story.

By now, so could I.

This hornfels was formed a long time ago when magma had punched into an ancient river channel. Subsequently—still a long time ago—during a period of uplift, that intersection got exposed and eroded. And the gold-bearing gravels mixed with broken-off chips of hornfels, and in the due course of time and travel downstream, the stuff got re-cemented by river sand and clay. And chunks of that conglomerate got scattered hither, thither, and yon.

And that was the source of the chunk of ore Robert Shelburne brought to our lab.

I pictured Henry standing here, telling himself the story. Yesterday? Day before? And then in a fever hunting around for that magical junction, that giant riffle in the old blue lead, that collector of gold.

Reburied, over the course of the years. Volcanic eruption, landslide, who knew?

Perhaps buried right here in this slim canyon, or in the hillside before me, or somewhere in the tunneled hillside behind me.

Perhaps right beneath our feet.

Right, Henry? How's it feel? To be so near, and yet so far. You can't just haul a water cannon up here and hose away the mountain.

So you look to the likely. To the drift tunnels.

You can't go in there yourself. Your brother disappoints. So you send me in, in hopes that the junction has been breached, in there. Tough luck, Henry. It wasn't. Although it's quite likely to be around here somewhere.

I shrugged.

Not my problem.

I turned to go.

There was a downhill path on the tunnel side of the sluiceway, an access route I guessed, reinforced with occasional rock steps. I crossed the ditch back to the tunnel side and took the miners' route down, stopping once to look for and find a piece of chiastolite-studded hornfels float.

And then, as I neared the intersection of Sluiceway Canyon and Enchantment Valley, all thoughts of cross-studded rocks and ancient gold went by the wayside.

I saw smoke.

31

GAIL HAWKINS SAW HER CHANCE.

She watched Cassie come out of the tunnel and poke around the mining area and then cross the narrow canyon to look at the big boulder and then go down the canyon and disappear into the little valley.

Gail tried to stay calm but her heart started pounding.

This was the place, wasn't it? Tracking Robert and Cassie and Walter--and that thief Henry--was going to pay off, wasn't it?

She had started the morning with the shock of the theft.

By the time she recovered, regrouped, and left the alcove, the others had a head start. So she needed to make up the lost time. She'd made her way up the canyon quickly, her wilderness fitness deeply ingrained, her foam-pad footwear guarding her feet against the rocks, and when a sharp pebble found its way through a seam, and lodged beneath her second and third toes, digging, gouging, she had endured it. She had felt the warm seepage of blood, and cursed Henry, but she'd kept going.

Here and there, there were bootprints. Four different hikers.

She'd identified Henry right away because his prints led in and out of her alcove. She'd been able to track him up and down the canyon, Henry Shelbure tramping this land as if he owned it, as if he didn't give a damn who followed him.

He should have.

The second hiker she identified was Robert Shelburne, by process of association. His tracks mingled with Henry's outside the tunnel shelter. What had they talked about? Did Henry tell Robert what he'd done, the theft? Did Robert now know about her? Was Robert, now, a worry?

Gail was able to pick out Walter's and Cassie's tracks outside the tunnel shelter--assuming the smallest bootprints belonged to Cassie, assuming the set that mixed with hers belonged to Walter. They had talked out there. Gail had heard them, faintly. Voices. Waking her.

She was able to track all four hikers up the canyon. They'd left a map in the mud for her to follow. And when she'd come to the little canyon that branched off this miserable rocky main canyon, she'd found bootprints again.

When she'd come to the little opening in the rock wall, she hesitated. What if one of them was waiting for her, on the other side? It would be Henry. With her Weatherby.

She'd waited silently. Watching.

Listening.

There were voices, faint sounds carried on the little breeze that funneled through the break in the rock wall.

She'd pulled the knife from the sheath on her belt, steadying herself, and slipped through the opening, a hair's breadth at a time.

There was nobody waiting on the other side.

There was a valley down below, a long wooded valley.

She inched forward, scanning, eyes sharp, senses alert.

Voices. Fractured words.

Another step, and then she saw them.

Chapter 31

She'd frozen, in shock. Robert and Walter and Cassie were lined up facing Henry. Henry was pointing a gun at them.

The bigger shock was that Henry's gun was a pistol.

What had he done with her Weatherby?

Why did he hold the others at gunpoint? She answered that, easily. He was fighting his brother for the gold, he was using the geologists. But what was he going to do next? She got her binoculars and studied him. He was looking sick. Sicker than ever. His hands, on the pistol, shook. Sick people were Level-5, untouchable. That confused things. Henry kept changing levels. He had been Level-3, and then, when he stole from her, hobbled her, a Level-1.

She'd grimaced. *Observe*. Where were they, what were they doing? She shifted position again and saw that they were outside the mouth of a mine tunnel.

They were all Level-2 now, necessary.

It wasn't until Henry made Cassie go into the tunnel that Gail had fully centered herself.

She knew what to do.

She'd ghosted along the flank of the valley and found her way to a ridge that gave her a view like a postcard, showing her where everything was, and then she'd found her way to the narrow canyon where the tunnel had a second exit, the place with all the mining junk. She had taken up position above that place, watching to see if Cassie was going to find her way through the tunnel and come out that way.

And she did.

Gail was right.

It was almost too easy.

And now as she watched Cassie disappear into the valley, she wondered what Cassie had found in the tunnel, what she was going to report to the others. Gail couldn't see the others through the cover of the trees but she knew they had to be there in the valley waiting for Cassie.

Henry would be waiting with the pistol.

It didn't matter.

All that mattered right now was getting into the tunnel.

Gail saw her chance and took it.

Her senses were sharp as she padded up the tunnel.

The overhead bulbs were lit. Her golden eyes saw everything.

Her heart rate was steady.

She was ready.

It was possible that one of others would decide to come into the tunnel, from the valley entrance. But she moved unseen and unheard and unexpected and if she came upon anybody she would be coming with her hunting knife ready. She was not going to allow anybody to take her unaware.

When she came to the reddish gravel layer, she nodded. She'd seen this before, in other drift mines. On other hunts. They had never taken her to what she needed. This time? She could sense it.

She moved easily, surely, at home in this tunnel. Nothing to hear but the beats of her heart, sounding in her ears, like the mine's own breathing. She always found home in the heart of a mine. She liked to sleep in the tunnels. She liked to feel the hard rock that, somewhere, hid the gold. Hard rock. Hard G for Gail. Hard G for gold.

She followed the oxidized gravel layer up the tunnel, and then, surely, as she had sensed, she came upon it. The light cast from overhead shined on a gash in the cemented gravel.

Cassie had cut out a piece of the rock, down to the blue.

Chapter 31

Gail strapped on her headlamp and blazed the wall. For a long time--it felt like hours--she studied that cut face. There were no flecks of gold. Only blue.

Cassie's gouged-out bits littered the floor below. Left there like trash.

This was failure.

Gail felt the whiplash, dizzied. Moments ago she had been so sure, and now she saw that she had been mistaken.

There came a whisper, soft, the mine breathing, words in her ear. You are a fool.

But she'd been so sure. The day had begun with failure--Henry's theft--but she'd rallied and crafted the foam-pad footwear and gathered herself and tracked the others, found this canyon with its mine--like dozens of other canyon mines she'd found during her years hunting, all of them failures--but *this one* promised more, she'd been led here by Henry and Robert and Walter and Cassie, tracking the source of that gold-studded chunk of ore, that legend made real.

She had been mistaken.

She stared down at the trash on the floor of the tunnel. Her feet ached. She wanted her boots. The foam-pad footwear gave no support. She'd removed the pebble that lodged beneath her toes, but the wound still ached.

Her pride still ached. Losing her rifle.

Her vision went red. Her heartbeats pounded in her ears and she wanted to scream, to drown out the drumbeat.

It took all of her fitness to bring herself back. She breathed, slowly, deeply. In and out. When she found her center, her hawk, when she saw clearly again, she straightened.

There was more to the tunnel. Cassie had come in from the valley entrance. Gail would track Cassie's steps.

She moved on, following the reddened gravel, up the tunnel and around a bend, and within a few yards she found that

Cassie was not a failure, after all. There was another cut in the gravel layer, and here Cassie hadn't littered the floor with the gouged-out bits. The floor was clean. Cassie had kept what she'd found. Cassie had prospected the length of the tunnel, made the first cut back around the bend, found nothing, come back this way, made this cut, and found something worth keeping. And then she had exited the tunnel into the narrow canyon and headed down to show the others.

This was it? This time?

Gail held her breath.

She put her light to the cut that Cassie had made, and found blue. A slash of blue. And nothing more. Not the color of the sun. Only blue. An ocean of blue.

Gail Hawkins stared until her eyes watered, and stung.

All right.

She would find her own way in. She opened her senses and tracked the gravel layer and came upon the right spot. She took off her pack and got her hammer and chisel and went to work. She dug into the wall of rock, through the gravel, deepening her cut, tearing the gravel away until she reached the blue, and when she studied this cut and found it blue as an eye, empty of gold, she widened her attack, slamming her hammer against the chisel, again and again, feeling the vibrations in her hands and arms and it was like a live thing had entered her body, turned her blood molten gold. But there was only blue.

Where was the gold?

Where was the gold?

She began to burn.

She didn't know how it happened but she had dropped her hammer and chisel and was now pounding the blue face with her bare hands.

A long time later she found herself slumped on the floor.

She was a fool. She'd been spellbound by Cassie's trail

through this trickster tunnel, wanting to believe. She'd fooled herself, wanting it so badly.

She slumped there on the rough floor until the burn left her, until she cooled. Then, with cold purpose, she vowed never to be fooled again.

She took off her parka and rolled up her left shirtsleeve and found the place on the back of her arm where, years before, she had cut herself on the sharp edge of a pyrite outcropping, which embedded a grain of itself under her skin. She fingered the hard nodule, the alien thing which she'd worn all these years as a warning.

She'd ignored it, here. She'd played the fool, lured by Cassie's excavations.

She drew her knife from its sheath and matches from her pocket and struck a flame, purifying the tip of the blade, and then she pierced the skin at the edge of the grain and began to dig. At first, it felt cold. And then it burned. She gasped. And dug deeper, until the knife point gouged out the little nodule.

Hot blood painted her arm.

She got her first aid kit and applied antibiotic cream and wrapped the cut in a bandage, then used the knife to cut a length of kinesiology tape--the bloodied knife point staining the gold material. She wrapped her arm in a pressure bandage. She put her shirt back on, and then her parka. She got her water bottle and washed down three Tylenols.

As the pain pulsed, along with her heartbeats, she practiced breathing. Slowly. Deeply. In and out. It took another twenty minutes before Gail Hawkins felt ready to go back on the hunt.

Gathering herself, to rise from the tunnel floor, she spotted the little kernel of pyrite, blood-red in the light of her headlamp.

She left it there, like trash.

32

When I reached the bottom of Sluiceway Canyon, the terrain leveled out.

I was back in Enchantment Valley.

Several yards beyond me was the campfire ring. Sitting around the campfire were the three men I'd left at the main tunnel entrance. Robert and Walter sat side by side on a log on one side of the ring. Their packs sat on the ground beside them. They'd brought mine, as well. Henry sat on a low boulder on the other side. Around his waist he wore a belt bag. His Glock hand rested on the bag.

The little fire struggled.

As he watched me approach, Henry picked up a ferny spray of dried mountain misery and tossed it onto the embers and the fire leapt to life. He explained in his fragile soulless voice, "The odor repels insects."

Holy hell it was some kind of bizarre camp-out.

Henry nodded at an unoccupied boulder and I came over and took a seat, so chilled that I hunched toward the fire and held out my hands.

My eyes caught Walter's eyes and I read caution there.

Chapter 32

Henry watched me intently, the way a kid who's built a campfire in the woods waits for Mom's approval. Mom nodded, cautious. Good work, Henry. Now let's go home and by the way you're grounded for life.

Henry spoke. "You look cold."

I nodded.

He said, "Put something warm on."

Shit, I thought, the gunman gives me permission. I opened my pack and dug out my green wool beanie and put it on. Now Henry and I both wore warm hats--a tiny connection, for what it was worth. I said, "Thank you." For the permission.

He said nothing.

Okay, worth nothing.

He said, "What did you find?"

I cast about. Where to begin?

He said, "You came all the way."

"How did you...?"

Walter cut in. "We heard you."

Yeah, tramping down along the sluiceway.

"What did you find?" Henry repeated.

I swallowed. Whatever I said in answer was going to have consequence.

"*What did you find?*" he said again, Henry the fixated kid who keeps on *asking asking asking*.

Be very careful, I thought. You've got to give him something.

As I hesitated, I noticed Robert's keen attention. He had to know I'd seen the place where he'd made a cut, down to the blue lead, the detritus of his work on floor below. He had to know I'd heard him lie to his brother--*found nothing, Bro*. I held his look. Don't worry, I've no intention outing you to your brother. Robert suddenly ran a hand through his hair--raking it further, mussing it further. Nervous. Well, that Glock would make anybody nervous. But he was watching me, assessing, not his brother.

Something else going on, Robert? He finally looked away, to Henry.

So did I. I had my own needle to thread. Impatient Henry was waiting for my answer.

What could I say? The gravel was not blooming gold. The miners had stopped, given up, run out of money to cover the costs. All I'd found in there was the ancient bearer of treasure—the deep blue lead. I thought, it's deeply risky to bullshit this life-long seeker of legends. Very slowly, I unbelted my field kit and opened it. I withdrew the chunk of cemented gravel that I'd hacked free.

I held it up so that all three men could see it.

In the pearly light the rock face looked blue-gray, like the cold face of an ice crevasse. For a flash I thought I saw Walter respond, thought I glimpsed the *Dogtown* boy who fell in love with painted nuggets and grew up to thrill to the geology of the deep blue lead. But Walter just jerked a shoulder in the direction of Henry and the gun, and gave me a look. Focus.

Henry sure focused. He was staring at the rock in my hand with a student's concentration. I wondered what more he had to learn. His face twitched, like a fly had buzzed him. Shoo fly. His hands began to shake. The gun bobbed on his knees. He said, "Please give it to me."

I could not reach him. I'd have to stand and take three steps to hand the rock to him. I thought that over.

"Please bring it to me, Cathy."

"It's Cassie," I said. Like that mattered.

"Cassie Cassie Cassie." He nodded to himself. "Cassie."

I glanced at Robert and Walter, who appeared to be on alert. Waiting for something? Waiting for me. I set my field kit on the ground and leaned forward and tossed the rock to Henry. It landed behind him.

Chapter 32

He did not turn to look. His hands steadied on the gun. "Only a child falls for that trick."

"It wasn't a ..."

"I'm not your brother Henry."

I twitched. Hard. Like I'd been punched.

"My brother told me about your brother who died. We have the same name. It's only a name, Cathy."

"Cassie," I said, automatically.

"I have trouble with names," he said.

So the fuck did I.

Still having trouble with Henrys. It was more than a name that linked the two Henrys, it was the fragility of a boy with hemophilia and a man with mercury poisoning, and it was guilt, Robert's guilt about his brother and my guilt about my brother, and isn't that a kicker that guilt trumps logic every time?

Oh boy, get a grip Cathy.

I watched Henry's hands on the Glock. Shaking again. One twitch and his finger trips the trigger and then he shoots *his* brother. Or Walter. Or me. Accidentally, on purpose, doesn't matter, shot is shot.

He said, "How did your brother..."

"Accident," I snapped.

He said, "What more did you find?"

Short attention span, Henry? My mind raced. I gave him the only thing I had. I jerked a thumb, pointing uphill. "I found an outcrop of chiastolite hornfels."

"Is that all?"

Well that answered that. He'd already seen it. And it wasn't enough. Okay then, I'd *make* it enough. "Somewhere around here, Henry, you've got hornfels intersecting an auriferous channel. Maybe near the existing tunnel, maybe a deeper or parallel channel. Maybe somewhere out here."

Henry listened.

Walter jumped in. "That's right, Henry. The channels were laid down in different ages. You can have later channels intersecting earlier channels, channels occupying different positions laterally as well as in elevation—all in the same general area. You understand the geology, son?"

Henry shifted his fevered gaze to Walter. "Not like you do."

"Nevertheless, you've had a few days to look around."

Henry said, "A few weeks."

33

A FEW WEEKS?

Walter and I exchanged a look. According to Robert, Cameron Shelburne had died three weeks ago. And Deputy Vicky Bleeker had brought a team to the South Yuba River to retrieve the body and assess the scene. And the next day, she had met Robert and Henry at the morgue, where they identified their father's body. And then the brothers had driven to their father's place, where Robert had spent the night. Where they'd gone through old family things. Where Henry had opened the letter from his grandfather, which led them to the ore specimen hidden under the floorboard in the attic. Two-plus weeks after that, Henry's landlord had contacted Robert to say that Henry had left him a message--along with the ore specimen, and the link to our lab.

According to that timeline, Henry had gone off hunting for the source of the ore *two days* ago.

According to Henry, himself, now, he'd been here for a few weeks.

Doing what?

Robert gaped at his brother, as surprised as we were.

Henry stared back.

"Hey Bro," Robert said, finding his voice. "What the hell?"

"What the hell," Henry echoed.

"You want me to put two and two together?" Robert looked at the sky, looked at the ground, taking the time to do the math, struggling to catch up. And then he faced his brother. "Well hell, Henry, looks like that equals four. You went looking for the source of that damned rock right after we found the rock in the attic. You've been here *a few weeks*? And then--what, three days ago?--you phone your landlord--you hike down to some place to get sat phone service?--and you say please check the faucet in your room, and it turns out the faucet isn't running, but there is something else there. Your note, half the rock, the links to Walter and Cassie. So of course the landlord contacts me. You expected me to follow you."

"You followed," Henry said.

"Damn straight I did." Robert jerked a thumb at Walter. "With help."

"You found me."

"Here I am."

"You know why I wanted you?"

"Oh, I read you loud and clear, Bro. I found the bandana on the hike in. I assume kicking the rocks over the edge was an accident. And then down in the pit, I found the dimes. I played it out. And then that flask in the river. I understand. It's all cool, Henry. I'm here now. I'm listening to you."

"And I'm listening to you," Henry said.

I thought, this is isn't going anywhere good.

"Why didn't you just *talk* to me, Henry? That day in the attic. We could have talked."

"No we could not."

"Meaning what? We need to play games to talk?"

"That's how we roll."

Chapter 33

Robert gave a short laugh. "Where'd you pick up *that* phrase?"

"From the movies."

"It's a little cliched. I wouldn't use it if I were you."

"How should I talk, R?"

"R?"

"You call me Bro, I call you R. It's cool."

"You're playing games with my *head*, Henry."

"That's right."

"So what's this game called? Bro."

"It needs a name."

"How about *brothers*?" Robert said.

"That's good."

"How does it start?"

"You apologize."

"No problem," Robert said. "I apologize."

"Do you know for what?"

Robert said, "For whatever I did to offend you."

Henry's hands began to shake. He shook out his arms, gun bobbing in his clenched fist like a jackhammer. He pressed his hands back onto his knees and steadied himself. Steadied the gun. He repeated, "Do you know for what?"

"I just *said* I..." Robert dipped his head, then nodded. "Sure, I know. For being a bully of a big brother. All the times I put you down."

"That's when we were kids."

"I don't recall being a shithead to you as an adult."

"Do you know for what?"

Robert said softly, "Not just being a bully. Enabling you to mess around with the mercury. I'm truly sorry about that, Henry."

"That's when we were kids."

Robert blinked. "Then I don't know what you want me to apologize for."

"Think."

"If I was a shithead as an adult, I apologize for that too. We good?"

Henry didn't answer.

"So why are we here?" Robert glanced around, spread his hands, encompassing the valley, the mine, the canyons. "Why have *you* been here for, what, three weeks? I mean, what..." Robert cut himself off.

"*What?*" Henry parroted.

Robert just shook his head.

And then Henry looked beyond us, to the hillside that bordered Sluiceway Canyon.

34

I LOOKED where Henry was looking, wondering what's over there?

I'd come that way, following the sluiceway path down the slim canyon. Up top, I'd found the hornfels. Down here, in Enchantment Valley, the hillside met the high southern wall that caged the valley and rose to a ridge far above.

I stared hard but could discern nothing remarkable about that hillside.

Henry stood and, with his gun, urged us to stand.

It seemed we were going to find out what was over there.

He steered us to the bottom of the sluiceway where the climb upcanyon began. This was the side without an established path, and the ground was rough. We carefully hiked a short distance and then Henry turned us to walk toward the hillside. We halted just short of it. The footing was uneven, the slope gradient noticeable.

We stood in a line, ducks in a row, me at the uphill end, Henry at the downhill end, with a fine position in which to cover us with his gun.

I examined the hillside. Now that I was facing it straight-on, I saw that its gravelly face appeared to have been eroded, perhaps by a hidden spring, some long-ago finger of flowing water. Indeed, a shallow trough ran out of the cavity and cut the slope between Walter and Robert. The cavity itself looked to be about twenty feet deep and twenty wide and ran a good twenty feet high. It was nearly overgrown by vegetation. It looked like a grotto. It looked like a good place to hide.

It looked, actually, like the miners had claimed it as a storage space. Old timber was piled in there, castoffs from the sluiceway.

Robert spoke. "Got a pile of dimes in there, Henry?"

"No."

I shifted. What, then? Not certain I wanted to know.

"It's under that... that..." Henry frowned.

"Bracken," Walter said.

"Bracken," Henry repeated.

I didn't know if this was another word Henry had forgotten or if he simply didn't know the proper name. I would have just said *fern*. Tufted ferns sprouted in crevices on the back wall of the grotto. It was a day for ferns, lacy mountain misery and spreading bracken and I could live happily for the rest of the day without encountering another variety of fern.

"Look under the bracken," Henry said. He added, "R."

Robert didn't move.

Henry adjusted the aim of his Glock so that his brother was squarely in his sights.

Robert Shelburne gave a shrug, as if he had no real worries—no expectation, certainly, of finding anything of note in there under cover of the ferns. Gold nugget, snake, turkey baster. Whatever. Robert strolled over to the grotto and stepped inside.

"Push the bracken out of the way, R."

The bracken was about chest-level. Robert yanked a fistful of

Chapter 34

ferns clean out of their crevice. For a long moment he looked at what he'd uncovered, and then he turned to face us. Uprooted ferns in his fingers. "What's up with *that*, Henry?"

I angled for a look but I could not see what Robert had found.

"Move out of the way," Henry said.

Robert gave a tight smile and stepped aside.

I didn't understand the meaning of what I saw. Sticking out of the hillside at the back of the grotto was a length of rusted pipe. A spigot was fitted to the end of the pipe. It looked for all the world like a tap in a garden wall for a hose. Given the lush vegetation, I wondered if it was indeed a water source tapped into a fracture spring in the hillside.

I said, to Henry, "Is it for water?"

"Go turn it on."

Actually, I didn't really care to do that.

"It won't bite, Cathy."

Robert stood very still, very quiet.

Walter said, "I'll do it."

Henry leveled the gun at me. "She asked about it first. *Cassie* did."

I thought, he got my name right this time. Like it mattered? Like it indicated clarity of mind? Reasonability?

I moved stiffly to the grotto, trying not to stare at the garden hose bib, instead scanning the walls and the floor, getting the lay of the land. It was like a roomy walk-in closet. Make that a roomy tool shed. Splintery sluice box planks and riffle blocks were stacked against the back wall and an overturned rusting bucket lay in a corner. The walls sprouted bracken, brush, greenery I could not name. There was no 'roof' to speak of. The cavity simply chimneyed up until it became flush with the face of the hillside. The floor was bedrock—the Shoo Fly Formation,

I noted, including the now familiar spotted slate. In the middle of the bedrock the floor was gouged, like a water-eroded pothole in bedrock exposed to the elements. I stepped down into the pothole. It was a couple of feet deep. I scuffed a boot across the rock. It was rough, not erosion-smooth. I wondered if it had been manually gouged. I stepped out and moved to the spigot. My homey comparisons died. I evaluated my task. The pipe extended maybe ten feet out of the compacted gravel wall. It was supported by a brace, a metal stand driven into the bedrock at the edge of the pothole. The pipe was rusted. The spigot at the end of the pipe was rusted. Perhaps it would not turn. I've tried that before—straining to open a corroding faucet. Might need a stronger hand here than mine. How about Robert's? I recalled his hands gripping the sluice box back at the pit when he'd seen the dimes, big strong hands. I glanced over my shoulder. Robert's face was white, pinched. As was Walter's. Henry's face was pink with the cold. With the poison. He gave me a nod. I turned back to the spigot, fearing that this was not a water source. I gripped the handle, hoping it was rusted shut. Hope died. The spigot turned. I let go like it had come alive.

Liquid metal began to flow, thin as a necklace.

Holy hell.

"Open it all the way," Henry said.

I twisted the handle. All the way.

I should have retreated then. Instead, I stood rooted. I grew a little dizzy, the way you grow a little dizzy standing on the edge of a cliff staring down at the sea. You know you should back up. Instead, a primitive part of you wants to jump.

A primitive part of me wanted to reach out and catch the flow.

Not smart, although in this cold air there was little risk of the quicksilver giving off vapor. Still, the flow was thicker now, more like a snake, and it poured into the pothole.

So that's what that pothole's for.

"Cassie Cassie Cassie," Henry said. "Move out of the way."

Yeah.

I turned and headed back to my place in line. As Robert and Walter gained the view into the grotto, their faces mirrored mine. Mesmerized. Spooked.

Robert found his voice. "Did you do that, Henry?"

"It was here."

"How did you find it?" I asked.

"In the supply room." He pointed. "There's a... There's a... It shows where things are."

A diagram. I looked up Sluiceway Canyon, up where the bunker was, the room with the old mining equipment, the room with the flasks. I looked back to the grotto, to the spigot. "So where's the mercury coming from?"

Henry pointed.

Walter glanced up, to ridge above the grotto. "Was there mining up there?"

"Everywhere," Henry said.

I got it. Mercury loss from the sluices. Hundreds of thousands of pounds of the stuff, over the years. And mercury being so very heavy, it leached down through the soils. The soils were saturated. And the miners came across the seepage and drove the pipe into the hillside to capture the free supply. And it's still here today. But in that case the stuff would still be oozing out of the hillside. I didn't quite get it. I said, "Hillside's not oozing mercury."

"Sequestration," Walter said. His place in line bordered the trough. He stepped down into it, scrutinizing it, no doubt running the hidden spring scenario. He looked up and scanned the entire hillside, examining the terrain with that look he gets in the lab when he's considering the provenance of a chunk of evidence on his workbench. "Most plausibly, the mercury has sunk down to an impermeable bedrock layer and collected there. A basin of sorts within the hillside."

I nodded. "Makes sense."

Henry said, "What do you think, R?"

"Why ask me?" Robert said, cautiously. "I'm no expert."

"You sounded like one, R. That day on the Yuba."

35

I WENT COLD. Which day on the Yuba?

Something happened there, which has brought us to *this*?

I took a few steps upslope, angling for a better look into the grotto, to judge the size of the growing pool. It came nowhere near to filling the pothole. But still, it grew. The silver snake kept sliding out, the pool kept swelling. It was like watching a faucet left running in the kitchen sink, and the person who left it running didn't notice the sink beginning to fill. I noticed. I'd left it running. My hands went slick with sudden sweat, with the need to turn off the damn spigot.

Robert finally spoke. "You want to help me out here, Henry? *What* day on the Yuba?"

"The day I saw you and Cam."

Robert stiffened.

Henry said, "Cam called me and told me to come."

Robert said, after a moment, "I didn't know that."

"The night before."

"That's when he called me."

I made a little sound. Getting it. Walter put a hand on my arm.

The brothers ignored us. They were studying one another, like they'd just met. Henry looked calm, for the moment utterly still. His hand on the gun was relaxed, as if he'd forgotten he held it. He cocked his head. He watched Robert with what I could only call curiosity. Robert looked uncertain. His narrow eyes narrowed further, as if he were squinting, not against the dull light, but looking for an answer, somewhere beyond us. In the dull light, the sharp angles of his face were softened, or perhaps it was just that his expression slackened. He looked like a man who was trying to catch up. Not the status quo for Robert Shelburne.

Then Robert found his way. He flashed a mirthless smile at Henry. "Family reunion at the river, huh, just like old times. I mean, Dad *did* have his gold pan in the water. So where were you, Bro? Were you hiding?"

"I was up on a ridge. Coming. I stopped... stopped... I stopped when I saw you and Cam arguing."

"Wait. *Wait*. Are we talking about a company Dad and I had going? What's that got to do with anything? That was a deal I helped Dad put together, that's a technology he came up with-- you know how handy he was--and I arranged the financing, that was *business*, that was..."

"That was my idea," Henry said.

"Yours? Hang on. I'm blindsided here."

"You heard me say it before. Cam heard me say it."

"Say what, exactly?"

"Clean it up."

Walter broke in. "Clean what up?"

"The quicksilver," Henry said.

The word hung in the air. In the mind. Harsh, then liquid on the tongue. A whisper in the ear. I swore I could hear the hiss of mercury straining through the spigot in the grotto. I took a step back.

"Robert," Walter said, "is that what your company does?"

Robert answered, curtly, "Planned to do."

"Clean it up how?"

"Dredging."

Walter's eyebrows rose. "That's a violent process--it can flour the mercury in the riverbed sediment." He added, "Just as storms do. Leading to methylation. As we discussed back at the river."

"I recall. My father was developing a technology to address that."

"I'd have been interested to hear about that. Back at the river."

"It's proprietary."

"Does it work?"

"We ran into problems."

Henry said, "What kind?"

Robert put up his hands. "Feels like I'm under interrogation here. Henry. Walter. Cassie, you next?" He shot me a look, gave a tight grin.

I said, "Maybe just answer Henry."

Henry repeated, "What kind of problems, R?"

"You just heard Walter explain the issue. *You* understand the issue. Dad and I were trying to correct it."

"But you didn't?"

"No Henry. Dad died. The project is in limbo now."

"Now what?"

"I don't *know*. Look, Henry, you had an idea, but that's all it is. You said clean it up, the way we all say somebody needs to fix something, and you're right, but Bro, just saying it is *not* how it gets done. You weren't around, you've been off on your wanderings for years, sometimes Dad and I didn't even know how to contact you, but..."

"He contacted me. He called me. And I came. That day on the Yuba."

Robert shook his head. "Camden Shelburne's game. Play one brother off the other. I don't know why he wanted you there, but... Maybe to take his side. Look, he and I had a disagreement. He wanted to scrap everything, start over. I said, how about fine-tuning the existing tech? And, you know him, he went nonlinear."

"He wanted to stop you."

"Right. Cameron Shelburne's motto. My way or the highway."

"You fought him."

"We didn't *fight*. He brought some water samples we'd already taken. He set the case on a boulder. Made a big show of opening a bottle, going to dump the contents in the river. I tried to stop him. We kind of tussled, and the case got knocked over and the bottles went rolling and..."

"You knocked him into the river."

"*No*," Robert hissed, "*I did not*. While I'm collecting the sample bottles, Dad goes full grandstand, he's going to start all over, do it right, so he takes the water bottle from his pack and wades into the river."

Walter and I exchanged a glance. *That* bottle. That buckle-clip bottle found downstream from Cameron Shelburne's body. The bottle Vicky Bleeker showed us on Zoom.

Henry said, relentless, "You let him drown."

"*I did not*. He was wading around cursing when I left. I assume he slipped on a rock, hit his head, got knocked out. Just as the deputy told us--the reasonable assumption. And you accepted that explanation. We both did."

"I didn't."

"You never said otherwise."

"I needed to think. To think...to *think*."

"For three damn weeks?"

"Yes."

"Henry." Robert expelled a long breath. "You said you were

watching. So you must have seen that I left before Dad went into the water."

"I didn't."

"You didn't go down to the river?"

"I waited a long time."

"What did you see when you *did* go down?"

"I didn't go all the way."

"Did you go far enough to see Dad?"

"Yes."

"Alive?"

"Facedown."

"You saw him facedown in the water? And you didn't check..."

"He'd been there too long."

"How do you know what's too long?"

"I looked it up. Afterward."

"Christ, Henry." Robert shook his head. And then he reached out a hand. "It was a tragedy, Bro. But it's done."

Henry ignored Robert's hand. "You need to apologize."

"*Christ*, enough. For *what*?"

"You know for what."

"You're like a damned broken record. I'm not apologizing for Dad's death. I wasn't there."

Henry said, "You need to go into the quicksilver now."

I thought, fiercely, it's symbolic. You'd float, not drown. I wondered how long the mercury would continue to snake out of the spigot. That depended on whatever the hell the pipe tapped into. That basin. However big that basin was. I looked to Walter, who was scrutinizing the grotto, face set in concentration.

Robert Shelburne turned his back on the grotto. He fully

faced his brother. He took off his parka and dropped it on the ground.

"What are you doing?" Henry asked.

Robert didn't answer. He pulled off the next layer, a fleece sweatshirt, and dropped it on the ground. He was stripped down to his green Club One Fitness T-shirt.

"You don't need to do that," Henry said. "Clothes don't get wet in quicksilver."

Robert lifted the green shirt.

Walter shot me a warning look but there was no need. I wasn't going to speak, move, do anything at all. It was all I could do to stifle my sudden hope. I'd forgotten that Robert was wearing his brother's belt. I stared at the big silver buckle with the curlicue lettering. Back at the lab, his display of the Quicksilver buckle was sure effective, sure worked on Walter and me. Sure helped get us to the contract-signing.

I wondered if it was going to work on Henry.

Henry's face was closed. Unreadable.

"Our father had the heart of a snake," Robert said. "It's just us now, Henry. Look, I'm wearing your belt. I'll take on every burden of Quicksilver."

He was silent.

"Or, you want me to take it off?" Robert began to unbuckle the belt.

"Keep it on," Henry said. "It won't get wet."

36

Robert Shelburne stood at the mouth of the grotto.

His hands were on his hips. His fitness T-shirt showed bare arms, muscles flexed. He looked ready to run. Or fight.

"I don't want to shoot," Henry said.

Robert said, over his shoulder, "You don't need to." He went in.

He skirted the pothole, hugging the south wall, leaving us a view of the works, putting as much distance as he could between himself and the flowing mercury. He tipped his head to follow the flow, down to the pool.

I tried to estimate how much mercury had accumulated. If that had been water it would drown a small animal. But it was liquid metal. Thirteen times denser than water. A small animal would float. A large animal would float. A full-grown man would float, buoyant as a cork.

Robert Shelburne was examining the pool as if doing his own calculations.

I glanced at Walter. He was frowning deeply. He watched the scene in the grotto, and then broke off to make a slow survey of the lay of the land. I figured my partner was estimating distances, angles of fire, places to take shelter. I assumed he was concocting a scenario in which Henry's attention faltered long enough for us to flee. That seemed unlikely. Get help, for Robert? That would take hours.

"Sit," Henry called to his brother.

Robert Shelburne did not have hours.

I watched him work up his nerve. He stamped his feet, one and then the other, like a guy preparing to wade into an icy river. And then he stepped down into the quicksilver pool.

The liquid lapped his thick-soled Asolo boots. The stuff was so dense it pushed them back. His feet could get no traction. His body revolved, trying to maintain its balance but every little move popped a foot out of the mercury, skittering for purchase, and then abruptly he gave it up and folded heavily down into the pool in a cross-legged sit.

Not into the pool. *Onto* the pool.

He put out his hands to brace himself on the surface. He flinched.

At the cold, I thought. At the clammy cold.

And then he found his balance. He sat very still upon the spreading silver pool. He folded his hands in his lap. For a moment he wore a childlike look of wonder and then he flashed us a tight grin. "Game on, Bro."

Some kind of inbred Shelburne bravado. He probably knew. Liquid mercury is poorly absorbed through the skin and he could probably sit naked on there all day and take in only point oh-oh something percent if I recalled correctly from Chem 101. I recoiled from my calculations, as if this was normal.

Walter stared in dismay, and then his attention snapped away, back to his escape scenario, or whatever he was grasping at.

"Kinda cold in here," Robert said. "This shit's cold."

Henry's hands began to shake. He jammed his elbows into his flanks and steadied himself.

Robert said, "We still playing the same game? Where I'm supposed to guess what to apologize for?"

Henry nodded.

"Give me a hint. Give me *something* I can work with."

"At the river," Henry whispered, voice softer than ever. Breakable.

"Little louder, Bro."

"*At the river.*" Loud enough to make Robert flinch. "At the river," Henry said a third time, "when I heard you and Cam talk about your company."

"Yeah?"

"Cam said, it was Henry's idea. We should have brought Henry in."

"Yeah?" Robert said, voice tightening.

"What did you say to that, R?"

"Some bullshit."

"What did you say, R?"

"You want the exact words?"

"That's what I want."

Robert hunched forward. He was shivering now.

Henry said, "What did you..."

"I *said*, Henry would not be an asset in my world."

My heart squeezed.

Henry unzipped his belt bag. "That's what you said."

Walter grunted and looked away, shifting from foot to foot, almost skittish.

Yeah, I thought, that's it. Game over. I waited for... I didn't know what. Henry to shoot? He didn't want to shoot. He'd said so. And he wasn't aiming the damn Glock, he was unzipping his belt bag and whatever he took out of that bag had to be better than the Glock. Better for Robert. Better for us. Better for Henry.

Henry wasn't a killer. Henry was a wounded soul, betrayed by his father and his brother, not an asset in their world, surely not an asset in anybody's world. Hurt to the core. A man in the wrong century. And all he wanted now, here, was an apology from his brother.

Robert just gave his brother that appraising look of his.

I waited for him to apologize, so we could all go home. He'd already said the words, how many times? Doesn't matter if he meant it. Spit it out, one more time. When it counts. Otherwise, I hoped he had an alternative.

Walter spoke. "I would like to sit."

I glanced at my partner. That's all you got?

Henry jerked a shoulder. Go ahead and sit. Or maybe it was just one of Henry's twitches. Didn't matter. Walter cleared pebbles from a space with his boot and sank to the ground and Henry kept his wounded attention on Robert.

Robert smiled. "You want an apology, Bro? You wander around the mountains like some kind of original man and you think you know what a business deal is? You think it's unfair I left you out in the cold?"

Henry flushed, a deeper pink than the pink of his peeling nose.

I tensed. Careful, Robert, you're insulting him.

Robert rolled his shoulders and put his hands flat on the surface of the pool. This time he didn't recoil from the touch. He relaxed into a more comfortable position. He looked like a man lazing on a raft waiting for someone to bring him a mojito. He cocked his head to appraise his brother. "Not a world where you'd thrive, Henry."

Henry blinked. "*You either.*"

"Oh but I do," Robert said.

I glanced down at Walter, seeking some kind of help here, some way to take this in a better direction than it was now heading, but Walter was hunched over staring at the ground, perhaps trying to come up with a word, an idea, with *something* and if the answer was there in the dirt I wished him good luck finding it.

Robert finished it for us. "Bottom line, Henry, I kept you out of it. Secure in your world."

Henry Shelburne laughed.

37

It was the laugh that did it, knocking the bravado out of Robert.

Knocking me and Walter to a new level of worry. Walter whispered something, so hushed that I could not make it out and I moved down into the trough and knelt beside him thinking *finally* he's got an idea.

Henry reached into his belt bag and tossed something in front of us.

I looked. It was entirely commonplace. It was unsettling as hell.

Now that I was on eye level with Walter, I turned to him—what now, because things are really going to hell here. He met my look and gave a shake of the head. *Don't.*

Don't *what*? I could think of a dozen things not to do. I could think of nothing useful *to* do.

"Cassie and Walter," Henry said.

We looked up.

"You need to sit ankles together," Henry said. "You need to do them first."

I froze.

Henry nosed the Glock in our direction.

Chapter 37

Walter took hold of my arm and tugged me down to sit beside him in the space he had cleared.

The package Henry had tossed was closer to me. So I picked it up and ripped the plastic open. Took out two cable ties. Passed one to Walter. They were heavy-duty, rated to handle a couple hundred pounds. I'd used heavy-duty ties like these to bundle duct hoses when I installed my washer and dryer, two years ago. Now, slowly, Walter and I began to bind our ankles. Threading the cable ties, a micrometer at a time. Sounded like a clock ticking.

"*Zip them.*"

We zipped them tighter than I'd wished. Sounded like a machine gun.

"Now you need to do your wrists," Henry said.

I took out two more cable ties. Passed one to Walter. We bound our wrists, zipped machine-gun tight.

Walter hunched over his knees and muttered, "Blast it."

I whispered, "You okay?"

He hiked a shoulder.

Henry crabbed close and retrieved the open package. He moved to the mouth of the grotto. He took out a tie and tossed it to Robert. It landed short, in the brush edging the pothole. He took out another tie. Hands shaking. He crabbed closer. "I don't want to shoot," he told Robert.

"You don't need to." Robert leaned forward and held out his hands.

Henry tossed the tie. It landed true. It floated on the pool like a stick. Robert picked it up and began to loop it around his wrists.

"Only do one hand," Henry said. "Thread it through the handle first."

Robert's face tightened. He had to twist his torso and stretch his arm to reach the spigot. He slid around the surface of the pool like it was ice. He gripped the spigot. He anchored there. And then with an effort he threaded the cable tie through a wheel cutout in the handle and closed it off around his wrist. He pulled the zip tight. He adjusted his position to face his brother. Awkward, now. No mojito on the horizon.

38

Henry turned and walked away.

I could hear my own heartbeat, the pulse in my ears. I could hear the distant cry of a bird, the crunching sounds of Henry's boots upon gravel, Walter's quickened breathing beside me. I could hear the hiss of the mercury through the spigot. Otherwise, the silence went on and on, excruciating.

I watched Robert Shelburne. One expression after another seemed to chase across his face. Worry, confusion, anger, calculation. No, what I saw was mounting fear. And then he started yanking his cuffed hand, trying to free it from the wheel handle of the spigot.

I glanced at my partner. He was doing the same. Bent over his feet, shifting position, trying to find an angle to work.

Good idea.

I followed suit, hunching over my own feet, positioning my ankles, hoping for a little give in the binding, a space between one foot and the other which could be capitalized upon. Maybe if I took off my boots I could slip one foot free. Hands bound at the wrists but that left my fingers free. I yanked the laces on my right boot, the boot with the torn tongue, didn't even feel the bruise anymore, that damage entirely inconsequential, and now in my haste I'd knotted the laces and I thought fiercely *pay attention* but already another thought had entered my mind. A geologist thought. How many times have I used a rock pick to pry out minerals deep inside a pocket in an outcrop? I didn't have my tools at hand but I sat in a field of rock debris. I started raking through the gravelly soil.

Walter hissed, "He's coming back."

I snapped my attention to Henry. He was indeed returning and what he carried chilled my bones.

Robert, too, had seen. Had frozen.

Henry Shelburne went straight to the grotto, went inside, skirting the pool where his brother sat stunned, squatting at the back of the grotto where the old timbers and riffle blocks were stacked in a jumble. Henry deposited the armful of kindling he'd brought from the campfire.

They were brown and dried with thick woody stems and shriveled leaves. And they must have still held their resin glands, I supposed, because when Henry had thrown that mountain misery kindling onto the struggling campfire, it threw off that nose-tingling odor.

That, and set the campfire fully ablaze.

Walter whispered, "Can you get free?"

Yeah, sure partner, if I can find a pointed shard. If it's pointed enough to do the job. I whispered, "Rock pick."

He nodded, and began to pick through the pebbles around his feet.

"Hey Bro." Robert's voice rang out. Strong, but without the gloss he'd put on *Bro* before. Strong and harsh now. "What do you think you're doing?"

Henry stood and opened his belt bag. He took out a box of matches.

Chapter 38

"Not fair," Robert said. "Not a fair fucking game."

I was transfixed. I'd seen Robert play this game back at the great mining pit, the void, the place where a mountain had once stood. I'd watched Robert standing in the mountain misery, striking a match, dropping it onto the resin-thick ferns, showing how quickly the stuff would ignite. Explaining how the brothers had played this game when they were kids, vaporizing the mercury to go after the gold. But Robert's demonstration for us was just a dog-and-pony show. This, here, now, was the real deal. This mountain misery was tinder-dry. This stuff was ready to kindle a bonfire of old timbers and riffle blocks—no doubt impregnated with mercury—and if that bonfire got lit it was going to heat the pipe coming out of the wall, through which the mercury flowed from some never-ending supply somewhere in that hillside.

I wondered at what point it would give off its poisonous vapors.

I glanced at Walter. He too was watching. Pebbles forgotten.

Henry opened the box and took out a match. Hands shaking.

"This game is fixed," Robert said. Anger flared off him like heat from a fire. "You've got matches. I've got nothing. What kind of game is that?"

Henry said, "No kind of game."

"The hell it isn't."

Henry struck the match on the side of the box.

I waited for Robert to scream. Once Henry lit the resinous ferns on fire and heated the mercury, Robert wouldn't be wanting to scream, wouldn't be wanting to open his mouth. In fact, he'd be needing to hold his breath.

The match was burning.

"You want to play poker, brother? Let's play poker." Robert sucked in a breath, then let it escape. "I'll see you."

I shook my head. *How?* With what? Robert had no moves, no hand to play. He was bluffing.

Robert twisted his head, underneath the spigot, and brought his face to the silver stream.

I sealed my lips. This was some kind of crazy-ass Shelburne bluff, ready for the fire to start, the mercury to heat, to vaporize, for the poison to pour out of the spigot. Ready to breathe in a lung-full.

Robert opened his mouth wide.

It was a moment before I understood.

He was not bluffing. He was drinking.

Henry, stunned, let the match burn down to his fingers. He jerked, letting the match fall. By the time it touched the ground it had gone out.

Robert turned away from the flow, and grinned, a crazy-ass grin. "Drink it today. Shit it tomorrow."

I gaped. Drinking elemental liquid mercury--who does that? Only a desperate Shelburne brother does that. I knew the stuff was poorly absorbed through the skin but who knew if it would freely traverse the digestive tract—well Robert clearly knew, or hoped, Robert who had read up on all things mercury, Robert who was anything but suicidal. But *still*. I swallowed hard, watching him open and close his mouth like a fish out of water, a fish who'd performed the wrong kind of respiration.

"We can..." Robert spat, "...play this game all day."

Henry recovered himself. He lit the next match. "I'll see you, R." He let the match fall. This time it stayed alight. The little flame kindled a spray of mountain misery. It crackled to fiery life. Henry kicked it aside.

Chapter 38

Robert stared.

The brothers locked onto one another, a poisonous face-off, waiting it seemed for someone to make the next move.

Henry did. "And raise you." Henry pulled the Glock from his holster and tossed it into the pool.

39

I THOUGHT IT WAS A MISTAKE.

Even as I watched the gun rise with the toss and then fall with gravity—dropping into, no, *onto*, the surface of the pool—even as I watched the game change I thought it must have been a mistake.

Henry's head tipped up and then dipped to follow the arc of the gun as if someone else had tossed it.

Robert's mouth opened, an *O* of surprise.

Walter grunted, a sound of disbelief.

And then the Shelburne brothers upped their game.

Henry took another match from the box. The fire he had kicked aside was already consuming itself but the main pile of kindling awaited the next match.

Robert's free hand stretched, reaching for the gun.

Henry smiled.

It was too late but I did the only thing I could think to do, went back to raking my hands through the rock debris, hunting for that shard, my mind racing—*what the hell Henry?*—and the ugly answer came. Suicide by brother.

Walter whispered, "Use your nail."

Chapter 39

It took me a very long time to get it, to understand what Walter meant, and then for a moment I wanted to applaud the beautifully absurd genius of it, but Walter was watching me with such fierce hope that I wanted to cry. Sure, it could work, but Robert was about to shoot the shit out of his brother and Henry was about to turn that mercury stream into vapor and we were relying on my fingernail?

He lifted his bound hands, clasped. "I'll buy you the time."

I gaped. You will?

Walter sat up ramrod straight and bellowed, "*Your grandfather was here.*"

I was taken aback all over again. I had to stop myself from actually turning my head to look around. The Shelburne brothers were doing just that. Henry's head swiveled, the match in his fingers forgotten for the moment, but still at the ready. Robert looked right, looked left, although his field of view from inside the grotto was severely limited. My field of view was just damn good enough to see the top of the mercury pool, to see Robert's fingers kiss the handle of the Glock.

"*Right here,*" Walter bellowed. "*Look at this.*"

I looked.

Walter held his bound hands high. His right hand pinched a small rock between thumb and forefinger. "*This* is what you came for."

Henry peered at Walter. Robert cocked his head. I looked from one brother to the other, from the brothers to Walter. Surely they could not see what I could see, could not make out the details.

I made out the details. It was a largish pebble, rough and

reddish, lumpy, bits of rock cemented together. A conglomerate, if anyone was asking. I wondered, could it be?

Walter shot me a look. Shot my bound hands a look.

Use your nail.

And then I understood, staring at the pebble pinched between Walter's fingers, staring now at *his* fingernails, a man's good-sized hands with a man's good-sized nails. His nails were too large to do the job--unlike mine, which just might fit into the locking bar of the cable tie. Yes, Walter. I get it. You do your bluff while I do my best to unlock this sucker.

And then what? And then we'll see.

"Listen to me, boys," Walter said, voice gone soft now, so soft that we all had to strain to hear. "Your grandfather saw that hillside. *Look at it.*"

They looked, scanning the walls, and while they looked I bent to my work. The heavy-duty cable tie binding my ankles had a big wide slot. And I had small unclipped fingernails. Doable?

"I give you this," Walter said, "a workable hypothesis. *Follow me.* A, you have a source of trapped mercury in that hillside. B, it is likely trapped in a bedrock basin. C, something created that basin. D, a long time ago a dike intruded a Tertiary gravel channel and acted as a giant riffle. It created a giant pocket, in which gold collected. That ore specimen you brought to the lab, Robert, originated in there. In that hillside. Right behind you."

I began to think it wasn't a bluff. As my mind followed the geology lesson, my fingers worked. I worked my right pointer fingernail into the cable slot and pressed down on the locking bar. Astonishingly, the lock opened. Not astonishing. The right tool for the right job, hey? I nearly laughed.

I stole a glance at Walter, and gave him the slightest nod.

He returned it.

"*In that hillside,*" he said, "there is what geologists call a frac-

Chapter 39

ture spring. It charges with winter rains that percolate through the soils. Over the years it eroded the material in the riffled pocket and some of it flushed out here."

And it eroded the trough where we sat. I thought, it's really not a bluff. I held my breath and very very slowly backed the loose section of the cable tie through the slot, making that ticking-clock sound.

"Some bits were larger than others," Walter said, voice loud again, "and at least one was a large enough specimen that it caught the eye of your grandfather. Most were so small they would catch nobody's eye. Unless one knew where to look."

Henry turned. "How do you...?"

"*Know?*" Walter glanced at me.

I nodded at the cable tie, now loose around my ankles. I went to work on the cable binding my wrists.

Walter's glance snapped back to Henry. "How do I *know?*" Walter boomed. "*Listen*, Henry. I deduce. I look at the geology, I analyze. I make a hypothesis. And because I understand what I am looking at, I know where to look."

"Is there..."

"*Yes.*"

Henry came out of the grotto, pausing at the entrance, eyes fixed on Walter. Robert leaned forward, his bound hand straining against the cuff. His unbound hand had captured the Glock. He held it loose, upended, and a thin silver necklace slid out of the barrel.

I wondered, chilled, if the thing could work.

"Come here, son," Walter said.

Yeah, I thought. Step away from the grotto, Henry. Step away from the kindling. Step away from your brother.

"Look," Walter said, "right in my hand is a bit of that gravel. This is the same stuff your grandfather found." Walter angled his bound hands, showing a different face of the tiny rock. "Look here. There is a visible grain of gold. *Gold.* You can see it but you'll have to come closer."

I stared at the pebble. There was color. Could be a flake of gold. Could be a grain of pyrite. Either way, my pulse leapt. With a tremendous effort I yanked my gaze from the pebble to look at Robert. His face was keen. Hopeful. His gun hand had gone slack.

I moved my feet, just slightly to the side, in preparation, keeping them together as if they were still bound.

"Come on, son," Walter said. "You should have a look at this."

Henry whispered, "No."

I heard the yearning in Henry's voice before I turned and saw it in his face. No? You don't believe Walter? You, the amateur geologist, don't believe the evidence before your eyes? Then come the fuck closer Henry, and *look.* Because I saw. Because I believed. Because Walter was talking geology. Not legend. Not wishful thinking. For the love of your soul Henry come and take the pebble from Walter and see for yourself. This is what you've hunted since your father fed you the legend with your morning cereal. This is what Camden Shelburne promised. Lured you with. Taunted you with. This is why your grandfather left you a letter that said look under the floorboard in the attic. It's your legacy. This is it, Henry. Your father wanted it but he never had a chunk of ore to follow. He had only a flowery letter with vague clues. And he grew frustrated and he berated his sons. Berated *you,* Henry. This is where you prove yourself to your father, who I fear is alive in your tortured mind. *You* found this mine site. You got here, you got us all here. And then you pointed a gun and hired yourself a couple of geologists. All you have to do now is take the pebble. And then you can say you won. All that shit with your father and your brother over the failing cleanup company doesn't matter. You can win now. Take it. You earned it,

Henry. You spent your life force hunting this. You want it. You're squinting to see what Walter is offering. You look like the kid in the Old West photo.

"*Henry,*" Robert said. "We can do this. *Together.*"

The hesitation was tiny, a clenching around Henry's mouth.

And then he stepped back into the grotto and struck the match and flung it into the kindling.

40

I HEARD THE CRACKLING, like corn popping. I smelled the bitter odor of mountain misery. And then I saw a black resinous tendril of smoke, and then an orange tendril of fire. The smoke rose thinly, up up up the chimneyed grotto. The fire spread laterally, licking along a plank, probing the jumbled pile of splintery old wood.

Henry squatted and blew on his fire. There was a fresh match in his hand.

Robert raised his gun hand.

Time turned squirrelly, stretching and slowing.

I was pushing to my feet, ankles and hands free, staggering up out of the trough, legs rubber, and then I stumbled my way into the grotto, surprising Robert in the act of aiming the gun in the direction of his brother.

Time turned so stretchy that I had all the time in the world to glance at Henry in the corner and see him smile.

To glance behind me and see Walter struggling to get onto his knees, an impossible task with his ankles and hands still bound.

Chapter 40

To stop myself at the edge of the pool and wonder if there was room for me.

To assess the growing blaze, to see the flames heighten, to feel the heat cast off, to swear I could smell the iron pipe heating.

To yank up my parka to cover my mouth, my nose, and collapse into position with my boots over the edge.

And then *whoosh* I scooted into Henry Shelburne's pool, crushed between Robert and the bedrock edge.

For a moment all the familiar workings of things were cast aside.

I sat on top of—*on top of*—the silver sea.

My knees were bent, my heels cupped into the liquid, and I braced my arms behind me, hands clutching the mercury like I'd clutched the silver heart back at the South Yuba River. It was cold and clammy and alien.

The heat from the fire was almost welcome.

Robert's face was inches from mine. His eyes were bitter green. We gazed at one another, me thinking is this how you'll gaze at Henry, if you pull that trigger?

I was dizzy, short of breath from my exertions, breathing into my parka, re-breathing air that smelled of nylon. It was sweet in comparison to the grotto air that was about to go bad.

I hissed to Robert, "Cover your mouth."

He couldn't, not with one hand bound to the spigot and the other holding the Glock aloft.

There came a sound like a gunshot, another match striking.

Robert aimed.

I screamed, "*Drop the gun.*"

And time that trickster speeded up. It moved like liquid mercury heating up, particles vibrating faster and faster until they escaped their fluid bonds and formed a gas. I speeded up, throwing myself at Robert, hitting his chest, losing the grip on my parka in the process. My parka mask slipped down, leaving my face naked, my nose and mouth unprotected, as I sent Robert spinning, me spinning with him. Together we spun on the mercury, without friction, and Robert's free arm whipped out, his hand opening like a flower, losing its hold on Henry Shelburne's weapon.

Walter shouted, struggling to get onto his knees.

Robert shouted. "The *gold*, Henry, you and me, *we can do it*."

Henry didn't answer. Henry was a kid playing with matches. The only answer was the thunder of the fire and the hiss of streaming mercury.

I yanked my parka back up. I yanked Robert's Club One fitness T-shirt up over his mouth, his nose, as Robert desperately yanked his bound hand trying to get free of the spigot.

I fumbled open the cargo pocket of my pants, fumbled out my field knife.

It took forever to move to the spigot, it was like a dream where I'm swimming through molasses, where my feet run but my body remains in place, and I calculated the time, how long it was going to take me to cut Robert free, for the two of us to slither our way out of this hideous pool and escape the fire and the heating quicksilver. And, damn me, I thought, or I could just slap the knife into his hand--leave him to it, let him fumble the knife open one-handed, surely Mister Gearhead could manage that, while I get myself the hell out and tackle Henry and stomp out the fire, or *no*, stomp the fire first and then tackle Henry...

Or I could try to jolt Henry off this track. Keeping an eye on the growing fire, on the box of matches in his shaking hand, I uncovered my mouth and shouted, "*You* need to apologize."

It took him ages to shift his focus from the blooming fire, to me, frowning, and then another age to ask, his voice gone fragile again, "For what?"

"Your dad was trying to make your idea work. He was taking a grab sample. And drowned." The words were knives, cutting my throat. I swallowed. I raised my parka and covered my face and took in hot nylon air. I didn't know if Cameron Shelburne had been doing a grab sample--that was my fevered dream. Maybe there was no water sampling. Maybe Robert had been spinning a story to convince Henry. Maybe Robert pushed Cameron Shelburne, drowned him. I didn't know, but Henry's attention remained on me. I lowered the parka, and shouted, "Who's cleaning up your mess, Quicksilver?"

It took him another age to turn back to the fire.

I was fumbling with the knife again when I heard a sound like salvation--Henry stomping out the flames, kicking apart the pile of wood.

And then another sound, a broken sound that was Henry's own. "You do it, R."

41

By the time I managed to cut Robert loose, by the time we fumbled ourselves out of the quicksilver pool, by the time I got to Walter and cut his ties loose, by the time Walter grabbed the rusting bucket from the grotto and filled it in the sluiceway creek in order to douse the embers of the dying fire, Henry had disappeared.

And then the three of us stood outside the grotto, all action at an end.

Rooted.

At last, I cleared my throat and asked Robert Shelburne where his brother would have gone.

Robert rubbed a hand across his soot-streaked face and said, "Fuck if I care."

I looked up Sluiceway Canyon and then up farther, above to the rim, and then back down to Enchantment Valley—what I could see of it. There was no insubstantial figure retreating into the woods, no flicker of a brown parka.

Walter cleared his throat. "None of us is in any shape to go searching for him right now."

Chapter 41

As if we had a plan, we gathered ourselves and headed down into the valley.

There, we paused. Disoriented.

At least, I was. It seemed like another time when Walter and I had sneaked through the notch and entered this valley and found anything but enchantment. Rather, horror.

Robert finally said, "His tent's gone."

We moved again, and stared at the little clearing in the trees where Henry's tent had stood, the tent I'd glimpsed from the notch in the cliff wall when I'd looked down into the valley. There was a tent-shaped depression in the leaf-littered dirt. It made perfect sense that he would have come back to his tent, after abandoning the grotto, that he'd break it down, pack it in his pack, take his belongings when he fled. To wander around in the wilderness like some kind of original man, I thought, retrieving Robert's description, and then I regretted that, the cruelty of it, but the alternative description of Henry Shelburne that came to my mind was *some kind of unraveling man*. And then I retrieved the feeling of cold clammy silver sea under my hands, and echoed Robert again. Fuck if I care. As long as Henry's gone.

We moved on, coming to the fire ring.

Robert stumbled to the boulder where he'd sat an hour ago, an age ago. His pack still sat on the ground, beside the boulder. He said, "Thanks for nothing, Bro."

But the fact of Henry leaving the pack for his brother, instead of hauling it away, was worth thanks, I thought. Anything undisturbed was worth thanks. Walter's pack and my pack were there, as well. I gave thanks for that, using up my store of thanks to offer Henry Shelburne.

Walter and I resumed our seats.

Walter opened his pack and dug out the satellite phone. He turned it on and tried for a signal and found none, no surprise, no service way down here in Enchantment Valley. He turned to Robert. "Try yours."

It took Robert a long moment to think that through.

I thought, damn. He's wrecked.

But he pulled himself together and got the sat phone from his pack and tried for a signal. Shook his head. Then sat there with the pricey Iridium device in his hands, like he was waiting for a call.

I said, "Robert."

He looked at me.

"I'll take it." I rose before he could struggle to his feet, crossed the little clearing and took the phone from him, and returned to my seat.

For a long while--minutes that felt like hours--we sat there, leaning toward the ashes of the fire in the pit, but if there was any warmth left, I didn't feel it. Funny, I thought. Just escaped a crackling fire in the grotto that scared the shit out of me and here I am hunting for red coals of mountain misery.

Not funny.

I said, "We should find a place to call for help."

It was decided that I'd take Robert's phone and climb up to the notch--higher if need be--and find a position with a clear line-of-sight to the satellites. Walter would take our sat phone and climb up to the ridge just above us, and try there. Meanwhile, Robert would rest and recover whatever energy that might lurk in his Club-One Fitness body,.

That decided, Walter leaned over to redo his boot laces. I followed suit. My laces were fine. They had not come loose in the mercury pool. Everything was fine, but for the silver droplets that had lodged in the eyelets, I guessed when I was thrashing around. They looked like tiny pearls. I wondered if there were more, if the stuff had oozed into the crevices where my socks did not quite meet the collars of the boots. Robert was suddenly in front of me, handing me a twig. I looked up. He nodded down at his own boots, his grimy Asolos also decorated with silver. He shrugged. For a moment, I thought we were going laugh. Isn't this something? We should get our phones and take photos. Post on Instagram. It would go viral. People would say we did it on purpose, with an eyedropper or something. People would say we were crazy. People would say it was cool. We might start a trend. People will do the stupidest things, if they see it posted online. Robert, I saw, had his own twig, and was heading back to his boulder, was sitting and bending down to dig out the pearls. Was finding a drop of Club-One energy. I turned to my own business. The twig was nice and sturdy. I dug out droplets, flicking them away. I caught Walter watching. He just shook his head. Isn't this something? Isn't this crazy? In the end, I took off my boots and shook them out and then ran the twig inside but it was too stiff so in the end I had to use my finger, running it along the insoles, along the little crevices, finding a droplet lodged up near the collar. I took off my socks and found droplets lodged in the weave of the wool.

When we'd finished, when both Robert and I were re-shod, Walter said, "We should go now." But none of us moved. We just sat and stared at the ground. It was littered with shiny drops. They would need cleaning up. As would the pool they came from, the pool that Henry Shelburne had filled, and left. As would the hillside basin soaked in mercury that fed the running faucet, that fed the pool.

We needed to tell Deputy Bleeker to call in a hazmat team.

I got to my feet and shouldered my pack. "I'm off."

Robert levered himself up, shivering, his bare arms puckered with goosebumps. "I need to get my parka."

Walter rose, shouldered his pack, and said, "We'll re-assemble back here."

We headed off, on our separate ways.

42

Two words.

Gail Hawkins turned them over in her mind. On her tongue.

As she pulled the balaclava over her head, down to her neck, turning herself anonymous, she considered the words.

Gun.

Gold.

She needed the one, to get to the other.

What she'd heard, and seen, from her lookout at the top of the sluiceway, was Robert and Henry and Walter and Cassie going crazy down below in the narrow canyon. What she'd heard was incomplete, but enough. Walter had shouted gold. Here? And Cassie had shouted at Robert to drop the gun. Gail had thought, then, her *Weatherby*. Robert had it.

The only question for Gail was, did Robert drop it?

He must have. Because after the craziness, she saw Henry walking away, unharmed. Fifteen minutes later, she saw Robert and Walter and Cassie walking down into the valley, unharmed. And then there was a long time when Gail couldn't see or hear anything.

Chapter 42

She waited. A hawk. She could wait for hours. While she waited, she brooded on her Weatherby. Gun. Gold.

She couldn't wait for hours. She was going *now*, while the canyon was empty. It was hers, now.

She pulled on her gloves. She checked her balaclava. She checked on her foam-pad footwear. No disguising that. Hell, it *was* a disguise.

She grew a feral grin, for Henry.

She shouldered her pack, and stood.

She ghosted down the canyon, hugging the wall, scanning the valley below, watching for movement. Ready for anything. If they somehow intercepted her, she would play the strange backpacker, shake her head at them, raise her palms, *stay back*, and they would obey, they would want nothing to do with this stranger in camouflage with a knife on her belt. Then she would leave—she was easily fit enough to outpace them, and they would let her go and count themselves lucky. And she would find another approach, another way to track them.

First, though, she needed to find her Weatherby.

As she ghosted down the canyon, her nose began to sting. Something burning. Mountain misery. She pinched the balaclava over her nostrils. She inched toward the place where they had gathered, and gone crazy. They were gone, now. From her new position, she had a narrow view of the valley. She saw nobody. But the valley spread further and she knew they could be outside her range of vision. She accepted that. She moved to the crazy place. She was a strange crazy-looking backpacker, repellent to anyone.

She looked around.

She looked toward the wall, where they had looked, and she saw what drove them crazy.

Her own heart lurched.

There was mercury filling a hollow in the canyon floor.

She was stupefied. Upended.

Two words: Mercury. Gun.

She needed to touch the one to get the other.

She regained her senses. It was a handgun, floating on the silver pond. It had to be the gun that Henry pointed at Robert and Walter and Cassie, outside the mine tunnel.

Why was it in this pond?

Did Robert throw it in there? When Cassie shouted drop the gun?

Then *where was her Weatherby*?

She heard something. A rustling. She pulled her knife and spun around but there was nobody. Her heart pounded. She breathed in. Breathed out. Centering herself.

The gun was there for the taking.

She turned and scanned the canyon again, uphill, downhill, down into the valley, and then her attention snapped back to the hollow in the canyon wall, nearly overgrown with ferns. There was a faucet feeding a stream of mercury into the pool. It was impossible. But it was there. Her nose stung. She shifted her attention to the stinking pile of ashes behind the pool.

They were crazy.

This pond of mercury was crazy.

She had seen plenty of it in drops, and sometimes clumps, in the rivers, and when she'd caught that drop in her gold pan, but she'd never seen anything like this. It was a silver mirror and she leaned over it wondering if she would see her face reflected. She did not. Too dark in this hollow. That didn't matter. The closer she leaned to the pond, the more she wanted to touch it.

It was hypnotic.

It was base, a tainted metal, and it pulled at her like the devil's own work—she'd heard that somewhere, she didn't believe in the devil but she could find no better words.

She was going to have to touch it, to pick up the gun.

She took off her pack and dropped to her knees and leaned over, stretching her right arm, extending the fingers of her right hand. Not her left hand. Her left arm ached, burned, where she'd extracted the grain of fool's gold. She didn't trust the fingers of her left hand.

With her right hand she touched the grip of the gun.

She touched the quicksilver. It was slippery. It felt alive. A living cold thing. She burned, for a moment, to hold it, to warm it up.

And then she shook off the hypnosis and pulled the gun out of the pool.

The mercury slid off the gun like a shedding snakeskin.

She pointed the barrel downward. Silver ran out of the muzzle. A tiny stream, and then drops. Silver bullets.

"Who are *you*?"

Gail Hawkins stiffened, tried to scramble to her feet, tried to see through the sudden blaze of red coloring her vision, tried to understand how she could have been taken unaware *again*, and she turned, swiveling on her knees because she could not rise to her feet, and she saw the shadow of the man standing in front of the hollow and she squeezed her eyes shut for just a moment, long enough to clear her vision, and when she looked again she saw Robert Shelburne standing there, haloed in her golden vision.

He reached down to grab her gun hand.

She jerked that hand away, so he grabbed her by the other arm, the left arm, where she'd purified, and the pain shot through her, and she brought the gun hand back to point at Robert and pulled the trigger.

43

Up at the notch, I could not find a signal with Robert Shelburne's satellite phone. Didn't matter how much it cost, how many bells and whistles it had, there was no line of sight available. The phone and I were struck mute.

I hiked down through Skinny Canyon to the confluence with Shoo Fly Canyon, hung a right, and climbed until I found a more promising location, but no luck there, and no luck at the location even farther up this way. The canyon was too damned narrow to provide enough unobstructed view from the ground to the sky above. That left three options. Hike all the way down to the river and follow it to a wider spot in the Yuba Canyon. Or, return to the others, see if Walter had any better luck, and if not, we'd all head up to the ridges above the valley and hope to find a signal there. Or, once Robert had recovered enough strength-- once we'd all recovered--we'd all hike out the way we came and keep trying for a signal on our way.

I figured we could put it to a vote.

I pocketed Robert's phone and retraced my hike to the notch, climbed back through, and re-entered Enchantment Vally.

There was nobody in sight below at the fire pit. I guessed

Chapter 43

Walter was still hunting signal, up some ridge. I guessed Robert had run out of oomph, and collapsed somewhere.

As far as could be seen I was all alone and I didn't like it one damn bit.

I picked up my pace.

The valley felt different, entering this time. Strange. All that had occurred here was already hardening into memory. All of it past tense, even the horror of the mercury pool. It felt like it happened hours ago, days ago, and then suddenly the memory flooded back and it was happening right now.

I guessed I was at sixes and sevens, a phrase Walter liked to use to describe that feeling of disarray when one thing comes to an end and the next thing has not yet begun.

By the time I reached the fire pit and collapsed onto my boulder, I was wrung out.

And not a little pissed. Where were the others?

I shouted *hey* a couple of times and got no response.

A new thought came. Maybe they'd caught a glimpse of Henry up on some ridge above the valley. Heard a sound. Had no time to write me a note in the dirt. Had time only to dash off and try to catch him. If Robert had gone, as well, he'd left his pack here. I didn't much care about Robert's whereabouts, right now. I was focused on Walter's.

Which way, then? Following Henry

Given the direction Henry had gone when he left us at the grotto, my best guess was that he'd reached Enchantment Valley and turned to the right, up the valley toward the far end where it narrowed and continued up toward the higher ridges.

Not yet alarmed, but beginning to feel unsettled, I moved with the intention of exploring the upper reaches of this valley.

Along the way, I approached the intersection of the valley and Sluiceway Canyon, and because I was here, I thought about Robert. He'd said he was going to retrieve his parka, discarded outside the grotto. I estimated the time. He'd had nearly an hour to do so. Then again, he'd been exhausted, when we all went our separate ways. Maybe he'd changed his mind. Too wrecked for even that short hike. Or, understandably, unwilling to return to the scene of the horror. In which case, why hadn't he returned to his seat at the fire pit and dug out some warm clothes from his pack and slumped there to await our return?

Speculation brought me to the intersection of valley and canyon.

I turned, and looked up.

Something caught my eye.

Something was on the ground.

I didn't panic. I grabbed the idea that formed like a cloud above me. Robert went to the grotto to retrieve his clothing, did not have the energy to take another step, and so he lay down on the ground to rest.

I shouted.

He didn't move.

I ran, my pack bouncing, my legs rubber, my heartbeat in my ears, and when I came close enough to assure myself that the man on the ground was indeed Robert, and not Walter, I sobbed my relief.

Robert Shelburne sprawled on his back with a gunshot hole in his chest.

Where was the shooter?

I swiveled and looked at the mercury pool and its surface was unbroken.

Henry. He'd come back and gotten the gun and lured Robert to the grotto to finish the job.

I spun around, looking for Henry.

Nobody.

Where was he?

Where was Walter?

Chapter 43

Twisting, turning, scanning the ridge tops, looking upcanyon, I stumbled over to Robert and dropped to my knees and put my fingers to his neck to feel for the carotid although I had no expectation whatsoever of finding a pulse. His open green eyes held no pain, no life. His soot-streaked face was slack. The wound on his chest was not actively leaking blood. It had done, though. Drying blood smeared across his green Club One Fitness T-shirt. The shirt was rucked up to reveal his lower abdomen. There was no rise and fall, no sign of respiration.

There was, though, the tooled leather belt with the big silver buckle that bore the name of Robert's killer. Quicksilver.

For a moment the relief I'd been feeling that it was not Walter lying here gave way to a stab of sorrow for the man on the ground. And, guilt. We shouldn't have split up, leaving Robert a sitting duck.

I crouched lower, making myself a smaller target, and turtled my head around, looking looking looking for some sign of Walter.

44

I ABANDONED Robert's body and found a dark spot in the grotto to hide. Peering out, I had no field of view to speak of, I was a ground squirrel, mostly safe, entirely stuck here.

I was dizzy with the need to get up and run. *Go.* Find Walter.
Go where?
Nowhere until I could draw enough breath to think straight. It took precious minutes and an act of monstrous will to slow my heart rate and focus my mind, to get a grip.

Okay.

What do you know?

To begin, wherever Walter had gone, he had surely gone with Henry, and not voluntarily.

What I needed to do now was understand what Henry wanted.

Okay, he had lured his brother here, seeking revenge. He had played out his revenge here, in the grotto. And then he had walked away. And then, I figured, the hatred for his brother still raged, it had not been quenched in the quicksilver pool, it had driven Henry to come back and finish the game.

And Walter tried to interfere?

Chapter 44

He would.

But if he had interfered, he would be lying beside Robert Shelburne.

So, he heard the gunshot and came running and Henry intercepted him. Took him.

Why?

I thought of the lure Henry used to bring his brother here--a legendary chunk of gold-studded ore showing a deep blue face. Henry's grandfather's ore, the family legacy.

Henry had finally gotten his revenge. His brother lay dead.

Now he wanted to get his gold? And for that, he needed a geologist. Henry figured that Walter would know where to look.

That's what I needed to know.

Okay, do what Walter taught me to do. Look at the evidence. Think it through.

The evidence was a chunk of ore, blue-faced in its heart, studded with grains of gold. The question was, what's its provenance?

The answer would be found in the angular dark pebble embedded in the ore--its heart pierced by a black Maltese cross. Chiastolite hornfels.

I thought it through. Where would I be hiding, if I were a gold-bearing seam in this neighborhood, a seam that had not yet been mined to oblivion? A seam that had produced the ore that caught Grandfather Shelburne's eye.

If I were a diorite dike intruding an ancient river channel, cooking up a sheath of chiastolite hornfels—in the process creating a giant pocket where gold collected—where would I be likely to *do* such a thing?

I stared out at the ground where Walter and I had sat bound with zip-ties, me hunting for sharp rock to release the ties, Walter looking for a pebble. I looked around me, at the canyon wall encasing the grotto. How about in here? Here's where

Walter said I would be. Somewhere in this hillside, a fracture spring eroded the material in the riffle I created. And some of those bits and pieces of rock flushed out. And Walter plucked up a piece of it—a magic pebble to distract Henry.

I shifted my thoughts upcanyon, up toward the outcrop of chiastolite hornfels that I had found.

Outcrop.

It was, I thought, just that—the visible exposure of bedrock, the rest of which was buried in the hillside.

The hornfels outcrop was created by the diorite dike.

The dike and the riffle were buried.

I thought I knew where to look. Maybe I even knew where the pocket of gold was. All I needed to know, now, was where Walter, at gunpoint, would take Henry to find it.

Well, they weren't down here.

So they must have gone up to the ridge above, where miners had dumped mercury into the ground, mercury that seeped down into this hillside.

Miners had been at work up above.

Had Henry Shelburne's grandfather been at work, up above?

There were two obvious routes to the ridge up above. Go to the upper end of Enchantment Valley and follow the continuation of Skinny Canyon. Or, go up Sluiceway Canyon.

If I were Walter, which way would I go?

Sluiceway Canyon was the shorter, more direct route. Walter liked short and direct.

I got to my feet and left the grotto and did it Walter's way, starting my trek up Sluiceway Canyon.

45

I'VE BEEN WATCHING YOU, Gail thought, like a hawk watches her prey.

She watched him right now in front of her on the rough path. He'd already stumbled twice. If he fell and broke his leg he would be of no use to her. She'd had to tap him on the shoulder with the barrel of the gun and when he turned to her, she'd given him a thumbs down. *Slow down*.

She wondered if he thought he could out-hike her, out-run her. He'd taken notice of her makeshift footwear, her careful steps. He missed nothing. It was good that he couldn't see her bandaged left arm under the shirt--he would have recognized that as a point of weakness.

She grimaced. Robert hadn't known, when he grabbed her left arm. The *pain*. But Robert paid the price. She hadn't planned to shoot. She hadn't liked that. She hadn't disliked it, either. It had been natural. She'd killed before--deer, pig--necessary kills. Food. Once, with a wild boar, defense. She'd learned about her prey. They weren't all the same. Some were stronger, some were weaker. Some were smarter. It didn't matter. In the end, blood was blood. Life was life and death was death. After that, everything rotted.

She'd killed Robert in the same way. Necessary. Defense. Some time later, in days or months to come, she might process it differently. But for now, she categorized it without trouble, dismissing him. Robert was a Level-0.

Walter, ahead of her on the path, was a Level-1. The center of her world.

She needed to take care of Walter. And she needed him to understand who was in control. She was younger and fitter, and although he couldn't see her age or her fitness through the baggy clothes and balaclava, he had seen her for what she was, when she caught him kneeling on the ground beside Robert. She had ghosted right up to him, behind him, tapped him on the shoulder, and when he'd startled and turned and seen her, he had gone rigid in fear. Looking up at her. Maybe he'd glimpsed a flash of her golden eyes through the balaclava eyeholes. Maybe not. Either way, he'd been shaken.

It had been easier than she'd expected to communicate with him. First, the tap. Then the pointing gun. Then, she'd produced the rock from the cargo pocket of her black hiking pants. His eyes fastened on that piece of ore, and he'd nodded. Recognition. Admiration, for her skills. She'd given him time to figure it out, to understand that she had found Robert's pack, that she had *known* to look. That she had been tracking them from the start, that she understood what they were after. What she was after.

And then she'd put the rock back in her pocket and motioned for him to stand.

He did it clumsily. Exhausted. Frightened. Playing the old man.

But she wasn't fooled. She'd watched him on the trails. She'd seen him move--slowly, yes, but surely. He was fit enough for Gail Hawkins to respect. And to watch like a hawk.

Now, he hiked up the path slowly, steadily. As she'd requested.

There was the chance, she knew, that he was leading her on a wild-goose chase. But she counted that a small chance. That had been established almost from the start. He had looked back, three times, spacing it out, trying to make it look natural, as if he was checking his way. He wasn't. He had been looking for Cassie. He had known that she would follow--just as Gail knew--and the only question was, when? Gail herself had looked back, two times, and seen nobody. That meant nothing.

What mattered was that Walter had understood.

If Walter didn't do the right thing, Gail Hawkins had an alternative geologist.

And so Walter and Gail continued their hike in silent agreement.

They were hiking along a ridge top now, following an animal trail. Deer scat. She kept an eye out for movement down below, in the canyon and the valley. She watched for Cassie. And for Henry. She mustn't forget Henry.

Suddenly, Walter stopped. He put up a hand. "Give me a moment."

He was breathing harder than she liked. She nodded. She allowed him to sit and take off his pack. She sat facing him, her gun hand resting on a knee. She kept her pack on; she had no need to drop it; she was fit. Walter took a water bottle from the side pocket of his pack, opened it, took a long drink. And then he reached out to her, bottle in hand, offering.

She almost laughed.

With her free hand she reached back to pull her own water bottle from its pocket, and then she unscrewed the top one-handed, and then she brought it to the mouth-hole of her balaclava, and drank. Didn't spill a drop.

All the while, he watched her. Assessing. Looking for an angle.

His eyes, she noticed, were the color of the blue lead.

She gave him four minutes to rest and then motioned with her gun hand--a flick of the wrist, of the barrel--and he understood. He stowed his water bottle and put on his pack. He got to his feet. Less clumsy than the last time. In synch with her, now.

Ten minutes into the continuation of their hike, he spoke to her, over his shoulder. "We can do this together. As a team."

Her eyes sharpened, but of course he didn't see.

"Whatever we find," he said, "you take what you want. And I'll take what I can."

She wondered what his angle was.

His voice was strong and clear for an old man. Not so old, after all.

She'd thought he was weak when she first tracked him yesterday, climbing up the rocky part of the slope. Now she had to change her thinking. Now she knew him better.

Walter turned to look at her, his blue-lead eyes searching.

She shrugged. He was bluffing, she knew, about the sharing, hoping to trick her into trusting him. Maybe he even thought she would put away the gun. That didn't make her mad. She would have done the same thing. Pretend to trust, pretend to be a team, pretend that they could share the gold.

"And then," he said, "we each go our own way."

Just like a Level-4, she thought. There was no level where trust lived.

She gestured with the gun, a sharp jerk. *Turn around. Move.*

They hiked along the ridge that on one side dropped down to Robert Shelburne's valley and on the other side flared out into an upper valley. A high spur led down from their ridge into the upper valley.

Walter started up again, talking at her, over his shoulder. "You see the rimrocks of slate and Shoo Fly schist exposed on each side of the valley?"

She saw the bedrock. She couldn't have named the schist.

"That indicates the course of the old channel through here," he said. "The bedrock still holds up the elevated riverbed."

Gail's golden eyes swept the land.

"But there's something you have to consider," he said.

Her attention snapped back to him, to his straight back and measured pace.

She waited.

He said, "I might not be able to find what we're looking for."

She thought, he's bluffing. He's studied the ore, he found his way here. And now he wants her to believe he's too stupid to find the source. She couldn't believe he'd be that stupid, to try a bluff like this. She had no more patience for this nonsense. She tapped him on the shoulder.

He turned to her.

Their routine.

She glanced over her shoulder. Put a hand to her brow, shading her eyes, a cartoon of searching. He caught it right away. He was anything but stupid. He knew what she meant. If he couldn't be of use, his partner would. And she'd be coming.

For emphasis, she aimed the gun straight at Walter's heart.

They took the high spur that led down from the main ridge to the upper valley. They passed a flattened piece of rusting pipe and then a crumbling stone foundation where a shack had once stood. On the far side, beyond the little creek, the black mouth of a drift tunnel showed through the trees and the brush.

Walter led the way to the base of the hillside that separated this upper valley from the valley down below.

Walter was steady. No more talk of not finding anything.

They hiked for awhile and then he stopped and told her they needed to backtrack along the deer path.

She cocked her head.

"Getting the lay of the land," he said. Staring at her, unafraid. Those blue-lead eyes held steady.

She jerked the gun, reminding him.

They backtracked.

Walter kept stopping to look up the hill. And then he'd shake his head and they'd go again.

While he did his job and looked for the gold, she did her job and kept watch for Cassie.

Neither one of them found what they were looking for.

Walter turned them again and took a different path along the hillside. He kept looking at it like he knew what he was doing.

And finally they came to a tangle of brush and Walter said, "Here."

She stared at the brush, then shook her head.

He said, "It's not going to stand up and announce itself. If it did, it would have been found long ago. What we have to do, now, is look for the detritus--the rocks and cobbles that show somebody mined here once. Found something here once."

She waited.

Walter looked at her carefully. "How much do you know, about the ore? You must know something, or we wouldn't be here."

She waved a hand.

He laughed. "Be easier if you talked. On second thought, it's

Chapter 45

better this way. Easier for us to go our separate ways, afterward, you keeping your anonymity."

She nodded.

"Very well, the gist of the story is that the Shelburne brothers' grandfather was a rogue. He didn't work the established mine over there." Walter pointed across this upper valley to the opening of the drift tunnel. "Whatever he found, he found on his own."

Gail stared at the hillside. It looked no different to her than any other parts of the hillside they had been exploring. She wished that her hawk eyes could see what Walter's blue-lead eyes saw.

"The gold is in there," he said.

Her mouth watered. It was close enough to touch. If she could trust him. She studied him. Standing there relaxed, like he felt at home. Confident. If she could trust him. She gave him a curt nod.

"I'm going to have to fight through the vegetation," he said. "On my hands and knees, close to the ground, so I don't miss anything."

She steadied the gun on him. No tricks.

46

———

THE KILLER WAS POINTING a gun at Walter.

My world froze.

"Please," I whispered, to nobody, to fate. Walter is the backbone of my life. Please stop this.

My heart was pounding so fast, so wildly, that my throat constricted, my vision blurred, I went light-headed, and there was a buzzing in my hands as if I were holding that gun and it was about to go off.

I was free-falling, and then I grabbed hold of a boulder and stopped short of a crash. When my vision cleared, I focused on the killer.

The killer wasn't Henry. It was a figure in camouflage: balaclava, gloves, baggy clothes. It was a woman and the reason I thought *woman* was the drape of the black hiking pants across the hips when she bent to get a closer look at what Walter was doing, the gun in her hand shifting to keep a steady aim on him.

Walter was on his knees, digging through a patch of low-lying bushes. His backpack sat on the ground, nearby.

All I could think was that she wanted something and

Chapter 46

ordered Walter to find it, and he dropped his pack in order to search the brush without the pack getting snagged.

And if he didn't find what she wanted, she was going to shoot him.

I couldn't think much further than that.

Could barely breathe, hiding behind the boulder, feeling dense as the rock.

I gripped the seam of sharp quartz that spined the top of the boulder, to hold myself in place.

Don't go stampeding over there.

If you go stampeding across the open ground from your hiding place here behind this brush-haired outcrop, she will hear you or sense you or see you and she will shoot Walter or you or the both of you, one and then the other, because her gun fires in microseconds and you move in geologic time.

I wanted to throw up.

I took in a long breath and fought my panicking self to get a grip.

The grip of the gun was wrapped in the woman's gloved hand but the barrel and the slide were visible in the light of the sun. The color was two-tone, black body with a silver slide where the finish had worn off--the color of quicksilver.

There was a woman pointing Henry Shelburne's gun at Walter.

I had a thousand questions.

First—what the hell should I do?

Answer: don't stampede.

Next question, the gut-twisting question: why did she shoot Robert Shelburne?

I knew how she got the gun, Henry's gun, because when I'd last seen it, it was lying on top of the mercury pool like a gift, and her target Robert Shelburne presented himself just outside the grotto, like a gift.

Why did she shoot him?

And what did that mean, for Walter?

I focused on the killer. *Who are you?*

A big brown backpack lay on the ground beside her. I recalled the glimpses of brown through the trees, on the clifftops, during our hike yesterday.

I'd thought that was Henry—Henry, who had his own brown pack, and brown parka, as I'd learned today. Maybe it was Henry sometimes and this woman sometimes. I'd had no idea there was somebody else out there to keep track of. I'd glimpsed brown and thought bear or deer or Henry. And now here was another one.

Oh shit. Oh shit. Oh shit.

I started to free-fall again.

I tightened my grip on the boulder's seam of quartz and caught myself.

What the hell should I do?

First, call for help. I pulled Robert's sat phone from my pack and tried for a signal but no luck, not here hidden in the brush. Maybe out there in the open valley. Out there where I'd be in full view. Shit.

Anyway, there's not time for help to arrive. You've got to do something *now*.

Okay. Okay. What do I know?

Whatever this woman wants with Walter, it made her follow us, brought her to Enchantment Valley, brought her to the grotto and the gun. And then she killed Robert. And then she marched Walter away at gunpoint.

Why?

The answer was pretty damn clear.

What did Robert Shelburne want with Walter? Track the ore sample that held the gold. What did Henry Shelburne want with Walter outside the mine—and with me by extension

Chapter 46

because Walter put me forward? Go into the tunnel and find the gold.

And why had this woman and Walter come here? The answer came, right or wrong: because Walter knew there was a fracture spring in the hillside, because he figured he knew where a dike intercepted an ancient channel and formed a riffle that lodged gold. I didn't know *how* she'd know that Walter knew that—maybe she'd overheard us—but that was the only reason I could unearth to explain the scene before me.

The woman in camouflage wanted Walter to find the gold.

That's what he was doing on his knees in the brush--looking for float.

My fingers stung. I relaxed my death grip on the sharp-edged quartz.

Okay.

You need a plan.

I walked slowly, heavy-footed, scattering rocks, making noise, with my hands in the air.

She heard me.

Her head snapped up and swiveled, facing my way. She took two steps backward, two well-planned steps to position herself so that she could point the gun at me and yet swing it in a flash back to Walter.

Walter noticed me, too.

He reared back on his heels and stared at me and slowly shook his head.

I nodded, in reply. Too late, partner. We're in this together.

I slowed even more, trying to leverage an understanding with the killer.

She nodded. Keep coming.

I kept coming, my hands high.

And then, up close, I looked down and saw one more detail that puzzled me. Instead of boots she wore some sort of foam padding taped around her feet. That made no sense. I guessed she'd lost her boots. Or, they'd failed, uppers separating from soles, old boots, but the rest of her clothing and her pack looked serviceable enough. Worn, but not at the point of failure.

I thought then, doesn't matter what happened to her boots. She won't be able to run in those foot covers. I filed that piece of information. At the moment, it was the only thing in our favor.

I said, as steadily as I could manage, "I'm Cassie." My name didn't matter. In fact, if she'd been tracking us, maybe overhearing us, she might already know it. What I wanted was a reply from her. A shred of human connection. A tiny wedge.

She did not reply.

Walter said, "She doesn't speak."

Shit.

We three were silent. We were a tableau—the woman with a gun held on the crouching man, and the woman with her hands in the air. I tested the boundaries. Slowly, I began to lower my hands, and when she did not object, I lowered them all the way. My shoulders ached. I hadn't noticed the aching, when I had my hands up high, I'd been too busy posturing as the captive. I also noticed, now, that I was squinting. The sun was fast breaking through the fog. I had to stop myself from raising a hand to shade my eyes. Don't do anything to startle her.

Walter seemed to hold his breath.

Me too.

There was nothing else to do but go with the plan I'd whipped up. I said to her, carefully, "You're wasting your time here."

Walter placed his hands flat on the ground, leverage, should he be required to shove himself up.

Chapter 46

The woman motioned with her gun hand to Walter and then to the bushes where he had been searching, and then she turned the gun on me.

Walter said, quickly, "I can use Cassie's help here."

He was buying time. I got it. But I had a plan that would buy us more time and give us a slight advantage. Or so I hoped. This wasn't normal, Walter coming up with a plan and me deciding I had a better one. He has the years and the skills and the wisdom, and I'm only just getting started on the path. But hey, he trained me. I kept my eyes on that gun and said, to the camouflaged woman, "I can show you where the gold is."

She shook her head, slowly, like I had deeply disappointed her.

I said, "It's in the mine tunnel. In the valley down below."

Walter opened his mouth to speak, and then shut it.

The woman looked at him, looked at me, then back and forth, pointing at Walter, then me, then giving a thumbs down. The message was clear. One of us was lying. Or maybe both. Then she made her choice, facing me. She raised her first two fingers and pointed at the eye-holes in the balaclava.

It took me a moment. I took a guess. "You've already looked in the tunnel?"

She nodded. Then drew a finger across her throat.

Shit.

"*Hey*," Walter said, "you might have looked but you're not a geologist--if you were, you wouldn't need us. Cassie is. She's explored the tunnel."

I thought *thank you Walter*, you're getting on board, and let's just hope she's not a skilled amateur like Henry, because he sure in hell spent enough time out here in this country learning what to look for, and he knew bullshit when he heard it. Let's hope she doesn't. Surely she's not good enough to find the gold on her own. That must be so, or Walter wouldn't be here, alive. But the question now became, is she good enough to have seen what I saw in the mine tunnel down there in Enchantment Valley, and understand that it was a bust?

Just how good is she?

I hadn't thought this through, I had a half-baked plan to get us all on the move, back down to the valley and the tunnel that I figured had become my stomping grounds, where I figured Walter and I would have some sort of home-field advantage. Two against one. Yeah, one with a gun. But better odds down there than up here with Walter on his hands and knees digging in the dirt, with the killer wondering if I was needed, here.

Everything hinged on the answer to the question. Just how good is she?

I gambled and said, "Did you go all the way?"

She went rigid.

"You wouldn't," I said, "unless you knew there was a fault block offset, in the tunnel. A buried side adit," I added, throwing in the mining term as if I knew my stuff. "The lead got richer in that direction."

She faced me, unmoving, waiting for more.

She wasn't good enough.

I rushed ahead, spinning the bullshit, telling the tale of a twice-buried blue lead marked by a fault block that only a trained geologist was going to take notice of, and I offered her a deal, we'd all go back down and I'd show her the way to the gold and in return she would allow us to walk away, and I knew she would never keep such a deal but if I got her down to the tunnel, then Walter and I might find the time and the place and the chance to remake the deal.

As she listened, she grew antsy. And then, suddenly, her gun hand moved to her left arm, touching the bicep with the heel of her hand, an unconscious move, I thought, because the gun now pointed at the sky, but then she quickly recovered and moved her gun hand back into place.

And moved her left hand to the sheathed knife on her belt.

Oh shit.

Her fingers wrapped around the knife hilt.

Walter was slowly and carefully getting to his feet.

My heart pumped so much adrenaline that I felt sick.

I watched her hand on the knife. Our best hope was that she would go for the knife and abandon the gun, because that would give Walter and me a chance to tackle her. Get cut in the process but that's better than shot. Still, the sight of that wicked blade sliding up from the sheath was terrifying.

She didn't withdraw the knife all the way. She unsheathed it just enough to expose the heel of the blade and then she drew her index finger across it, gently, as though testing its edge. She pressed too hard. Blood oozed.

I went a little faint, with fear. I said, steadily as I could manage, "Use that knife on the pay gravel I found and you'll draw gold."

She sheathed her knife.

Gave a thumbs-down to Walter.

Pointed her bleeding index finger at me.

Okay, I thought, my show. My bloody show.

47

We went single-file, first me and then Walter and then the woman with the gun, following the ridge that would lead to the spur trail down to Sluiceway Canyon.

I spun the scenario awaiting us ahead in the tunnel.

A dozen ways to spin it.

Too many ending in gunshots. Or a knife blade.

I heard Walter behind me softly say, "En echelon."

Say what? En echelon meant parallel stepped fractures in a rock and I was thinking it must be some wild-ass plan he was cooking up for the tunnel, and then I heard the clattering sounds from the woman behind me--kicking pebbles, coming to a fast halt on the steep path--and another meaning of en echelon came to me, some kind of military flanking maneuver Walter had read about, telling me with a joke about double meanings, and the meaning that had to count right now was *get ready to flank me.*

As I turned I heard a shriek from the woman.

It was almost an animal sound.

And as I moved up to flank Walter and saw her staring up at

Chapter 47

the ridge across the canyon, her animal sounds resolved into words, high-pitched, words that made no sense. *My weatherby*.

What?

Reflexively I looked for an answer where she was looking, up on the ridge across the canyon. I tipped my head back and looked. And froze.

There was a man with a rifle, aiming down at us.

A shadow of a man backlit by the sun, a rifle silhouetted.

The woman raised the Glock.

Walter lunged for her gun hand.

I had no time to think. I was already coming around Walter, all *en echelon*, and then trying to come around the killer with the gun but her big brown backpack was like an outcrop, crowding the trail, giving me no room, and I had to navigate while trying to keep an eye on her gun hand and the rifle hand of the man on the ridge, expecting a shot from one or the other or both.

And then the shots came.

The woman was firing, aiming at the ridge.

And then Walter got hold of her wrist, trying to yank down her hand, but she was strong and fighting and her hand with the Glock would not be forced all the way down.

I started to panic, adrenaline again, she was going to wrench free of Walter and turn the gun on him. I couldn't get close enough to help him, and I couldn't get around her to flank on the left side, couldn't get past that monumental backpack, and then knowledge came, muscle memories--thousands of steps on uneven ground wearing my own monumental pack, the feel of it snugging there, joined at the spin, at one moment a part of me and the next moment, with the wrong step and the misplaced boot, the pack becomes its own entity, takes possession of my balance. Free falling. I knew that feeling in my bones.

She was moving, a little side-step, turning away from Walter.

She was moving wrong. The foam lashed to her feet was slipping on the thin soil.

The wrong step, misplaced. *No boots.* No grip.

I put my hands on the only thing within reach, giving her big pack a yank.

There was forty pounds at the least on her back.

It took her down.

She went down flailing, onto her back, the fall broken by the pack just enough to allow her to hump her body to the right. She was so strong that it seemed she was going to regain her balance and then her momentum.

But not fast enough.

She was slow enough for Walter to disarm her.

Slow enough for me to glance once more up to the ridge across the canyon and see nothing but trees.

We got her to her feet.

Walter provided cover with the gun while I helped her up, hard to do with the big pack tugging her down but we wanted that pack on her, wanted her unbalanced. I had to grab her arm to get her upright, and she gasped, a gurgling sound, and I thought, hurt yourself falling down? Tough.

I withdrew the knife from the sheath on her belt. There were small smears of blood on the blade, on the handle. I got an evidence bag from my kit, and stowed it.

We headed back up the path--the woman without the gun leading the way, Walter second, with the gun, me third, a backup in case she managed to kick back or turn and somehow manage to throw Walter off-balance.

We did not remove her balaclava, figuring leaving it in place might limit her field of view.

Chapter 47

Up in the high valley, the woman sat in the dirt, hands and ankles bound with ace bandages from our first-aid kit. Heavy pack still on her back, helping to anchor her to the ground.

I noticed dried blood on the kinesiology tape she had used to bind her foam-pad footwear--blood from whatever wound she had acquired during her journey tracking us. Tough.

The only words spoken were mine, asking, "Who the hell are you?"

She raised her middle finger.

For a moment, I was free-falling into fury, but Walter put a hand on my arm and I gave him an all-clear nod.

Walter got his sat phone and--hallelujah--got a signal and called Vicky Bleeker, whose phone went to voicemail, and he unleashed a torrent of words until the message timed out. He got a call-back from Jean in the sheriff's office--everybody but Jean in a meeting, she's just back from vacation and unfamiliar with the case but she'll get hold of everyone and get everyone moving, don't worry, help's on the way. Another torrent of words that Walter summarized for me after he'd hung up.

And then Walter and I settled to the ground, using our packs as backrests.

We drank from our water bottles.

Walter got the water bottle from the woman's pack and put it to the mouth-hole in her balaclava.

And then we waited. A silent tableau.

48

THE HELICOPTER LANDED close enough to spin up dust and we ducked our heads.

I stole a glance at the woman, wondering if dust could get through balaclava eye-holes, mouth hole. I thought, may you choke on it.

When the dust settled, I turned my focus to the response team debarking the helicopter. Relief washed over me.

The last to exit was Deputy Vicky Bleeker.

Vicky split her team, sending three down to Enchantment Valley to assess that scene, stationing two with us, to monitor the camouflaged woman, and to keep watch on the ridge top for a man with a rifle.

I'd been checking the ridge top, myself, but I didn't think Henry would show. He could have shot us at the grotto, and didn't. I wondered if he'd found his brother's body. Maybe he'd been hunting Robert's killer. Could have shot the woman who'd used his Glock on Robert, but didn't. Bottom line, I thought,

Chapter 48

Henry Shelburne was a wounded soul with a damaged mind, but that didn't make him a killer. Still, we all kept an eye on the ridge top. Simple prudence.

Meanwhile, Vicky asked us her questions. We gave what answers we could.

"The only thing she said," I jerked a thumb at the woman, "was 'my weatherby'. When she saw Henry on the ridge. Screamed it, really. Whatever *weatherby* means."

"It's a hunting rifle," Vicky said. "Half the people in the county have one."

Ah.

We moved to the woman on the ground.

"I'm going to release your hands," the deputy said, squatting beside the woman, "and then you're going to remove that face covering." She added. "Unless you would like me to do it."

When her wrists were free of my Ace bandage, the woman peeled the balaclava up from her throat, up over her face, yanking it off her head. Her hair lifted, then fell. It was sweat-soaked, lank, some kind of punk 'do, ragged and randomly streaked blond. Her face was a leathery brown, mottled here and there where the fabric of the mask had pressed tight. She had a small nose and wide mouth, almost a little girl face. The look she gave us was pure grown-up malice.

Vicky rose, gazing down at the woman. "I am placing you under arrest. You have the right to remain silent..."

I watched the woman listening to the Miranda warning, impassive.

Vicky ended it. "Do you understand the rights I've just explained to you?"

The woman spat in the dirt.

Vicky asked for her name.

The woman remained silent.

Vicky said, "I'm going to need identification. In your pocket? In your backpack?"

The woman remained silent.

"You need to remove your backpack," Vicky said. "Unless you would like me to do it."

The woman unbuckled her hip belt and shrugged out of the padded shoulder straps. The heavy pack fell to the ground behind her.

I thought, that must feel better. But she made no sound, no sigh of relief. Her face was a mask. She was playing tough. Or not playing--she'd been damn tough when we tangled with her. Well, tough didn't matter now.

Vicky opened the pack, poked around, and fished out a small transparent case. It held a set of keys and a wallet. She opened the case, withdrew the wallet, opened it. Read the ID. "Her name is Gail Hawkins. Address..." Vicky made a sound, surprise. Her face showed surprise, when she looked at us. "I know that address. We collect that kind of information as part of a case. We needed a way to contact the Shelburne brothers, in regard to their father's remains." She held up the open wallet. The driver's license showed through a window. "This address," she said, "is the same as Henry Shelburne's."

It took me a moment before the pieces snapped into place.

Walter let out a low whistle.

I stared at the woman on the ground. "You're the landlord."

49

WE WERE WAITING for the team to return from Enchantment, and for a second helicopter to arrive.

Meanwhile, Gail Hawkins had already been loaded into the chopper here. Her face was at the window, looking out on the valley where she had hoped to find gold.

I was still trying to wrap my head around her identity. Gail Hawkins, also known as Henry's landlord. She would have observed him, year in and year out--for however many years he lived in her building, in her home—heading out, with his backpack, off to the wilderness. She might have guessed what he was hunting. A word dropped here, a flicker of interest shown there, let's say when the landlord mentioned her own interests. And then, Henry's father drowns in the South Yuba River, Robert comes, and the brothers head off. Next day Henry returns from his father's place--wound up--and then he heads off to the wilderness yet again. Gail Hawkins is getting *very* curious. Would she have snooped? Of course. She'd have his room key. She'd have all the time in the world to dig through his papers, his files--and let's say she finds his grandfather's letter, and learns about the family legacy. Then, weeks later, Henry phones and asks her to check if he left the faucet running. She does. And she finds a chunk of gold-bearing ore on a table--split in half! Along with Henry's laptop open to our Sierra Geoforensics website, and the link to Walter's old blue-lead articles. Along with the call-Robert note, with its cryptic 'rogue route' postscript. So she consults Henry's maps. And Henry's grandfather's letter. And she's good to go.

The question is, how does she know if, or when, Robert will enlist us? If we do sign on, how does she know when we three will set off on the rogue route in search of Henry? I guessed she gambled. This was a chance not to be missed. So she headed off and set up camp, to wait. And her gamble paid off. We came. And she had guides to the source of the legendary ore.

Lost out, though, in the end.

I shifted my attention to Vicky, who was in deep conversation with another deputy. They were talking about Henry, about sending a search team after him. Walter and I had told her what we knew about his last location, but we had little idea where he might have gone from here, if he'd gone, if he wasn't still lurking in this neighborhood. Deeper into the wilderness, I presumed.

"While we're waiting," Walter said, to me, "I'm going over there for one more look."

Over there was the spot where he had been on his hands and knees digging through the brush, hunting for float, with Gail Hawkins holding him at gunpoint. Where I had joined them.

I came along, now.

I expected my partner to again get down to eye level with the ground, put his nose again to the scattered rocks and cobbles. Take his one more look. He didn't. He just stood there scanning the slope, head cocked.

Finally I said, "You see something?"

He turned a smile on me.

Chapter 49

I said, "Tell me this was all a bluff. You bringing Gail up here. Tell me there's nothing here of interest."

He swept a hand, encompassing the rimrock, the exposed seam of cemented gravel, the creek, the hillside in front of us. If there was a visible outcrop of chiastolite hornfels in this valley, I had not spotted it, and I doubted that he had either, but that didn't matter. I'd pinpointed the hornfels outcrop down below in Sluiceway Canyon--it could very well extend into this upper valley. And the story I'd figured down below held true up here. The old channel got exposed and eroded and the auriferous gravels mixed with chips of hornfels and then the lot got re-cemented by river sand and clay. And then got buried again in the hillside in front of us.

I said, "Are you talking theory, Walter?"

He put his hand in the drooping cargo pocket on his left pant leg and pulled out a small cobble. He held it out to me.

I didn't take it.

He said, "It won't bite."

Yeah, right. One could say that about the chunk of ore Robert brought to our lab day before yesterday. That sure did bite.

I sighed and took the rock from Walter and held it up to the sunlight, taking a long look. It was smaller than Robert's specimen, but otherwise surprisingly similar. Alarmingly so. It was rough and lumpy, a gravel of pebbles cemented together, quartz and diorite and black chips of hornfels. Unlovely. It fit like a plum in my palm.

I did not need my hand lens to spy the buttery gold grains embedded in the plum. They were about the size of kernels of wheat. Coarse gold. Nuggets.

Damn me, my heart leaped.

I turned to my partner and asked, "Where?"

He pointed in the bushes.

"When?"

"Before you made your entrance."

I went a little dizzy. "What if she'd *seen*? Were there more? *Are* there? In the bushes there? *Did you find more?*"

He smiled. "Got the itch?"

"*No.*" Well, maybe a tiny miserable itch. I said, "What I have right now is a question. Why did you lead her to it? And, by the way, how did you know?"

"Why?" He shrugged. "She was holding a gun on me and I was running low on diversionary tactics. How?" He smiled. "More years than I care to count of study, of poking around in the field." He added, "And the evidence of a fracture spring."

"But what if she'd *seen* what you found?"

"I pocketed it."

"What if she got impatient and demanded you produce something?"

"I would have played for time."

"What if she got down there with you and found one of those suckers herself?"

"That was a possibility I kept in mind."

"Well shit Walter, then she wouldn't have needed you any longer."

"Oh, but she would."

I wanted to shake him.

"Give me some credit, Cassie. I wasn't wild-ass guessing—I had a Plan B."

"This better be good."

"You be the judge." He pointed to the hillside above the thicket of bushes where he'd been hunting. "Do you see that spot, about half a dozen yards up?"

I looked. The slope there was steep, not holding much in the way of vegetation. I said, "Yeah."

"Do you see the slight cupping?"

I looked. If he hadn't pointed it out, I would never have taken notice. But yeah, there was a spot on the flank of the hill, where it cupped. Like the flank of a dog lying in the sun, taking in a deep breath.

I was beginning to get it.

"As a hypothesis," Walter said, "let's say that Grandfather Shelburne found the mother lode of his dreams up here, that he ran a glory hole into the Tertiary channel around here and hit a riffle where a dike of diorite intruded, where it formed a gold-catching pocket. And he took out whatever he took but the ground was unstable and, at some point, his one-man operation collapsed. His glory hole caved in. And so he went home with his diggings, and spun tales and gave hints and played his games and wrote his flowery letter, and at some point he decided to entrust his discovery to his antisocial grandson Henry, and so he buried a chunk from his diggings under a floorboard and wrote a letter to his grandson." Walter paused. "You with me on this?"

I nodded.

"Which brings us here." Walter pointed at the hillside. "The only signs left here are some mined-out cobbles and the cup-shaped indentation that shows where there was once a cave-in of some past miner's excavation."

I stared up at the flank of the dog.

Walter said, coolly, "Plan B, had it come to that, was to tell Gail Hawkins that we had some searching to do, to go looking for evidence of an old tunnel around here. At some point I expected to be able to take my chance, to distract her. To get the jump on her. But I didn't have to move to Plan B." He eyed me. "Instead, you came onto the scene."

Yeah. Plan C.

50

WHEN WE RETURNED from the Yuba wilderness--two hours and one helicopter ride later--Deputy Bleeker requested a debrief. She listened intently. And then she requested our help.

She was talking murder.

She wanted to investigate the project that had caused a rift among the Shelburnes. She wanted to find out if there was motive, there, for murder. She wanted evidence.

She got the warrant late that day; small town; she knew the right judge.

Meanwhile, Walter and I got rooms at a cheery motel, on the river. We cleaned up, got takeout, then settled in for a good night's sleep.

Next morning, Vicky drove us across town.

Cameron Shelburne's house appeared to date from the 1800s. It was a rambling Victorian with a steep gabled roof, a round turret with an awning window, deep balconies, a wrap-around porch, and bay windows with scrolled trim. It was bright blue, the paint peeling.

I wondered if the turret housed the attic, if that's where Grandfather Shelburne hid the chunk of ore beneath the floorboards. Now, I imagined Henry Shelburne in the turret with Gail Hawkins' Weatherby pointing out the awning window.

A uniformed deputy emerged from the big front door and gave Vicky a thumbs-down. No Henry in the house. No Henry on the property.

Good to go.

We bypassed the house and headed to the large shed situated at the far end of the spacious acreage.

This building looked to be all business--polycarbonate panel siding with steel reinforcements, a sloped steel roof, two shuttered windows, and a large roll-up door. To the right of the door was a cast-metal sign--AquaHeal--in high-tech font, no Victorian curlicues there.

The door was rolled up.

We went in.

Inside was bright as day. The deputies had left the overhead lights on, long fluorescent tubes that lit every nook and cranny.

There were workbenches and shelves, a file cabinet and several tables. There were Thermo-scientific laboratory bottles in various sizes, an optical microscope, plastic five-gallon buckets, trowels, shovels, rock specimens, and a bookcase that looked to be stocked with spiral-bound manuals. In the center of the shed was a dredge, maybe three feet long, sitting on a big table.

Vicky waved a hand. "This is what Robert and Cameron argued over?"

Walter answered, "So Henry implied."

More than implied, I thought, recalling Henry with his shaky gun hand and his broken words, interrogating his increasingly nervous brother. I added, "So Robert confirmed."

"All right," she said, "my warrant allows us to search for any evidence that could implicate Robert, or Henry, in their father's death."

The warrant gave us the shed.

We set to work.

Vicky moved to examine the shelf with the cases of sample bottles.

Walter was drawn, like a moth to the fluorescent lights, to the dredge.

I took the file cabinet. There were folders of schematics, folders of maps, a folder of company brochures. And there was an application for a permit--not completed, not submitted--requesting the Bureau of Land Management to allow AquaHeal to conduct a pilot test project looking at the feasibility of removing Hg-contaminated sediment at the SYR/HC confluence in the northern Sierra Nevada of California, by using standard suction-dredge technology, enhanced with a new apparatus to capture fine-grained sediment with elevated mercury concentrations.

All right, here it was in legalese, what Robert had told us up at Enchantment Valley. His dad was developing a technology to recover the floured mercury.

I glanced at Walter, who was engrossed in the standard suction-dredge technology on the table.

I reread the permit application. It took me a moment to decipher SYR/HC. I double-checked a map. I googled the SYR/HC confluence + mercury. Then I said, "Hey guys, they were planning to apply for a permit to test some new technology at the confluence of the South Yuba River and Humbug Creek."

Vicky turned. "Humbug Creek?"

I recalled the steep hike down from the great pit of Malakoff to the Yuba River, following that creek, which was named by hopeful miners who had struck out. Bah, humbug.

Chapter 50

I explained, to Vicky, what I'd learned from Google search. "The confluence gets drainage from the big hydraulic-mined site. It's a known hotspot for mercury contamination."

She looked again at the bottles on the shelf. "There's six here full of murky water, with labels. SYR/HC. That the spot?"

"Evidently." But something nagged at me.

I joined Walter, at the dredge. It looked like a portable sluice, with pontoons on the sides, with long snaky coiled suction hoses, powered by a compact engine. I asked my partner, "How does it work?"

"Pretty simple," he said. "The intake hose suctions material from the riverbed, and that gets processed through the sluice box. Samples of slurry material from both the intake and outlet are bottled up, to be analyzed and compared. Ideally, you've extracted a high percentage of mercury from the riverbed."

"Ideally. But Robert said they had problems."

"Well, *this* certainly isn't new technology. It's a portable dredge--you can backpack it. You can buy one online--I just checked."

"Then where's the nifty apparatus that captures the floured mercury?"

"Not here. Perhaps," he added, thinly, "it's still in development."

I bent closer to examine the ribbed sluice box, which still held a smudge of sediment, multi-colored mineral particles. My eye caught on a few greenish grains. Familiar. I moved over to the shelf, beside Vicky, and gazed at the specimen bottles. Yep, murky water. Full of sediment. I picked one up, examined it. Couldn't tell much without an analysis. I put it back.

Walter said, "Something wrong, Cassie?"

Yeah. Not sure what, though. I turned. "Remember, up at Enchantment Valley, when Henry forced Robert to explain what happened with his father at the river? About the failed project?

And Robert said that Cameron had brought the case of sample bottles. Robert made a big deal about Cameron's temper, about Cameron grabbing a bottle and starting to pour the contents into the river. Then Robert stopped him, they tussled, and the bottles scattered."

Walter said, "I certainly recall."

Vicky nodded. We'd described it to her in detail, yesterday.

"So," I said, "six sample bottles at the river." I jerked a thumb at the six bottles on the shelf. "Not a stretch to assume, same bottles?"

"I can buy that," Vicky said.

"Meaning?" Walter watched me, appraising.

"Meaning Robert told us he collected the scattered bottles, and left. So let's say, sometime in the three weeks between his father's death and his hunt for his brother, he brought the bottles here. Put them on this shelf. Everything all neat and tidy. Maybe he was planning, at some point, to continue the project."

Vicky said, "It's not surprising, is it?"

"No," I said. "Robert was a businessman. What's surprising, to me, is that Cameron--in business with Robert--made a point to invite Robert to their old family gold panning site. That he took the trouble to pack in the case of specimen bottles, that while arguing with his son about the problems with the project, he started to dump the contents of a bottle in the river. Why *there*? How about, because *that's* where the samples came from."

The deputy pointed to the bottles on the shelf. "Labels say the samples came from SYR/HC. That confluence."

I said, "They're just labels. I could write the coordinates on a label for the riverfront motel we stayed at, and slap it on a bottle. Wouldn't mean the contents came from that spot on the river."

She frowned. "So they did their tests at the family site, instead of the confluence? And mis-labeled the bottles. Why do that?"

Chapter 50

I had an answer, a wild-ass onageristic estimate. But I looked to Walter, to see what he was making of all this.

He rubbed his chin. "Why? Because the confluence is the big-time. The hotspot, according to Cassie's Google search. But cleanup there would be challenging. Easier, for the Shelburnes, to run their tests at the family site, where the mercury concentration is going to be much lower--fed by smaller mines. Much easier to get impressive results."

Vicky said, "If there was intent to misrepresent, we're talking about fraud."

"*If*," Walter said. "Then the question becomes, who was AquaHeal planning to defraud?"

I looked around the shed. A lot of equipment. Money was spent. Money was a venture capitalist's domain. I recalled Robert explaining to Henry that he'd arranged the financing for the company.

I said, to Walter and Vicky, "Hang on."

I returned to the file cabinet, rifling through the folders, looking for the high-gloss brochures I'd noticed earlier, and passed by. I found them. I yanked one out of the folder and gave it a gander.

Walter and Vicky flanked me, crowding to see.

The brochure was slick, colorful. There were more photographs than text. The photos were of a rocky river site. The caption read *SYR/HC Confluence*. It was the site of the not-yet-submitted permit application. I thought I recognized the dredge floating in the shallow water; there was no 'apparatus' attached. I didn't recognize the worn-looking man in the floppy hat and khaki clothes standing on the river bank, but I had no trouble identifying the grinning man beside him, with a companionable arm around his shoulders. He was Robert Shelburne, looking as wilderness-stylish as I'd seen him on our own wilderness trek. I assumed the man he hugged was his father and business partner, Cameron Shelburne. Another photo showed a golden-tanned gray-haired man in a white shirt and black slacks and white sneakers, looking more stylish than Robert but less appropriately dressed for the river. He too grinned for the camera. The accompanying text said, *CTO Jerry Wilcox checks out Western Petroleum's latest venture.* Said, *in years past, attempts to recover mercury from the river ran into problems, enhancing mobilization of Hg downstream.* Said, *now AquaHeal is developing a revolutionary apparatus to capture all the mercury in the sediment.* The next photo was taken right here in the shed, in front of the dredge, partially obscured by Robert, Cameron, and Jerry Wilcox crowding together, with those triumphant grins. The caption read: *Today's technology cleans up yesterday's calamity.* The piece went on to promise great things. I didn't read all the way. I got the gist.

I thought of Henry, shut out of this grand project, listening to his brother's bullshit. I said, "It doesn't matter."

Vicky asked, "What doesn't matter?"

"At Enchantment Valley, during the standoff with Henry, Robert said 'it doesn't matter' in reference to the company's problems. At the time I thought he meant, his father was dead and the company had no future."

"What do you think now?"

"I think 'it doesn't matter' could explain this." I tapped the brochure, the glossy photos. "However well the dredge project did, or did not, or will not, perform, it doesn't matter, because it *looks like* a solution."

She swept a hand, encompassing the workshop. "Then what's all this for?"

I shrugged. "Something to show oversight agencies, on a site visit?"

"And when they want to analyze the results?"

I tried to channel slick Robert-talk. "Robert reminds them it's a pilot project. AquaHeal has had a few problems, not uncommon. They're doing some tweaking. Not ready for prime time."

Walter cleared his throat. "We don't know that it was a fraudulent scheme. If it was, perhaps Cameron was in on it from the start, but eventually had enough. Or perhaps he was duped, and finally learned that his son and the Western Petroleum CTO had a different business plan. So he invites Robert to the old family site, calls bullshit, starts dumping the specimen back into the river it came from. And when Robert stops him, Cameron takes his own water bottle into the river for a grab sample. Grandstanding--he's going to start from scratch and do it right. But he loses his footing, hits his head on a boulder, loses consciousness and drowns." Walter added, "The scenario you presented on our Zoom conference, Vicky."

"That's when I thought he was out there alone, panning for gold." The deputy folded her arms. "Now we have three people at the scene. Robert, alarmed at his father's turnabout. Henry, resentful, shut out of the company. Either one has motive." Vicky eyed us, one by one. "You two have thoughts on that?"

I didn't. I thought of Robert, on our journey up the river, so eager to have Walter and me help him find his brother, and then when he succeeds, he writes a note saying thanks, we're done, all is well, go home. Gives it to Henry to deliver to us, at the Shoo Fly mine tunnel, proving the brothers have come together. I'd thought, then, Robert wanted time alone with Henry. I thought, now, he was worried about *us* spending too much time with Henry, his unstable brother who just might bring up the subject of the family meet-up that day on the river. Who might accuse Robert of shutting him out of the mercury-cleanup project. Which might get us asking questions--what the hell's going on with your company? And then we do show up, and we all end up talking about the very thing Robert feared. Poor Robert, stuck between a rock and a hard place, between two nosy geologists and a vengeful brother with a gun. Poor Henry, wanting a real apology from his brother. And then things escalated to the pool of mercury.

I recalled what I'd said to get Henry to put out the fire so that I could get myself and Robert out of that silver pool. I said, now, what I'd said to Henry. More or less. "I think Cameron wanted to redo the mercury-remediation project. He made a grand gesture, and drowned." I added, "For what it's worth, I don't think either brother is a killer."

Vicky said, "Henry threatened you."

"He did. And in the end, he walked away."

"Huh." She turned to Walter.

"I'll agree, about Henry. As to Robert--he had the arrogance, and perhaps the motive to protect his scheme. But evidence of murder? Do you see it?"

"No. Evidence of fraud, at best." The deputy's folded arms tightened, fingers bunching the sleeves of her tan uniform shirt. "Even then, I'd say insufficient to make a case. I'd say we're finished here."

I said, "Not so fast."

I went to the dredge. Scanned the sluice box. Found the dark-green mineral grains. Got my hand lens. Focused in on a grain. Under the twenty-power, the mineral was finely textured, with a waxy luster. I got the geologic map from my pack. Confirmed what I'd recalled. I turned to Vicky and asked for permission to take samples from the dredge, and a bottle of that murky slurry.

Walter's eyebrows lifted.

51

THE CONFERENCE ROOM WAS JAMMED. The press up front on the right. Company officers up front on the left.

Walter and I got here early enough to grab seats five rows back. The room was upscale minimalist, in colors of gray and black with accent slashes of red. We fit in. We'd dressed up, Walter in his flannel jacket, me in my wool blazer.

I angled in my seat to scan the room.

Walter put a hand on my arm and I straightened. Nerves jumping. Not good at this.

And then the tall blond woman in gray silk at the podium--the CEO--tapped her microphone and welcomed all of us shareholders, and the members of the press. Behind the podium, a screen showed a slideshow of workers at consoles, workers in hard hats, workers in T-shirts with the company logo playing pickleball.

I half-listened. Words floated by. Dividend growth. Energy challenges in a changing world. New opportunities to lower carbon footprints. I got the gist.

Onscreen, now, a virtual tour of Western Petroleum's facilities, sites marked by a star, the biggest star in Sacramento, headquarters, where this annual meeting was taking place.

And then it was question-and-answer time. Shareholders raised their hands to ask about dwindling returns, share buybacks, a new company logo, emissions targets, and I got enough education, I figured, to apply for a job.

And then Walter stood and raised his hand. "I have a question for Jerry Wilcox."

In the front row of the left-hand section, a tanned gray-haired man stood and turned to see who knew his name.

Without waiting for permission, Walter and I rose and headed up the aisle to the front of the room, to the information table. We carefully moved aside stacks of press releases, to make space. And then we opened the small cases we'd brought.

Wilcox put up a palm. "What's all that?"

"Evidence," Walter said.

Reporters raised cameras.

Wilcox appeared to think twice.

We had our go-ahead. We set out specimen dishes, bottles of murky river water—evidence from the AquaHeal shed. We set out comparison samples we'd gathered when we returned to that catch basin at the gravel bar on the Yuba.

I focused hard on the green mineral grains--the one that had caught my eye in the AquaHeal dredge sluice box, and the one that I had found on our return to the Shelburne family site. Both of them float from the parent rock, just upriver. Could be twins.

The serpentine settled my nerves.

Walter whispered, "Time for the dog-and-pony show."

Chapter 51

We got far enough to establish that the AquaHeal pilot test took place at a site miles from the hotspot SYR/HC confluence cleanup promoted on the Western Petroleum website. And then Jerry Wilcox stopped us, saying we'd used up the allotted minutes for shareholder questions.

It didn't matter. We used up another couple of minutes packing away our specimens, straightening the press releases.

Time enough to shift attention to the man at the back of the room.

People were taking notice. There was something about him--not just the outdated clothing, the high-collared white shirt, the vest with shiny silver and black stripes, the woolen pants. What they noticed, I thought, was his hesitant pace up the aisle to the front of the conference room--like he didn't belong, and knew it.

In fact, Jerry Wilcox was staking out a spot to intercept Henry Shelburne.

Henry glanced at Walter and me at the info table, then drew to a stop in front of the CTO. Henry held out a hand. From my position, I could see the state of his palm, red and blistering. Wilcox saw it, too. He stared. Henry withdrew his hand.

Video cameras caught the moment.

Wilcox spoke. "I'm afraid this meeting is restricted to shareholders."

"I am a... I am one," Henry said, in that broken voice of his. "Shareholder," he finished.

There was no credible way for Wilcox to challenge that.

Henry withdrew a piece of paper from his vest pocket and held it out.

"What's this?" the CTO asked.

"You need to read it."

"I don't know who you are and I don't have time to read your letter."

"My name is Henry Shelburne."

Wilcox drew back.

Oh yes, I thought, he knows the name Shelburne.

Henry said, "It's easy to read."

Wilcox recovered. "Leave it with the attendant at the door."

"You need to read it now."

Reporters moved closer.

Henry looked down at the paper in his hand, hair falling in his face. First time I'd seen his hair. Up in the mountains, I'd only seen him wearing the Sherpa-style hat with earflaps. Now I saw that his hair was auburn, curly, almost pretty. And it was noticeably thinning, an effect, perhaps, of the silver vapor.

Henry looked up. "You need to... You need to read it."

Wilcox blew out a dismissive breath, snatched the paper, and scanned.

"You need to read it out loud."

Wilcox snapped, "You're out of order."

"You need to."

Over in the left-hand section, the CEO made a sound and when Wilcox looked, she circled her hand. Just do it.

Wilcox lifted the paper and read it out loud.

I pretty much knew it by heart so my attention shifted to the company officers, to the shareholders angling for a view. I watched their faces as Wilcox rushed through the words. *Laboratory results. Yuba River. Mercury contamination. Fifty-nine percent recovery. Concomitant flouring of the Hg during dredging.* Dismal results. It didn't matter if people in the room didn't get it. Reporters would do their homework and pinpoint the coordinates as the site miles upriver from the hotspot that Western pledged to clean up.

Wilcox stopped reading and tried to return the paper to Henry.

Henry said, "Read the rest.... At the start."

Wilcox shook his head. "Your time is up."

"Please read the part that says your name."

"That's irrelevant."

"*Jer.*" The CEO was on her feet.

He stiffened, and read. "*To,*" he said, "*Jerry Wilcox, at Western Petroleum. From, Robert Shelburne, at AquaHeal. FYI.*" Wilcox shot the CEO a this-is-on-you look.

There were whispers in the room. I couldn't hear from my spot at the table. I did see a man mouthing *who's Robert Shelburne* to the woman next to him.

"Now read at the bottom," Henry said.

Wilcox looked for an out. Didn't find one. He shrugged. "It's handwritten, a scrawl. I can't read it."

"I did." Henry pointed to himself. His hand was steady. He said, in his frugal voice, "It says, *round-file it*. That means throw it away. And there's a comma. And then there's a *J*. There's the… the initial. *J.*"

Somebody, somewhere in the room, whistled.

No question, I thought, they got it. J, for Jerry. As in, the Jerry Wilcox who'd been sent the laboratory analysis. As in, the CTO of Western Petroleum who told Robert Shelburne to throw it the hell away. But Robert didn't. Robert had paid a private lab for the analysis, and then tucked it away in a lockbox that held the kind of papers you don't want to lose. This paper, I figured, was his insurance, in case something went wrong, in case Western tried to disavow all knowledge of AquaHeal's deception. And of course, something did go wrong, something Robert wouldn't have anticipated. Not least being his brother finding the key to the shed after their father's death, snooping around, as Robert would no doubt have put it, finding Robert's lockbox, breaking into it.

Wilcox spoke again, now into clean-up mode. "This so-called association was drawing-board. Western Petroleum briefly considered the work of a company that we hoped could further our efforts to be good stewards of the environment, but we could not..."

Henry interrupted, raising that blistered palm. "You took my idea."

Wilcox recalibrated. "*Your* idea?"

"To clean up the quicksilver."

"We promote good ideas. I'm afraid this one didn't work out."

"You say it does. On your... on your website."

"An oversight. We'll remove that link."

"And you need to apologize."

Wilcox laughed.

Henry shrank back. I tried to catch his eye, but he was already moving down the aisle, slipping away.

Outside the conference room it was a sunny winter day in Sacramento, the sky a mellow blue.

We left the meeting early, hoping to beat the crowd out of the parking lot, keeping an eye out for Henry, spotting instead Deputy Vicky Bleeker leaning against my Prius. She wore her uniform. That took me aback. I thought things were settled. Two and a half months ago, a search team had located Henry and returned him to Yuba City. Arrested, arraigned, probation, medical care, counseling.

A few weeks later, Henry emailed Walter and me to say he'd found Robert's lab analysis. To say that he mourned his brother, to say that he was sure his brother was not a killer, but his brother did something bad. And so we explained our findings, by return email. And it came together. We back-and-forthed entirely by email, Henry more comfortable at that distance than face-to-face. When it suited him, he chose to live in the modern digital century.

Chapter 51

Now, I wanted to tell him that he was going viral. As Walter and I left the meeting, I'd heard somebody's phone on speaker, and caught the words *mercury contamination*. I'd got my phone, googled, and found a YouTube clip of Henry in his Old West outfit, titled *Quicksilver teaches CTO some manners.*

I wanted to tell him he'd got the word out. Been an asset in this world.

Walter and I drew up to the Prius, joining Vicky.

"You looking for him? You just missed him," she pointed, "heading for the bus stop. Probably on the way back to Cameron's house. *Henry's* house, as soon as the estate gets settled. Or who knows, back to the mountains."

I'd had a half-baked idea of catching Henry before he left, taking him to lunch. Just the three of us, Walter and Henry and me, breaking bread.

Now, it was Walter and me and Vicky, and I wondered why she was in uniform. I asked, "You here on official business?"

"This?" She smoothed the tan shirt. "It gets me in. I wasn't going to buy a piece of their stock to get a ticket to their meeting."

Walter said, "We're glad you came."

"They use my river for green cred? Hell yes, I came."

52

The morning after our return from Sacramento, I came into the lab to find Walter just ending a phone call. I waved a hello. He hung up and went to our mini-kitchen and returned with a steaming mug of coffee and set it on my workbench.

I regarded the mug. Whatever the call was, it required coffee to deal with? I said, "Thanks."

He returned to the kitchen and brought back his own mug and a nearly empty box of donuts.

I declined. Weaning off the sugar.

He chose a cinnamon coil, his favorite. He settled at his workbench with his coffee and donut.

My partner liked his drama. I caved. "What's this about?"

"Gail Hawkins' rifle was found by some hikers--in the area where Henry thought he'd lost it."

"Oh." The Weatherby. Vicky had told us she'd found a photo in the boarding house, Gail cradling a hunting rifle in one arm, standing over a gut-shot pig. I'd thought, well, the Weatherby ended up in safer hands than Gail's. I envisioned--not for the first time--Henry on the ridge with the rifle, drawing her furious attention. Could have shot her. Didn't. Could have shot us.

Didn't. Just stood there holding onto that rifle. Hands shaking, no doubt.

And now the Weatherby is recovered and out of anyone's hands. And Gail Hawkins is in custody for the murder of Robert Shelburne.

I said, "So, it's all over."

Walter dissected another cinnamon coil.

I raised my coffee mug. "Here's to a quieter future for Henry."

Walter fixed me with a sharp blue stare. "To Henry Shelburne. Yes."

I didn't get it.

And then I did. Henry Oldfield. That is not over. I said, carefully, "I know I got myself a little twisted about my brother, I conflated one damaged Henry with another, and I will likely get twisted about my brother again in the future, but you don't have to worry about me."

"Let me ask you something," my partner said. "Why do you do what you do?"

"You're jumping around like a frog. Okay, easy answer. Right the wrongs."

"And why did you sign on with me, to begin with?"

"You mean, way back when?"

Walter nodded.

"Aside from the fact that playing Sherlock Holmes with rocks looked really cool?"

Walter allowed a small smile.

"Something more?"

He took a bite of his donut, and waited.

I raised my coffee but sensed no warmth in it. I saw where he was going with this and I didn't want to follow. Back to my eleven-year-old self, babysitting Henry, ignoring his pleas to read him *Where The Wild Things Are* for the umpteeth time. Instead, I was looking out the window, yearning to join my older brother and his buddies setting off bottle rockets in the backyard, paying no heed when my little brother jumped up and down on his bed to get his own look out the window. Jumped and fell and crashed into a table and broke his skull. If I'd been watching, maybe I could have caught him. Nobody blamed me, so I was left to blame myself. And then along came Walter Shaws and his lab, where wrongs got righted, where I found the chance to start balancing the scales for an act of inattention.

"Okay," I said, "I actually do get it. You get a phone call about the rifle Henry was holding up on that ridge, and you're thinking Cassie is going to get all metaphorical about wounded souls named Henry. And you're hoping she'll call off her own search for justice in the case of her brother."

"Something along that line."

I said, "It's a work in progress."

I waited until the next day to mention the plum-sized rock that had been sitting on his workbench ever since we returned from the Yuba wilderness, the chunk of ore he'd dug out of the hillside in the upper valley. I didn't invoke the coffee ceremony, I just blurted, "How long are you going to leave that thing there?"

Walter didn't pretend to misunderstand. "Speaking of obsessions?"

"Speaking of something that had a hold on you."

"Wasn't I clear enough up at the diggings? At that grand pit. The cost of that obsession, to lives and the land, is way too steep."

"You were clear. But then you found that." I jerked a thumb at the glittering ore.

He sat back and folded his arms. "I'll put it another way." He picked up the rock and held it on his flat palm, so the gold grains

Chapter 52

caught the light. He said, in the resonant voice he adopted when quoting poetry, "*Gold, gold, gold! Bright and yellow, hard and cold.*"

I said, "I don't know that one."

"It's titled *The Grip of Gold.*"

"You intend to recite the entire poem?"

He shot me a flint-eyed look.

"I'd love to hear it. Go ahead."

"One more line will do," he said. "*Price of many a crime untold.*"

A vision rose, along with the steam from my coffee. Me, on that gravelly sandbar on the Yuba, hands in the water, digging through the gravel, looking for dark hornfels float, and then my heartbeat ramps up and I find myself looking for another color--bright and yellow. Instead, I find that riffle pocket in the water and plunge my hand down and my fingers close on that soft cobble of mercury--the clammy silver heart of the gold country.

Walter rose and moved to the shelves where we store interesting specimens. He placed the gold-flecked rock beside an ice-white slab of bull quartz.

He went to the kitchen and returned with a mug of coffee and settled to his workbench. "To be clear," he said, "the *Dogtown* boy is still in here." He tapped his head. "We carry all our past selves."

Yup. "Gets crowded in there."

He found a smile. "Shall we all get back to work?"

I gave him a thumbs-up. "We shall."

THE END

I hope you'll join Cassie and Walter on their next adventure. For a preview, please turn the page.

PREVIEW OF BOOK 2: BADWATER

The figure coming down the dark road was bulky, and it took me a moment to realize he was dressed in hazmat.

I suddenly felt a little naked out here.

Walter, beside me, crouching to stow the donut bag in his field pack, had not yet noticed.

We were at the intersection of the highway and an offshoot side road that climbed uphill, and our view from here was limited. The only thing visible, way uphill, were emergency spotlights cracking the night.

"Our man's coming," I told my partner. "And he's in hazmat."

Walter looked up. "*That* wasn't mentioned."

"No kidding."

The oncoming man was moving slowly—perhaps due to the muddied condition of the graded road. I glanced at the sky, where a cloud roof glowed faintly beneath a hidden moon. Presumably, there'd been a summer thunderstorm here, wherever precisely *here* was.

It had been clear an hour ago in Mammoth, our home base in the eastern Sierra Nevada mountains. We run a two-person lab called Sierra Geoforensics and what we do for a living is read earth evidence at scenes of crime and crisis. This job had begun truly in the dark--it was four a.m. when Walter picked up a call on our after-hours number from an FBI field officer who urgently requested our services. Walter had then phoned me, jolting me out of my four a.m. stupor. It took us ten minutes to consult, speculate, and sign onto the case. Fifteen minutes later an agency helicopter collected us and we headed east from Mammoth and crossed another mountain range, which meant we'd passed from California into Nevada, then bellied down to this dark desert highway, coming in well short of the scene. The pilot deposited us with a *good luck* and then the chopper lifted off and disappeared into the night.

And here we waited.

"One good thing," I said, "our man's not wearing a breather."

Walter peered. "You have young eyes."

"Hey, it's more a question of what jumps out at you."

"Cassie, what jumps out at me in the dark belongs in the realm of bad poetry." He added, "Night vision goes to hell as one ages."

I nudged his arm. "Yeah, you predate the dinosaurs."

"At times I feel I do."

We fell silent, as the Special Agent drew up to join us.

Indeed, he was bare-faced. The hazmat suit encased him from booties to plastic collar line. Above that, he was unprotected. He had graying hair in a salon cut and a beaky face with aristocratic lines. He gave us a nod. "I am Hector Soliano with the FBI." The voice had a faint Spanish accent. "Mr. Walter Shaws, Ms. Cassie Oldfield, I appreciate that you have come on such short notice."

"The situation appeared to warrant it," Walter said. He added, "And your colleague should have informed us that we would need to suit up."

"When she contacted you, there was no need."

"And now?"

"A precaution. The situation evolves."

A vein began to throb in my neck.

"Mr. Soliano," Walter said, "I don't guess well. Not on five hours sleep. A cup of coffee would help. Barring that, I would like to know what the devil is going on."

Hector Soliano gave a curt shrug. "And I, who have had three hours sleep, would wish to know this as well."

Walter's eyebrows lifted.

"On the surface," Soliano said, "the attempted hijacking, the shooting...my colleague should have explained this."

"She did," Walter said. "And the evolution?"

"And the evolution has led us to err on the side of extreme caution."

And it's like pulling teeth, I thought, for the FBI to share details with non-agency people. I said, "And?"

"It is best you see for yourself. But first I am most anxious to have you suit up." Soliano started up the side road.

We fell in.

Walter said, "Where, precisely, are we?"

We were, as best I could tell by the castoff of emergency lights, on an alluvial fan leading into the hacked-up foothills of a gaunt range that loomed above.

"We are just off Nevada state highway 95," Soliano said, "southwest of the town of Beatty. A passing motorist saw what appeared to be a vehicle chase turning onto this road and notified the Beatty Sheriff, who investigated and notified federal responders. I came out here and determined that we wanted a forensic geology consult. We have you on file. I am told you are worth your fee."

"We are," Walter said. "Let's go put our eyes on the scene."

As we tramped uphill we topped a small rise and got a better view. Ahead, big vehicles clogged the road. Adjacent to the road, the scene was spotlighted. Yellow rope zoned off a large chunk of desert where a semi-trailer truck lay on its side. It appeared to have tumbled down an incline and come to rest in the desert scrub. Well uphill of the crash site was another roped and spotlighted area, occupied by a hulking crane.

On the road directly ahead of us there was a big white van, lettered RERT, and Soliano led us toward its open door.

I asked, "What's RERT?"

"An acronym..." Soliano touched his brow—the difficulty of acronyms in a non-native language. "With the Environmental Protection Agency."

My attention jumped back to the spotlighted crash scene, which was uphill of us and the white van. Suited figures had now come into view, poking around the scrub brush near the truck. The figures wore hoods and masks and air tanks.

Soliano snapped his fingers and turned to me. "R-E-R-T. Radiological Emergency Response Team."

I nodded. Made sense.

And then some.

Emergency evolving.

FROM THE AUTHOR

Thank you for reading—I hope you enjoyed the story. You might also like other books in the series, all standalone novels that can be read in any order. See a complete list with descriptions on my **website:** tonidwiggins.com

NEW RELEASES
If you would like to be notified of new releases, you can sign up for my mailing list: http://eepurl.com/GtdZn

JOIN ME ON FACEBOOK
facebook.com/ToniDwigginsBooks

LEAVE A REVIEW
Reader word-of-mouth is pivotal to the life of a book. If you enjoyed reading this story, please consider leaving a review. It would be much appreciated.

ACKNOWLEDGMENTS

"Writing is easy. All you have to do is cross out the wrong words."
— Mark Twain

I had some help identifying the wrong words.

I want to thank the following experts in their fields for information, reading the book, and giving me terrific suggestions: Tom Colby, G. Nelson Eby, and Raymond C. Murray.

If there are factual or technical errors in Quicksilver, they are mine alone.

Thanks to the following for reading and commenting on the drafts: Gerald Hornsby, Clare Midgley, Catherine Thomas-Nobles, JZ O'Brien, Kay Podboj, Emily Williams.

You are all golden.

To Chuck Williams, for support, patience, and wisdom—thank you. Seven houses full.

No book is complete without a cover.

I'm fortunate to work with a talented cover designer—Shayne Rutherford at Wicked Good Book Covers. She has created extraordinarily wicked good covers for my books.

Many thanks, Shayne. I look forward to working with you on the cover for the next book in the series.

Printed in Great Britain
by Amazon